SUGAR AND VICE

"One of the bakers from the contest was found dead on the Augustin Marina's property," Warren said.

Sherry clutched the handle of her cart to steady herself. She shuddered. "Dead? Who? When?"

"I realize you were familiar with many of the contestants, so I hope the news isn't too much of a shock. Remember the man with the story about baking his cookies for a homeless shelter? His name is Crosby Currier. He went by the last name Banks in the bake-off. Crosby Banks."

Sherry took a moment to process the name. "Oh, no. Crosby?"

"You did know him. I'm sorry."

"Barely, but yes. That's awful. What happened? When? Where?"

"I know you have a lot of questions, but I don't have all the answers. The police said his time of death was not long after the bake-off."

"I'm so sorry for the man and his family. Was there an accident or did he have a medical condition of some sort?"

"Neither. I'm afraid he died from neither of those. Police said they have every reason to believe he was murdered . . ."

Books by Devon Delaney

EXPIRATION DATE

FINAL ROASTING PLACE

GUILTY AS CHARRED

EAT, DRINK AND BE WARY

DOUBLE CHOCOLATE COOKIE MURDER

Published by Kensington Publishing Corp.

A COOK-OFF
MYSTERY!

Double Chocolate Cookie Murder

Devon Delaney

KENSINGTON
PUBLISHING CORP.

www.kensingtonbooks.com

This book is for Chris and my daughter, Jesse, who support my urge to wander away to my happy place—my writing desk. And for my granddaughter, Isabella, who I didn't know I needed so much.

Chapter 1

"You should have worn a warmer coat. Are you in denial that winter's around the corner?" Mrs. Nagle, bundled in a boiled wool coat and a plaid scarf, returned her attention to the door handle. "I really must replace this confounded mechanism. My hands are too cold to wiggle the key this way and that to get the blasted thing to work."

"Let me help." Sherry wedged herself between the woman and the storefront door. She handed Mrs. Nagle two dog leashes and took hold of the door handle.

"Two dogs today?"

"My friend and coworker, Amber, is out of town, so I'm watching her dog, Bean. He's my Chutney's best friend." The door to Augustin Dry Goods opened sluggishly as Sherry applied pressure with her shoulder. "There you go." Sherry collected the leashes from the owner of the store. Sherry was reminded and amused by the fact no one addressed Mrs. Nagle by her first name, Penny, as she watched the woman enter the doorway. She introduced herself as Mrs. Nagle and offered no alternative. Her husband, on the other hand, was Tony from the first introduction.

"Dear, would you mind helping me in with the box of holiday decorations?" Mrs. Nagle pointed to a cardboard box on the sidewalk, the size of a small steamer trunk. "Tony was in a great hurry this morning to get to the Black Friday TV sales. On one hand, I'm glad stores in Augustin don't open until nine for Black Friday; on the other, we may be losing customers to the early bird deals the malls offer. In his rush to get to the mall, Tony left me on the curb with this monstrosity. I don't know how I could ever lift it. We do such a good job packing up the holiday goodies after New Year's, I always forget how much stuff we fit in the box." The woman looked Sherry up and down. "You're such a strong young woman. Must be all the good cooking you do."

Sherry considered Mrs. Nagle's description. She was strong, in a casual-exerciser sort of way. She was young, in a midthirties sort of way. She handed the leashes back to Mrs. Nagle. "Of course. Where should I put the box?"

Mrs. Nagle swept her arm forward, indicating anywhere inside the store was appreciated. Sherry grunted as she hoisted the box. She put the container inside the door before her frame collapsed from the strain. She had to remember to either take a different route from the parking lot the day after Thanksgiving next year or get in better shape.

"Phew. Glad we keep our holiday decorations in-store." Sherry straightened and turned toward the open door. "Have a nice day."

"You too. Don't forget these guys." Mrs. Nagle returned the leashes. "I'll stop by to see what you and Erno have on sale for Black Friday."

Without looking back, Sherry tossed Mrs. Nagle a farewell wave. "What are we putting on sale? Good question. Dad is so dead set against Black Friday sales he won't even work the day," Sherry mumbled.

"I'm sorry. I couldn't hear you. Can you repeat what you said?" Sal, performing the same exercise with his key and door as Mrs. Nagle, turned his attention to Sherry as she neared.

"Hi, Sal." Sherry nodded a hello to the elderly man who'd owned the Shore Cleaners for over fifty years. His tiny wife stood vigil over two canvas bags, presumably stuffed with laundry. "I was muttering to myself. You didn't miss a thing."

"Talking to yourself. This crazy time of year will do that to a sane woman."

Sal's wife, Effi, let loose a high-pitched giggle. "Sal!"

"I saw you helping Mrs. Nagle with her box of decorations. That woman is as precise as clockwork. The day after Thanksgiving on the nose, every year, her store goes from autumn's harvest theme to winter holiday extravaganza, and we're all expected to follow suit."

"Guilty," Sherry said. "I'm putting up our decorations today if there's a slow time. Can't help myself. Dad's not working today so I want to surprise him."

"I'm amazed he's not working on Black Friday. I can't resist a good sale, whether I'm on the giving or the receiving end. The cleaners is running a one-day special.

Two items cleaned for the price of one. Some exclusions may apply, of course." Sal opened the door, stepped over the threshold, and held the door open for his wife.

"Dad says he can't witness his rugs sold at a discount, even if it's only one day a year. Says they weren't crafted with half talent, why should they be sold at half price."

"Makes sense," Sal added. "Erno's as proud of his rugs as we are of our family business. Can't say the same for most businesses these days. We're a dying breed."

"I'm sure having the store decorated for the holidays will brighten his mood when he comes in tomorrow. At least, that's what I'm hoping. Have a good day," Sherry called to the couple as she walked away from the cleaners.

As she headed toward the Ruggery, Sherry thought about the Thanksgiving meal she'd served the day before. As wonderful as it was to cook for most of her family, she was still sad her brother, Pep, and his new wife, Charlotte, couldn't attend. They didn't want to travel too far with their infant, but a smile danced on her lips as she visualized the rest of her family seated around the dining room table. Sherry's sister, Marla, Marla's husband, Grant, their father and his girlfriend, Ruth Gadabee. Sherry was thrilled when the lively group gushed over her menu. Well, almost all of the menu. The roasted butternut squash panzanella hadn't come out exactly as she'd liked. How could she enter the recipe, as she intended to do, in the upcoming Holiday Sides Recipe Contest if her own family was lukewarm on the dish? Lost in thought, Sherry found herself at a dead stop in front of a stocky man in uniform.

"May I help you, ma'am?"

Sherry took note of the nameplate pinned to the man's

lapel: *Hans*. She lifted her gaze to his ruddy face, then up to the building sign etched in stone above a massive door behind him. "Oh my gosh. I wasn't paying attention and I've walked too far. While I'm here, I'll introduce my-self." Sherry stuck out her hand. "I'm Sherry Oliveri. To-morrow I'll be a judge in the bake-off here." She shook the man's gloved hand.

"My name is Hans. I'm head of security for the Media Center." Hans cracked a broad smile. "Very nice to meet you. You and your dog have been walking by the building for years. Glad to finally, formally, be introduced. We are very excited to be host to the Story For Glory Cookie Bake-off. I'll be providing security for the event." Hans enunciated the words slowly and deliberately, with a slight Dutch accent, as if he'd practiced hard to memorize the long contest name. "Personally, I'm excited about any leftovers. I've been told to expect fifty-plus contestants bringing their cookies in the morning. I think I'll skip breakfast, just in case I get to taste some of the baked goods."

"You've got the right idea. I'm usually the contestant in a cooking contest rather than the judge, so I'll be get-ting my first chance to taste all the entries this time around."

"How lucky are you?" Hans's eyes brightened as his bushy eyebrows lifted. "Even at my age I'm still a cookie monster. I have tea and cookies with my five-year-old granddaughter every time she visits."

"This bake-off is an interesting one because the cooks prepare their recipes at home. That is a challenge all in it-self, to be able to recognize when you've made your best batch. No time limitations like in the usual bake-off, but you might drive yourself crazy striving for perfection.

The contest is also about the story behind the cookie recipe. To hear where the cooks got their recipe inspiration is what I'm most excited about."

"Sherry. How nice to see you. Good morning, Hans." Patti Mellitt, in a beige overcoat, approached. She was carrying a briefcase and a slouchy tote bag. What appeared to be celery stalks protruded from the bag.

"Patti, hi." Sherry glanced at the greens. "Thanksgiving leftovers?"

Bean and Chutney strained at their leashes to get a whiff.

"Exactly. The reporter who sits next to me in the *Nutmeg State of Mind* newsroom texted she needs celery and did I have any. If I never see another celery stalk until summer, I'll be happy. I made pounds of my famous sausage stuffing with it yesterday for the homeless shelter."

"That's why you're the best food journalist around. You share and you care," Sherry said.

"I'll see you tomorrow at the bake-off, right?" As Patti spoke, she flashed her credentials at Hans, who nodded the okay for her to enter the building.

"Right. Sorry you're not on the judging panel with me. It's my first time being on the judging end rather than the contestant end of the contest."

"That's a story I'd love to write about. How you're making the transition from contestant to judge," Patti said.

"No, no. This is a one-time deal. Competing is my passion. Judging others makes me uncomfortable. I was honored to be asked, and I'll give it my best effort, but I've already got my sights on the next contest."

"Okay, I understand. I'll see you tomorrow. I'm covering the contest for the newspaper and my podcast. May the best baker and cookie backstory-teller win."

"And would you mind writing up a blurb for my Town Hall newsletter also?" Sherry asked. "I'll need your input by Sunday, please."

Chapter 2

"Brace yourselves. Black Friday is about to begin," Sherry told the dogs as she unlocked the Ruggery's back door. She unhooked the dogs' leashes. Habit dictated they remain at her feet until she rewarded them. She treated each to a crunchy biscuit from the jar she kept just inside the kitchenette. A moment later, they were on their way across the store to find a place to wrestle. She flipped on the light switches, took off her coat, and delivered her lunch sack to the kitchenette. She made her way back to the front of the store to unlock the front door and rotated the window sign to "Open." Immediately, a group of potential customers entered.

"I'm so excited to see what you have on sale," one woman said as she surveyed the store. "Where are your sale rugs?"

"I haven't had a chance to put a sale sign up." Sherry

pointed to a small, handmade sign across the room. "Over there. Next to the demonstration table."

The shoppers flocked toward the stack of area rugs, following Sherry's lead. Along the way, she was asked if the larger, hand-loomed rugs were on sale. She delivered the bad news that only the smallest rugs were discounted. Disappointment turned to excitement when they reached the sale rugs. Sherry beamed with pride as the customers complimented her on the treasures they found for less money than at any other time of the year.

By noon, all the sale rugs had been purchased. The last morning customer was gone, so Sherry went to the kitch-enette in the back of the store to retrieve the turkey cran-berry panini she'd brought in her lunch sack. As she savored her first mouthful, the dogs' chorus of barking alerted her that she wasn't alone. She peered out of the arched doorway, then swallowed the bite of sandwich and called out, "Hello. I'll be right there."

"I'm sorry. You're in the middle of lunch. Must be im-possible to get a moment to yourself." A man made his way closer to Sherry. "Please, take your time."

"A bite here, a bite there, and, by the end of the day, somehow, I've finished my lunch." Sherry laughed. She dabbed her mouth with a napkin. "Excuse me one sec." She turned and took the sandwich to the small kitchen counter, well out of reach of the inquisitive Jack Russells' jumping range. She wiped her hands on the kitchen towel and made her way to where the man stood waiting.

"How can I help you?" There was something familiar about the man dressed in a camel-hair blazer and blue jeans. At first glance, she estimated his age to be some-where in his forties. Possibly he was a customer who hadn't been in the store for years. If so, Erno would know the man. Her father never forgot a name or a face. He often attached a nickname to a customer to help jog his memory. The man in front of Sherry would fit the nickname Questioning Man, for the lift in his voice at the end of his sentences, making each sound like a question.

Before he had a chance to respond, the front door burst open. The bell over the door tinkled, and Bean and Chutney raced to greet the visitor. From the dogs' reaction, Sherry knew who had arrived.

"Sherry," shouted the woman. "Your favorite sister's here."

"Over here." Sherry returned her attention to the man. "I'm sorry, my sister is visiting from out of town. May I show you a rug?"

The man stuck out his hand. "You're lucky to have family visiting. My name is Crosby Banks. You must be Sherry Oliveri?"

Sherry shook Crosby's hand. "Yes, that's me. Very nice to meet you. You look familiar. Have we met?"

"Hey, Sherry. I've come to help out for the afternoon. Grant has some things he wants to get done, so I'm flying solo." Marla neared.

"Marla, this is Crosby Banks. Crosby, this is my sister, Marla."

The two smiled at each other.

"I was telling him he looked familiar. If only Dad were here, he'd help me out with where I know you from."

Marla squinted in Crosby's direction. "Nice to meet you. First duty is to walk these two pups. I know you probably haven't had a minute to do that, today being Black Friday and all. Be right back." Marla clapped her hands to herd the dogs her way.

Chutney and Bean trotted toward the leashes hanging by the front door.

Sherry turned her attention back to Crosby.

"Tomorrow, I'll be in the cookie recipe contest. I saw the advertisement in the paper and decided to enter. I read you're a judge. In the same newspaper, I also saw your rugs were on sale today, and I know that's very unusual, so I had to rush in. Lucky me, you're on duty today. I can kill two birds with one stone."

"Ha. You're right. I'm counting on the fact my dad is okay with the rugs I chose to set at sale price. The rugs aren't inexpensive, and this is such a great opportunity for everyone to own one. How could he not like that notion? Speaking of the sale, though, I'm afraid you've missed the chance to own an Oliveri original at a discount. They sold out about an hour ago."

He lowered his head. "My idea of rushing here took a few detours. I regret my lack of punctuality. There goes one bird I can't kill."

"We do have plenty of full-price beauties to consider. Right this way." Sherry swept her hand forward.

Crosby didn't budge. He raised his head, and the overhead lights picked up the pronounced creases around his eyes.

"I had a second reason for coming today. Any chance I could run my cookie recipe backstory by you? I know it's an important part of the recipe contest and while I think I've got a great story, I'm not sure its worthy of a grand prize. Any chance you'd have a listen?" Crosby flashed a shy smile.

Sherry peered around the store to make sure they were alone. "Being a judge in the cookie contest, I can't give any advice one way or another. You understand. If you read the contest rules, you'll get a good idea of what we're looking for in terms of showcasing the origin of your recipe. Beyond that, the ball's in your court, so serve us up something special."

"I came up with the recipe to entice my girlfriend into becoming my wife," Crosby blurted out, as if he hadn't heard what Sherry just said.

"That's a nice story. I imagine there'll be a wide range of stories, so be genuine and you're automatically a contender. That's all I can say." Sherry silently willed him not to pursue the subject any further.

"You haven't changed a bit," Crosby added. "Nice as can be. Even when you were a teenager, you were so kind to your fellow students. That's really saying something. Teens are a tough bunch."

"You knew me when I was a teenager?" Sherry examined Crosby's face.

His graying hair and day-old scruff disguised how he may have looked decades ago.

"Where would you know me from?"

"I was your home economics teacher for a year at Augustin High."

"Mr. Banks? I'm sorry, I don't recall a Mr. Banks." Sherry's head turned in the direction of the tinkling front doorbell.

Marla and the dogs walked in.

"I cut the walk short when it occurred to me where we know you from," Marla called out. "Did you teach at Augustin High?" Marla unhooked the dogs' leashes and freed the pups. She made her way across the store and parked herself next to Crosby.

He nodded. "Sure did."

"Home ec. Not my favorite class but required, so I showed up. I took it as a freshman. Sherry took it as a senior the same year and, surprisingly, almost failed. Right?"

"That's right. Good memory," Crosby replied.

"I didn't recognize your face or your name, to be honest, but your voice is incredibly distinctive," Marla said.

"In a good way, I'm hoping," Crosby said.

"You have a way of ending each sentence with a questioning lilt. I remember the tone of your voice when you lectured so vividly," Marla added. "The students imitated you all the time. Not sure if you knew that or not."

Crosby winced. "Comes with the teacher territory, I'd say. Picture me with brownish hair, a lot more of it, and clean-shaven. Usually with a whisk in my hand, pointing to a recipe on the chalkboard. Teaching that course was my first real job out of college." He put air quotes around the word "real."

Sherry considered Crosby's description of his younger self, and an image of a class of disengaged teens, giggling and goofing off, emerged. Home ec was one of her favorite classes back in the day, and she knew she was alone among her peers in that sentiment. It was considered a waste of time by most students and parents and, years later, eliminated from the curriculum. The class had a revolving door of teachers placed there against their will by the school principal. The joke was, teaching the class was some sort of punishment for a misdeed. Sherry had kept her love of the course content to herself, or so she'd thought.

"Sherry, you said the class was your favorite in four years of high school, remember?" Marla said.

The joys of having a sister with no filter. "It was." Sherry's cheeks heated up.

"I wasn't going to mention the connection to anyone, because Sherry told me, a few minutes ago, she's a judge in the cookie cook-off I'm in tomorrow. Don't want to be under suspicion for favoritism." Crosby flashed a sympathetic smile in Sherry's direction.

"No worries there," Marla said. "Sherry knows most of the competitors, one way or another. Augustin's a small town, and someone's been after her almost every day since the contest opened for entries, for tips and advice on how to win. At least, that's what she told me."

"I was wondering if Sherry thought my cookie recipe backstory was interesting enough, not that I can change it anyway. I can't seem to persuade her to give her opinion, being an impartial judge and all, so would you mind if I ran it by you, Marla? I have a firm recollection of you being someone who isn't afraid of giving your opinion." Crosby laughed cautiously.

Sherry raised her hand, as if she were back in the classroom. "I'm feeling like a fly on the wall, listening to you two talk about me. I'm standing right here, you know."

"Yes, sorry," Crosby said. "In case you don't want to hear my recipe story now, this is your chance to escape. Otherwise, I'm running it by your sister."

Sherry liked Crosby's sass. Her recollection of him as a teacher was vanilla and bland. She had no memory of his wit. She had taken his class because she had to, to fulfill her graduation requirements, despite the fact that, in her early teens, she was already a better cook than most of her friends' parents. To her surprise, the class became her favorite one of the school week. The final examination was to create the perfect meal to serve a family of four. The students didn't actually have to cook it, merely jot down the menu on paper. The only cooking they were required to perform was to present the class with a dozen home-baked cupcakes, and that nearly cost Sherry her diploma. Sherry blinked away the unfortunate memory.

"I'm going to have one more bite of my lunch while you tell Marla your story. Excuse me." Sherry headed to the kitchenette. A few minutes later, she returned as the discussion of Crosby's cookie story was winding down.

"Do you still make the cookies for your wife, for romance's sake?" Marla asked.

"The romance ship sailed long ago. I doubt she'd eat anything I baked at this point. Can't even get her to taste test my cookies for the contest. She's out of town anyway at the moment." Crosby lowered his head slightly.

Sherry brushed a sandwich crumb from her forearm. "Would you like to come over for dinner tonight? The menu is Thanksgiving leftovers, so I don't promise a gourmet meal. Marla and her husband, Grant, are invited, as are my dad and his girlfriend." As soon as the invitation left her lips, Sherry realized the scenario sounded too coupled up. She side-eyed Marla for help.

Marla didn't return the glance.

"That's awfully nice of you. How could I resist a meal from the famous Sherry Oliveri, a former student who has gone on to greatness from humble beginnings in my classroom?" Crosby gave Sherry a respectful bow.

Chapter 3

"All in all, I'd say Black Friday was a success." Sherry inserted the key in the Ruggery door's lock. "That being said, I'm looking forward to enjoying a good meal without having to discuss design, color, and rug dimension."

"Will it mess up the numbers now that Grant won't be joining us?" Marla asked.

Sherry was in a struggle with Chutney and Bean, who were yanking on their leashes to get a whiff of something enticing under the nearest lamppost. "Boys, stop pulling."

Marla scooted the dogs closer to the door with a whistle, and Sherry was able to pull the key from the lock.

"As much as I love Grant, I was relieved he couldn't make it tonight. I was worried Crosby thought everyone was a couple, including him and me. Now the situation is downright awkward, because Dad and Ruth changed their plans and won't be joining us. It's a cozy threesome. You, me, and Crosby."

"And you don't want to have the conversation centered on high school or the cook-off. That's a tall order. Those are the only two subjects we three have in common."

"On second thought, can we persuade Grant to join us?" Sherry asked.

Marla lowered her gaze. "Grant's decided to head back to Oklahoma early and let me have some family time. I haven't stayed in Augustin for more than three days at a time for years. Which leads me to my next question: Is your guest room free for the next couple of nights, starting tonight?"

Sherry studied the face of the athletic, loving, sometimes stubborn woman she'd shared so many childhood memories with. "Yes, of course. Is everything all right between you and Grant? I may be overstepping sisterly boundaries when I say I'm getting a feeling you two aren't enjoying spending time together as much as you used to."

"As you know from your own experience, marriage has its ups and downs, and sometimes when it's been down more than up, a little time off isn't a bad solution." Marla turned and led Bean down the sidewalk.

"In my case, a little time off led to divorce court. But it was for the best." Sherry picked up her pace and caught up to her sister. She paused when she reached the Shore Cleaners red-brick storefront. Sal was stationed opposite the lime-green neon sign announcing the cleaners was open for business. A moment later, the sign went dark.

"Hi, Sal. How was your Black Friday?"

"Hi, Sherry, and Sherry's sister." Sal's well-earned

wrinkles complicated his delicate facial features. "Black Friday. A necessary evil, I'd say. I know how your father feels. We gave away so much free business today, I'm going to have to stay open Sundays and holidays to make up for lost revenue. All in the name of customer appreciation. How about you?"

"I'm very happy with how the day went."

"Before my wife comes outside, let me ask you a question." Sal leaned in toward Sherry's ear. His short stature meant he had to raise up on his tiptoes to best reach her. He whispered, "Effi is entering the cookie contest tomorrow with her Korean fortune cookies. My fear is she'll be crushed if she doesn't win. Despite her tiny exterior, she's a strong, proud woman. Her closely guarded recipes mean more to her than me and our four adult children. What do you think? I have one of our kids on standby to feign sickness and keep her home to play nurse, if need be."

Sherry caught sight of Marla shaking her head ever so slightly. "I would never discourage anyone from entering a cook-off. I bet Effi has a fantastic story to go along with the cookies. Recipe contests are fun, challenging, and, yes, sometimes disappointing when you think you're entering your best effort and you don't win. Tell her to go for it." She backed away from Sal.

"Thanks. I'll take your advice. We'll see you at the contest tomorrow," Sal said.

As Sherry, Marla, and the dogs headed toward the car park, Marla commented, "Good job back there. Aren't you tired of fielding questions like Sal's?"

"I don't mind. This is the first time I've ever judged. I'm getting a better appreciation for the work the judges do and the contest hasn't even happened yet." Sherry laughed. "I'm finding out the job starts way before the contest. I'm a bit worried about what happens after the bake-off. There will be a lot more losers than winners, and they all know where I live."

A voice, bellowing from behind the women, startled Sherry. She reeled in the leash when Chutney began to bark.

"Sorry I didn't get to the Ruggery today," Mrs. Nagle called out from her doorway. "The customers were loading up on holiday lights and extension cords and what-nots. I didn't even get a moment to eat my lunch."

"Must be a good time of the year for your business. Do you have trouble keeping inventory with the wide variety of possible odd requests this season may bring?" Sherry reached the Augustin Dry Goods storefront.

"Actually, no. I have a system that's served me well over the years. I have a list from last year of repeat purchases from November through December. Customers love to be reminded what they may have forgotten to put on their shopping lists. I also keep a separate list of customers who have made very unusual purchases, ones that stray far from their normal tendencies. You'd be surprised how appreciative people are to be looked after this way." Mrs. Nagle beamed a brilliant smile. "I feel like the dry goods grandma to most of Augustin."

"I appreciate you, that's for sure. You and Tony are the ones we count on when we run short of thumbtacks, edging tape, scissors, you name it," Sherry said. "I'll see you at the cookie contest tomorrow?"

"Definitely. Keep a look out for s'mores sandwich cookies. Those would be mine. And if the cooking contest needs batteries for some reason, the Dry Goods store just received a full-assortment shipment."

"Okay, thank you, Mrs. Nagle. I don't foresee needing

batteries, but I'll keep your offer in mind. And tomorrow I'll keep a special eye out for you and your creations."

"Goodbye, ladies," Mrs. Nagle called out.

"Was that a battery bribe?" Marla asked.

Sherry snickered. "Very possibly."

If the drive home was indicative of how many people were returning home after shopping for post-Thanksgiving deals, Sherry was happy she had the role of merchant rather than customer. The local roads were jammed, presumably by cars returning successful bargain shoppers home.

"Shopping isn't my thing, unless you count grocery shopping," Sherry commented. "I'm so relieved the Oliveris have put a ban on exchanging holiday presents."

"I agree. Surprisingly, Grant likes shopping. Or maybe it's his excuse to get out of the house."

Sherry took her eyes off the road long enough to see the frown on her sister's face. She withheld any reply to Marla's comment and, instead, turned the conversation in a more comfortable direction.

"I was thinking of making my Cowboy Turkey Shepherd's Pie for dinner. I was going to try to spruce up the roasted butternut squash panzanella leftovers, but I've changed my mind. I think the recipe needs a total overhaul. I need to figure out how to make it contest-worthy. The contest deadline is looming."

"Hold that thought. We're getting a group text." Marla held up her phone. "From Dad. Says he can come for dinner after all, and Ruth is coming, too. Do you have enough food? Total's up to five now."

Sherry steered the car into her driveway. "Should be fine. Do you think I made a mistake inviting Crosby to dinner? I mean, we barely know the man. He seemed a bit sad. What if he's in the middle of some midlife crisis?"

"Too late now. We're committed. And he may not be the only one having a midlife crisis."

An hour and a half later, dinner was in the oven. Sherry was upstairs, changing out of her T-shirt with the gravy stain down the front and about to begin a search for a clean shirt to match her jeans.

"Sher, your phone's ringing," Marla called from downstairs.

Sherry bounded down the steps with one arm in the sleeve of a sparkly shirt, the other unclothed. "Thanks."

"My hands are wet." Marla pulled the phone out of a kitchen towel. Her sister's sly smile gave Sherry some indication who was calling. "I'll finish the cleanup." Marla made no effort to return to the kitchen.

Sherry took the phone, wriggled past her sister, and made her way to the living room couch, while contorting to fit her arm into the sleeve of the shirt.

"Hi, Don. How was your Thanksgiving?"

"A bit quiet, but enjoyable."

Sherry pulled the phone away from her ear. A blaring horn pierced the earpiece. "What was that?"

"Sorry. I'm at the Augustin Marina. A fog is rolling in. Should be gone in a few hours. Are you free for dinner? Looks like I won't be back on the water for a while, until the weather clears up."

Sherry lowered the phone to her side. She took a few steps toward the kitchen and nearly bumped into Marla, eavesdropping around the corner. "He wants to have dinner. Tonight."

"Invite him over. I need to meet this fellow."

Sherry nodded. "How'd you like to come to my house for dinner? In, say, twenty minutes?"

"A cozy date?" Don asked in a suggestive tone.

"If you call a group of six cozy, then yes."

"Oh no. You had plans. We can do it another time." Don's voice trailed off.

"And those plans include you, so I'll see you soon. Do you need a ride?"

"Nope. Thanks. I'll grab a cab and see you soon. I'll bring wine."

Sherry dropped her phone to her side.

"You look happy," Marla said.

They returned to the kitchen.

"Any guy Sherry Oliveri meets at a cook-off and captures her fancy is a match made in heaven. That is where you met, isn't it?"

"Yes. Don was his sister's sous-chef in the Augustin Fall Fest cook-off. Cooking isn't his field of expertise. He's more of a wine connoisseur. We bonded over his choice of merlots for my recipe."

"How romantic," Marla teased. "It works out better that Don's coming. Crosby won't feel outnumbered by all the Oliveris." She bundled the kitchen towel into a ball. "Can't wait to meet your new fella. I'll take a quick shower and see you in a few."

While Marla was freshening up, Sherry set the table. Her new seating arrangement was to place Don on one side of her and Crosby on the other. She had high hopes the two would find something in common to talk about. Desired subjects to discuss didn't include Sherry's days in high school. Her domestic tendencies might scare Don off. Who would be excited to date someone whose past included trading Rolling Stones concert tickets for a Julia

Child cooking demonstration, as she had in her senior year?

As the last of the napkins were tucked under the forks, Marla descended the stairs. "Guess what? I found our old Augustin High yearbook from the year you were in home ec. No wonder we were fuzzy on Crosby. He was Mr. Currier back then, not Mr. Banks. Wonder why the name change."

Marla tilted the open yearbook in Sherry's direction.

Sherry leaned in and ran her finger across the page. "Mr. Currier, of course." As she studied the photograph of the young teacher standing behind teenagers dressed in cooking aprons, the dogs began to bark.

Knocking sounded through the canine commotion.

"I'll get it. Put the yearbook aside and we'll look at it later. I don't need to be reminded all night how long ago my youth was." Sherry opened the front door and greeted Erno and Ruth.

"We brought pie." Ruth handed Sherry a twine-secured box. "In case you didn't have any dessert leftovers from yesterday. From the Black Friday pie sale at Pinch and Dash, my favorite bakery. Bourbon Pecan Pie." She hugged Sherry, then Marla. "Should be plenty for the four of us."

"Chef Buckman's bakery," Sherry said. "Love that place. He's a judge with me tomorrow at the cookie bake-off. One of the prizes is to have the winning cookie featured at the bakery for a month. That's always so exciting for the home cook, to see their treat for sale."

Knocking resumed on the other side of the door.

"By the way, the head count has increased to six." Sherry saw two silhouettes through the sidelight windows. She reached for the door handle.

When the door opened, Sherry saw the look on Don's

face was somewhere between shock and embarrassment.
Next to him stood Crosby.

"Good evening, Sherry." Crosby placed a bottle of
wine in her hand.

At the same time, Don's hand jutted out, clutching a
bottle of wine. He retracted the gift when Sherry, bottle in
one hand and a pie in the other, shrugged her shoulders.

"Thank you, everyone, for your gifts," Sherry said.
"Marla, can you hold Crosby's gift?" She handed Marla
the bottle of wine.

"Good evening. I hope my last-minute phone call isn't
spoiling your plans. I'm so embarrassed." Don gave a
slight head tilt Crosby's way.

"Don't be. Come in. It's chilly out there. Coats this
way." Sherry collected the bottle of wine from Don.

"It's not too late to disinvite me." Don side-eyed
Crosby.

"Nothing was planned except eating with Marla, and
the number of guests grew from there."

"Okay, you've lost your chance. I'm staying." Don
smiled broadly.

"Good. Don, this is my sister, Marla."

The two exchanged greetings. Don turned his attention
to Crosby.

"Did you two gentlemen introduce yourselves outside?" Sherry asked.

"I was afraid to, in case I wasn't welcome," Don told
Crosby as he extended his hand. "I'm Don Johnstone.
Friend of Sherry's from the cook-off world, and beyond."

"Don, this is my new friend and old teacher—that
sounds odd, Crosby, um . . ." Sherry paused and looked
to Marla for assistance. None came. "I'm sorry, do you
go by Crosby Banks or Crosby Currier?"

Crosby lowered his head and seemed to examine his shoes for a moment before meeting Sherry's gaze. "That's the problem with meeting up with people from my distant past. Too much to explain. Rather than bore you all with a tedious story, I'll simply say my name is Crosby Banks."

Despite her curiosity, Sherry let Crosby's story stay untold. She moved forward with further introductions to her father and Ruth.

"So nice to see you again, Don," Ruth said. "Glad to see you're becoming a fixture at more of Sherry's get-togethers. You know you've finally made her A-list when she includes you in her recipe contest taste testing parties. Right, dear?" Ruth sent a smile in Sherry's direction.

"I can't wait to achieve that status," Don replied.

Ruth shook Crosby's hand and didn't let it drop. "A lovely family named Currier used to live next-door to my dear friend Frances. Are you the same little boy she used to find in her garden loading up his pockets with her award-winning pickling cucumbers? I was at her house at least three times when we escorted you home."

A rosy hue developed on Crosby's cheeks. "I'd wager if two pretty ladies didn't hold my hands and talk so sweetly to me as a reward for ravaging the garden, I wouldn't have done it so many times."

"A man learns early the rewards of bad behavior," Erno commented.

Sherry's guests followed her into the living room, where she took drink orders. When she returned with a tray of full glasses, the topic of conversation was recipe contests. Marla was finishing the story of Sherry's first foray into cooking competitions.

"So impressive you won the first recipe contest you entered." Crosby shook his head.

"I second that," Don added.

"Dumb luck," Sherry said. "I found an advertisement for the contest, whose theme was what can you make with a piece of bread. I've always loved French toast, so I made Orange-Dusted French Toast Fingers with Maple Dipping Sauce. Typed up the recipe and mailed it to the listed address. A few months later, they sent me two thousand dollars and I was hooked on recipe contests."

"Amazing. When I moved to Long Island for a few years, I lost track of your successes. But since I've moved back, I've on the Sherry cook-off bandwagon." Crosby took a sip of his beer.

"Where in Long Island did you live? I live in Pine Needle Point," Don said.

"I lived for a brief time in Canopy Cove. Couldn't be any closer."

"If you still lived there, I could have given you a ride home. I've got my boat in the marina. If the fog's lifted, that's how I'm getting home. Otherwise, I'll hop on the train and have to return for a boat pickup," Don explained. "I should probably keep one boat on Long Island and another in Augustin for just these circumstances. I'm just kidding, but it is food for thought."

"If you're serious about the idea of two boats, I may have an offer for you. Let's talk later," Crosby said.

"How exactly did you meet up with Sherry after all the years since high school?" Erno asked.

"At your store, actually." Crosby beamed a smile in Sherry's direction.

"More important, did you purchase a rug? I'm told

Black Friday is the day to get a bargain." Erno cleared his throat and glared at Sherry.

"I took a look at your beautiful rugs. Now's not the time, because I'm between addresses. But I will certainly have an Oliveri masterpiece in my home once I'm settled."

"I like the sound of a potential sale." Erno laughed.

"I sought your daughter out for some advice on the backstory of my bake-off cookie recipe. She couldn't divulge any information, but it got me a dinner invite."

"Speaking of dinner, it's ready," Sherry said over the ringing of the oven's timer. "Take a seat in the dining room, and Marla and I will serve."

Chapter 4

"Hey, Marla, I'm leaving you this message because I didn't want to wake you when I left this morning. I peeked in on you, and you looked so content. Help yourself to anything you find in the kitchen. So happy you're staying on a few days. My house is your house. If you want to meet me at the Nutmeg News Media building in about two hours, the cook-off should be winding down by then. Or I'll be at the Ruggery in the early afternoon. I'm rambling. Text me. See you soon." Sherry clicked off her phone and placed it in her purse. She fished her driver's license out of her purse.

"Morning, Hans." Sherry held up her license to Hans's square-jawed face.

Hans studied the license, glanced at the clipboard he was holding, and penned a checkmark. "Yes. Sherry

Oliveri. Second to arrive. Take the elevator to the third floor. The entire floor is an enormous meeting room, where the contest will be held."

"Thank you." Sherry stuffed her license back in her purse.

"Save some leftovers for me, please. I'd say, 'good luck,' but I'm sure you don't need it."

Sherry took a moment to reply. "Oh, I think I'll need it." Sherry softened her tone and leaned in toward Hans. "Between you and me, I'm pretty nervous. I'm not really sure what to expect, being on the other side of the decision-making process. I have the sudden urge to declare all the contestants winners."

"The bakers know there can only be one winner," Hans said in a soothing voice.

"Technically, a winner and a runner-up. Doesn't make my job any easier." Sherry headed inside the building.

"Okay, then. Good luck," Hans called after her.

Alone in the lobby, Sherry pressed the button for the third floor. As the elevator doors opened, Sherry was reminded of the baking contest she'd entered on a whim, years ago. Back then, her hope was that her baking skills had improved as her other culinary skills blossomed. Wrong. The theme of the baking contest was creating innovative recipes out of a boxed baking mix. Simple, she thought. Most of the dry ingredients' measurements were premeasured and contained in the box. Easy. All she had to do was put the Sherry spin on the ingredients after pouring them into a mixing bowl. Some ground almonds, condensed milk, lime, toffee bits. Sounded delicious on paper. Sherry felt confident enough to not even practice her creation one time. Big mistake. She served the contest judges a gooey, sloppy mess drizzled with broken, seized chocolate. Years later, baking still wasn't Sherry's forte, and here she was, judging others' baking skills.

"Sherry Oliveri?" A voice echoed through the cavernous room.

Sherry blinked away the memory of her baking disaster. She scanned the room to locate the voice. At the far end of the room, three tables were set up to form a horseshoe. A down vest was slung over the back of one of the chairs. Another table sat alone off to the side. A man in a white Oxford shirt, crisp, cuffed dark pants, and a bow tie waved in Sherry's direction.

"Judges' table is down here." The man waved until she lifted her hand in acknowledgment.

Sherry's flats tapped across the shiny wooden floor as she made her way over to the beckoning man. Sherry was met halfway across the room.

"Warren Yardsmith, editor in chief." Warren extended his hand and shook Sherry's. "Hans alerted me that Sherry Oliveri was on her way upstairs. I'm honored to have you join our judging panel today."

"Thank you for the invitation."

"My colleague, Patti Mellitt, food journalist extraordinaire, sings your praises constantly. If it were up to her, we'd have a section of the paper dedicated to following your every move." Warren pointed out one of three chairs. "Here is where the magic happens. If you'd like the middle seat, it's all yours. The cooks, their creations, and their wonderful stories should be ready to go in about thirty minutes. Take some time to check out the prize table in the alcove around the corner. The contestants are welcome to take a photo in front of it before the competition begins, for a bit of last-minute motivation. Excuse me." Before Sherry could respond, Warren was on his way across the room.

Sherry settled in her chair and took in the scene. It wasn't long before he returned, accompanied by a robust, bearded man in a chef's coat. Sherry rose out of her chair.

"Chef Buckman, this is . . ." Warren began.

"Sherry Oliveri, of course." The chef kissed both of Sherry's cheeks. "You put Augustin on the map in the cooking competition world. So nice to meet you. Please, call me Barry."

Sherry had no idea the award-winning pastry chef would know her from anyone. Unable to formulate an appropriate response, she greeted the chef with a broad smile. After a moment she responded, "Thank you. So nice to meet you. Your bakery put Augustin on the bakery map." She grimaced at the lame statement, in all its lack of originality. Her subsequent thought was, did the chef know how inadequate she was at baking?

She had no time to ponder the question as Warren asked the judges to take their seats. People were filtering in and filling the open space in front of the judge's table.

"My secretary, Gina, will hand out the score sheets and a printout of the contestant recipes. And pens, too." Warren waved a woman forward.

Her long skirt swooshed from side to side as she moved her slight frame toward the judges. She lowered her eyes to see through the reading glasses poised on the end of her nose. "Take a look at each row on the score sheets. For each cookie and story, assign a score of one to five in the corresponding box. One sheet per entrant. Keep the score sheets upside down in a pile until the final contestant. You will then have a moment to organize the sheets from highest to lowest scores. You will find a copy of the recipes in the papers in front of you."

Sherry received her pile of score sheets from Gina. "Thank you."

She scanned the rows of judging criteria: whimsical recipe title, overall taste, mouth feel, crumb texture, eye appeal, use of interesting ingredients, and the story behind the cookie. Her stomach fluttered. "I'm going to have to put aside all my empathy for what the contestant went through to get to this stage of the contest," she commented to no one in particular.

One glance from Barry's kind eyes gave Sherry the calm she needed. "Just be your honest self."

By the time Sherry finished reviewing the score sheet, a crowd of bakers and their cookie trays had filled the spacious room. The bakers took seats in a designated section of chairs. The room quieted down when Hans brought a microphone to the judges' table.

Warren received the mic from Hans. "Good morning, bakers, and those who love baked goods. Welcome to the Story For Glory Cookie Bake-off. I am Warren Yardsmith, editor-in-chief of the *Nutmeg State of Mind* newspaper, and one of the contest judges. To my left is esteemed judge Sherry Oliveri, reigning National Mushroom Cook-off champion, reigning America's Good Taste Cook-off champion, and Augustin's reigning Fall Fest Cook-off champion, to name a few of her titles. That's a lot of reigning, Sherry."

The audience agreed with a round of applause.

"To my right is our third judge, Chef Barry Buckman. He's been recognized for his series of dessert cookbooks and has appeared on multiple televised cooking shows.

His local bakery, Pinch and Dash, is currently rated number one in all of New England.

"At last count, we have fifty-three entrants who have brought their best cookie creations to be judged. Along with their cookies, the bakers will share the story behind the recipe."

The crowd murmured in hushed tones.

"Sounds like you're all as excited as I am to hear those stories."

The crowd clapped.

"The prizes today will include a total of three thousand dollars, trophies, plaques, having the winning cookie featured at Chef Buckman's fabulous bakery, and a ride on a float in the holiday parade down Augustin's historic parade route."

The crowd erupted into more applause.

Warren received the loudest applause when he concluded with, "May the best cookie recipe and story win."

With the introductions out of the way, the fifty-three contestants stood in silence as the first baker was called up to the judging table.

"Justine Deloise. Please bring up your Salted Caramel Tassies and tell us your cookie recipe's story of origin," Warren announced over the mic.

Sherry welcomed Justine and her platter of cookies with a warm smile. Justine offered each judge a cookie from her platter before taking her position in front of the trio. Sherry examined the cookie. Her discerning eye immediately noticed the cookie edges were a tad overbaked. She made a mark on her score sheet in the row labeled "visual appeal." Or, she suddenly considered, did a burned edge fall into "recipe execution?" The problem with pens, she thought, was the lack of an eraser. She crossed out the number two assigned to the improper box and made a decision not to score further until Justine's full presentation was complete. Maybe the burned edge was part of the backstory.

Barry tipped his head toward Sherry. "Please hold off on scoring until after the contestant leaves," he whispered.

Sherry moved her hand over her score sheet, obscuring the crossed-out section.

Warren stood and positioned the mic under the baker's mouth. "And how did your recipe originate, Ms. Deloise?"

Sherry listened closely to Justine's complicated story. Each judge simultaneously took a bite of the cookie they held. The baker described how elements of the recipe came from her grandparents, her travels during college, which must have been many years ago, and the loss of a parent. After Justine's voice broke when describing the therapeutic effect of pecans and caramel, Sherry saw the cloyingly sweet, overbaked treat in a different light. Considering the roller coaster of emotions Sherry had been put through after only the first contestant, she resigned herself to the fact this morning was going to be intense.

"Thank you. If you'll step over to the waiting area next to Hans," Warren pointed to the edge of the room, "we will score your entry." He sat back down.

Sherry set pen to paper. When the judges put their pens down, it was time for the next contestant.

Warren passed Sherry the list of contestants. He pointed to the second baker.

"Effi. Effi Forino. Your turn to bring up your cookie and your story." The room hushed, but no one came forward. After a moment, Sherry called the name again.

"She's a little nervous. May I walk her up there?"

Sherry recognized Sal's voice. For a petite man, he could project his voice like a trained actor.

"Of course," Sherry answered without consulting Warren. She leaned Warren's way as the couple stepped forward. "The Forinos are a lovely couple who own the oldest cleaners in town."

"But will her cookie clean up?" Barry added with a playful lilt to his voice.

"Sherry, Effi is really nervous. Would it be okay if I stand next to her? I won't say a word. Promise." Sal's arm was around his wife's shoulders.

Sherry glanced at Warren, who nodded.

"Mr. Buckman, your cleaning is ready. I had the dickens of a time getting your chef's coat clean. You'd be surprised how much pomegranate juice I clean out of white garments this time of year. You must be running a special on pomegranate desserts. Your coat was especially challenging, but the Forinos never give up on a stain."

"Thank you, Sal. That's why you're the best," Barry replied. "Sherry, would you hand Sal the mic, please? He can hold it for his wife."

"These are my Peppermint Snowballs." Effi offered the powdered-sugar-dusted white clouds to the judges. "I was going to prepare Korean fortune cookies, but I had a sudden revelation to go with a holiday recipe."

When her story was done, Sherry had a tear trickling down her cheek. Escaping her native country as it was racked in turmoil, with nothing but the shirt on her back and her family recipes tucked in her pocket for good luck, brought the room to silence. Only sniffling could be heard as the judges gave Effi's story its due consideration. Sal returned the mic to Warren.

"Thank you to you and your husband," Warren said. "Please join Justine over on the side."

Sherry smiled at Effi and handed the contestant list to Barry. As he perused the list, Sherry scanned the waiting contestants for any sign of Mrs. Nagle. There was none, but it was hard to see through the milling crowd from a seated position. When the list came back to Sherry, she'd check to see if the woman was among the bakers.

"Crosby Banks. Please bring up your Tropical Dream Bars," Barry announced.

Crosby offered the plate of bars to Sherry first. His expression appeared grim when a smile should be what greeted the judges. Barry on one side, and Warren on her other, leaned back in their chairs and traded hushed comments behind Sherry. Was she missing some important observation they were getting from the cookie's appearance?

Sherry turned her attention to Crosby. His expression was somber. Must be nerves. Sherry hoped to catch Crosby's eye and send him a "smile for the judges" subliminal message, but he was fully focused on his cookie platter. Sherry read the printed recipe from the pile of papers stacked in front of each judge before examining the cookie bar.

"Coconut, macadamia nuts, oatmeal, lime. Can't get much more tropical than that," Barry commented. "We sell a bar like this in our bakery."

"Not much risk being taken here, but it's quite tasty," Warren whispered between bites. "And the story behind the cookie bars is?" Warren stood and held the mic for Crosby.

Crosby assumed a rigid stance. The crowd hushed.

"These cookies changed my life. I was in a dark period

when I wasn't feeling fulfilled. What I realized was missing from my day-to-day existence was giving back. So, I went down to our county's homeless shelter and talked to a few of the patrons."

Sherry's line of sight tangled with Crosby's. He gave her a subtle nod.

"I'd always loved to bake. I even taught home ec for a short time, many years ago. Now, I teach business classes, but baking is still how I share the love. I'm not afraid to experiment in the kitchen, so I invented a recipe to transport those homeless folks out of their tough situation, if only for a few minutes. I choose my ingredients with care. The coconut is to inspire travel beyond your dreams, the white chocolate represents thinking outside the box, which people should do to achieve success, the macadamia nuts are an example of breaking out of your shell so great things will find you. The bars were a hit at the shelter. I gave back, but received more in return than I can say. Thank you." Crosby bowed his head.

The judges turned to one another. Sherry listened as Barry and Warren spoke over each other in quiet tones about the backstory.

"Anything you want to say, Sherry?" Warren asked.

"Interesting story." Sherry mulled over her score sheet choices until she felt the gazes of the other judges on her. She gave all aspects of the cookie high marks. She gave the story behind the cookie recipe a two. She pushed the contestant list toward Barry. "Next."

Sherry nodded to Tia Garcia as the mayor's personal assistant responded to her name being called. A moment later, the woman was facedown and sprawled out, her cookies crumbled across the floor.

There was a collective gasp among the onlookers.

Sherry stood. "Tia, are you okay?"

Tia sat up gingerly. She winced as she took in the sight of her cookies in bits all around her. "I'm fine. Slipped on something."

"We'll take a break while we get this attended to," Warren said. "Judges, this might be a chance to use the restroom, if need be. Hans and I will help Ms. Garcia."

"I'll run to the restroom and be back to help with the cleanup."

"Thanks, Sherry." Tia rose from the floor. "I'm so embarrassed."

Moments later, the contest resumed, with Eileen Weisberger called up to the judging table.

"That's my neighbor," Sherry whispered as Eileen winked in her direction.

"You know everyone." Barry laughed. "Someone's not going to be happy there's only one winner."

Sherry pinched her eyes shut to fend off the guilt creeping in. She reopened her eyes. "Toughest lesson in cooking competitions is not taking the judgment personally."

An hour and a half later, the Story For Glory Cookie Bake-off presented the last contestant. Penny Nagle. The woman carried her cookie tray forward and gave each judge one of her s'mores concoctions. While Sherry was happy to see Mrs. Nagle, she eyeballed her cookie with trepidation. Her waistband had grown so snug she had to unfasten the first button on her pants. The glass of water she had refilled twice sat empty in front of her. How was she going to get this sweet treat into her mouth and give it the consideration it deserved, knowing her dislike of s'mores? She was brought back to the time when, as a child, she'd eaten so many of the campfire cookies in one sitting she became ill. The sight of them turned her stomach.

"I hope you like it. Everyone does," Mrs. Nagle said with an air of confidence.

Sherry nibbled the corner of the cookie and was pleasantly surprised when the bite went down smoothly. Mrs. Nagle never took her sights off Sherry, making the process less about scoring the cookie and more about willing a happy face to mask Sherry's growing nausea. To Sherry's relief, her cookie's backstory was brief. Warren thanked the baker and she left the table.

Having signed off on the last score sheet, Sherry rearranged her papers in order of highest score to lowest. As she waited for the next step in the process, she mentally weighed the pros and cons of being a judge versus a contestant in future cook-offs. The cons came easily to mind. She preferred being a contestant. Before she settled on the first pro, Warren asked for her score sheets. At the same time, Eileen caught Sherry's attention by waving from the back of the room. Not wanting to appear biased before the results were made public, Sherry returned Eileen's wave with a slight grin.

Sherry rotated her chair to join the judges' huddle. This was the portion of the contest Sherry and all her fellow cooking contestants were most curious about. She had always wondered if the debate got testy, as opinions most certainly differed. Not everyone likes dried cranberries in their cookie. Some liked crisp texture, while others preferred chewy. Dark chocolate or milk chocolate preferences—the recipe creator's choice could make or break the recipe. She let the other two judges begin the conversation.

"I have a clear winner," Barry blurted out with no

preface. His expression challenged the other two to present the same conclusion.

The back-and-forth Sherry was bracing for never materialized.

"Me, too." Warren's nonchalance made Sherry question whether either of the men had considered all the aspects of the judging criteria spelled out in the contest rules. "And you, Sherry?"

Sherry cleared her throat. It was difficult to sound authoritative in a hushed huddle, but she attempted to do so. "I have narrowed down my choices to three."

"If it's the homeless shelter story that got you, me, too," Barry said. "I just found his recipe too safe. He didn't make my final three."

"Exactly my feeling," Warren said. "I had him in my final three, but he was eliminated based on lack of innovation. If anyone thinks cookies can't be reinvented, think again. That's the beauty of recipe contests. The creativity that is born from people's stories gives new life to stale recipes." He pointed to the tables of cookie platters beside the judges. "Cookies with black pepper, potato chips, pretzels, avocado—we got 'em all. And if the story can match or exceed the cookie, we have a winner."

Sherry shook her head. "No, he wasn't in my final three. I found his story overly dramatic, almost unbelievable, but I really enjoyed his bar," Sherry said.

"Effi Forino's story was heartbreaking and inspirational. Unfortunately, she fell short on the cookie execution," Barry added. "She was in my final three, but I eliminated her."

Sherry made a quick scan of the crowd in the room. "Okay. I've made up my mind. Taylor Underhill. His story about how he baked Mocha Java Whoopie Pies for

DOUBLE CHOCOLATE COOKIE MURDER   41

his kids' bake sale while his wife recovered from a difficult childbirth won me over, as did his cookies. They were fantastic."

"My choice is Eileen Weisberger," Barry said. "Her Gingerbread Pawprint Cookies captured the essence of the holiday season. Her touching story of how her newly adopted, curious kitten trampled the just-baked cookies, creating a pawprint indentation perfect for a filling she didn't know the cookie desperately needed, was magical and otherworldly."

Warren held up a score sheet.

"And I see she's Warren's choice, too. By a vote of two to one, I'd say she's the winner, with Taylor Underhill as runner-up."

"Eileen's going to be thrilled." Sherry paused before saying softly, "Although I don't really want her to know I didn't vote for her to win."

Chapter 5

Warren pushed back his chair and stood. He lifted his hand over his head, catching Hans's attention. Sherry and Barry stood beside him. Hans made his way to the side of the judge's table and lifted his arms. The room quieted down. Mic at his lips, Warren extended a second greeting to the crowd of people.

"Thank you all for attending the Story For Glory Cookie Bake-off this year. We hope to make it an annual event. We're certain there are many more bakers with creative recipes and stories to share. Everyone did a fantastic job making this year's contest a success. Give yourselves a round of applause."

Warren passed the mic to Barry. "It was a difficult decision, but we have chosen a winner. The winning cookie and story were presented by Eileen Weisberger of Augustin, Connecticut. Our runner-up is Taylor Underhill from Westerly, Rhode Island. You all heard their stories and you'll have to take our word for the fact that their cookies were glorious. Let's give these two bakers a warm round of applause."

The crowd cheered and a woman shrieked. Barry handed the mic to Sherry.

"I'm assuming that's you sending up a whoop of delight, Eileen."

A round of laughter traveled throughout the room.

"Come on up, Eileen and Taylor, to receive your prizes." Sherry looked at Warren when she realized there were no prizes in sight. She lowered the mic. "Where are the prizes?" she whispered.

Warren beckoned Hans with a curled index finger. "Hans, would you roll in the prize table, please?"

Hans left the room through a side door. While he was gone, Eileen and Taylor made their way to the front of the room. Congratulations was offered by the judges in the form of hugs and handshakes.

"We have plaques for the winners, and two cash envelopes, one containing a check for twenty-five hundred dollars and the other containing the runner-up check for five hundred dollars. Also, a trophy depicting the holiday parade float Eileen will be riding on, and the certificate stating Eileen's cookies will be featured at Chef Buckman's Pinch and Dash Bakery for one month."

The audience burst into a hearty round of applause.

"Sherry! I'm so excited. I've never won anything based on talent in my life, except maybe bingo." Eileen leaned across the judges' table and took both of Sherry's hands.

"Remind me how you two know each other?" Barry asked.

"She's my neighbor," Sherry shared. "No bias involved in my judging, though. I take impartiality very seriously."

"Obviously. You didn't even pick hers." Barry's eyebrows lifted when Sherry winced.

"Well, someone did. That's all that matters." Eileen leaned in closer to Sherry. "I'll ask you later why I wasn't your choice." Eileen dropped Sherry's hands and took Taylor's, raising his with hers above their heads.

Hans grazed the edge of the table as he sprinted to Warren's side, knocking the stack of recipes to the ground. "Sir, the prizes aren't where we discussed they'd be," he announced when he was able to catch his breath. "Did someone move them without notifying me?"

Warren's smile drooped. "I knew we should have hired a second security guard."

Eileen stepped back from the table. "Our trophies are gone?"

Hans nodded.

Warren lowered his voice to a whisper. "Hans, call the police. And please have Gina continue the search." He returned his attention to the audience. "In the meantime," Warren lifted the mic to his lips, "congratulations, Eileen and Taylor. Thank you all for participating in the contest today, and I hope to see you next year. Our apologies for the prize mishap. It may take some time to locate the prizes, so we may present them at another time." Warren lowered the mic. "We will contact you both as soon as this is straightened out. Again, congratulations."

"Do I still get to ride on the holiday parade float?" Eileen asked.

"Of course. And we'll reissue your prize checks if the mislaid prizes can't be located. I can't imagine what's happened to them," Barry added. "Let's give Hans and Gina a chance to see what they can come up with."

After a few minutes of the judges and the winners trading ideas for next year's bake-off, Hans returned to Warren's side.

"Mr. Yardsmith, no luck. And the police are here." Hans tipped his head in the direction of the door.

Sherry could make out two uniformed officers scanning the crowd by the room's entrance.

"I'll have a word with the police, although I really have no idea what happened to the prizes," Warren said. "Someone must have miscommunicated procedures. The police are here as a formality, in case it's more than a mix-up." Warren left the table and was soon swallowed up by the crowd.

Eileen and Taylor were poised to accept directions from either Sherry or Barry, but none were forthcoming. After an extended silence and an exchange of puzzled looks, Sherry instructed the contestants to collect their cookie platters and enjoy the remainder of the day.

"Do you need a ride anywhere?" Barry asked. "I have my car in the municipal lot."

"Thank you. I'm all set. My car's in the lot, too. It was nice working with you. A strange ending, but hopefully it will sort itself out and go down in the history books as a success."

"I agree." Barry pushed his chair toward the table. "Big success, despite the kinks."

Sherry collected her purse from under her chair. "Cooking competitions always have a snag or two. That's what makes them a challenge. I remember at the National Chicken Cooking Contest, the oven I was using to bake my Maple-Sriracha Chicken blew a fuse and . . ."

"Excuse me, Sherry?"

Sherry turned to face an approaching woman. She didn't recognize her as a baker in the contest. As the woman neared Barry, he leaned close to her ear and said something Sherry couldn't make out. He backed away and waved goodbye without expressing interest in hearing the conclusion of Sherry's story. He'd heard one too many personal tales today, she concluded.

"Yes, hi." Sherry studied the woman's face, which was lined and stained by sun exposure, yet very pretty at the same time.

"Hi, my name is Rachel Currier."

"Nice to meet you, Rachel." Sherry paused. "Currier. We had a contestant named Crosby Currier today. Crosby Banks, actually. But I knew him as Crosby Currier many years ago. Any relation?"

"Yes, my husband. I believe you might have had him over to dinner last night, isn't that right?" Rachel said with an edge.

Sherry glanced over the woman's shoulder in hopes of locating someone she knew who might provide an excuse to escape this awkward conversation. No such luck. Before she could ask why Crosby had told her Rachel was away when clearly she wasn't, Rachel took the conversation in another direction.

"I'm so glad you didn't choose Crosby's cookie as the winner because it's not his recipe. It's his long-suffering mother's. I don't know where he came up with the story that he baked the cookie for the homeless shelter. If he did do that, he's a changed man." Rachel tucked her highlighted blond hair behind her ears, revealing stunning diamond earrings.

Between absorbing the woman's revelation and taking

in her showy ear accessories, Sherry's tired brain left her speechless. She had no desire or strength to enter into a conflict.

After a moment, a reserve surge of energy kicked in. "As judges, we have no way to verify the stories the bakers told us. All we could do is sit back and enjoy them. You know, that wasn't his first story about where the cookie recipe came from."

"I'm not at all surprised he may have changed his story," Rachel replied. "How do you know he had another story?"

"At dinner, he told me a completely different one, despite the fact I asked him to please not tell me before the contest. He said he baked the cookies to woo you to become his wife."

Rachel lowered her gaze to the floor and sighed.

"Is Crosby still here?" Sherry asked. "I wanted to congratulate him on his delicious cookie, even though he didn't place. The competition is always tough at a baking contest. I'm so envious of the bakers who can master baking these delicious treats. I'm still trying to master baking a decent chocolate chip cookie."

"Huh," Rachel scoffed. "I don't believe you're not a wonderful baker. And no, Crosby's left the building. He's on his way to his car, pulling his carryall behind him."

"Sherry, can you join us over here?"

Sherry scanned the room to locate who was calling her name. Warren was waving from the front of the room. A sense of relief flowed through her when her excuse to end the conversation materialized.

"Excuse me, Rachel. I'm being asked to join Warren Yardsmith. Was there anything else you wanted to say?" Sherry backed away from Rachel.

"I'm going to stop into your store soon," Rachel said.

"Please do. If you've never been in, you're in for a wonderful experience."

Rachel's eyes widened, as if searching Sherry's words for something beyond a simple answer. "See you, then."

Sherry made her way through the thinning crowd. She found Warren sandwiched between two police officers. Barry stood a few feet away.

"No sign of the prizes," Warren said, "but the officers would like to know if you have any information to add. Like, did you notice any disgruntled contestants? Barry already gave a statement."

"No disgruntled contestants at all. Maybe Eileen and Taylor, when they didn't get their prizes." Sherry laughed.

The officers held their steely gazes on Sherry. She put on a serious face to match their demeanor. "Honestly, the mood in the room was happy and festive. I can't imagine what happened to the prizes. Every possible place in the building was searched?"

"Still searching as we speak, but why would the prizes be out for public viewing one minute and gone the next, without a trace?" Warren shrugged. "They were there when the bake-off was about to begin. I saw them. They were definitely stolen from the table."

"We don't have much to go on, but we'll do our best," one of the officers said. "Thank you for your time."

"You're welcome. Wish I could be of more help." Sherry shifted her attention to Warren. "Thank you again, Warren. I'll be checking in to see how the search for the prizes plays out." Sherry headed to the elevators. She joined the line for the ride down and immediately realized she was standing behind Effi and Sal.

"I hope you two had a nice time this morning. Your cookie was fabulous," Sherry said.

The couple turned around and gave Sherry a warm smile.

"I almost fainted from nerves," Effi said. "Now that it's over, I can't wait until next year. I can see why Sherry loves recipe contests."

Sal kissed his wife on the cheek.

Chapter 6

The next day, Sherry awoke with a renewed sense of purpose. The alternative perspective that she'd gained from being a bake-off judge had given her a feeling of untapped creativity just waiting to be put to use in future recipe contests. She was also excited to spend the day with her sister. Sherry was rinsing out her coffee mug and cereal bowl when Marla came into the kitchen.

"Good morning." Sherry greeted Marla with a big smile. "Help yourself to coffee and cereal. Guess what we're doing today?"

"Good morning to you, too. I can't imagine what you have in store for me."

"We're going grocery shopping because you're helping me make a new and improved version of roasted butternut squash panzanella for the Holiday Sides Recipe Contest. The entry deadline is in four days."

"Hasn't your motto always been, if you've tried a recipe for a contest a few times and it's not coming together, time to scrap it?" Marla asked with a note of caution.

"I thought about moving on to a new creation, but I'm not a quitter. Seeing all those people yesterday who'd baked their hearts out inspired me the way people tell me I inspire them. And I'm a tad bit competitive. It'd be like giving up on a problem child. Can't be done. Just ask Amber, the family therapist. This recipe is a problem child, and it demands special attention."

"You're never going to slow down, are you?" Marla's tone was more a statement of fact rather than a question. "I thought that was your goal for the new year."

"Definitely. Just let me get past the holidays. I promise to lighten the load."

"You don't have to promise me. You're the one complaining about lack of sleep, difficulty with decision-making, and exhaustion. To me, you're describing just another day in my life."

"I really do need to pare down my schedule. Three part-time jobs at last count, and more hobbies than Martha Stewart. Poor Chutney's not getting the attention he needs, and I barely have time to figure out this recipe. I think I've got a cook's version of writer's block, because I try to get too many things done at the same time."

"Changing the subject," Marla made a slight grimace, "would you mind if I stayed on for maybe the entire week instead of a few days?"

Sherry's enthusiasm stalled. She took a good look at her sister's expression. The worry lines across Marla's forehead had become pronounced.

"Is something the matter? Why have your plans changed?"

"Grant and I aren't agreeing on anything. A few extra days apart is our holiday present to our relationship. Plus, I'm feeling a sudden case of the Augustin homesicks."

"Here I am, talking about my silly problem of being too busy, and you've got real problems. Of course you can stay here as long as you like. Absence will make the heart grow fonder between you two, mark my words."

"I don't really want to talk too much about the situation, if you don't mind. I'd love to do whatever you had planned," Marla said in a soft voice.

"We don't have to make my contest recipe. What was I thinking? Only about me, obviously. What would you like to do today? Let's do something you'd like to do."

"It wouldn't be a visit to your house without a recipe trial. I'm all in. Give me a minute to eat something and brush my hair and I'm good to go."

Sherry sat with Marla as she ate her breakfast. "Haven't seen Eileen outside all morning, which is unusual. She's a fixture outside, weeding, planting in her front yard, or walking her cat on a leash. Hope she's not too upset about the missing prizes."

"She'll be fine. She's such a lovely person. I'd think she'd be happy with a win and a handshake. Plus, from what you told me, she was most excited to ride on the holiday parade float, and no one can steal that away from her."

"You're right. And she gets her cookie featured at Chef Buckman's bakery. She had a good story and her recipe was really tasty. I'm so proud of her." Sherry beamed. She took one last glance across the street to Eileen's empty front yard. Sherry checked the time on her phone. "Would you like anything more to eat or drink before we get going?"

"No thanks. I can tell you're chomping at the bit to get that recipe sorted out. I'll take my coffee to go." Marla laughed.

"In that case, let's get going."

At the market, the sisters decided on the divide-and-conquer approach to knocking off the items on the grocery list.

Sherry handed Marla her assigned portion of the recipe ingredients. "See you in a few."

Marla disappeared behind a display of seasonal baking ingredients. Sherry pushed her cart up and down the aisles, looking for Dijon mustard, balsamic vinegar, and the best extra virgin olive oil. The final item on her list was pumpkin seeds. She scanned the pouches of nuts and seeds in aisle eight until she found what she was searching for. She waited for a man to finish sorting through walnut pouches so she could reach the pumpkin seeds.

When he stepped aside, Sherry did a double take. "Warren?"

The man turned and faced Sherry. "Long time no see. The grocery store is the last place you'd think we'd be after eating all those cookies yesterday. I'm still not completely rid of the sugar rush." Warren held Sherry's gaze longer than she was comfortable with. He lowered his voice. "Quite a coincidence to see you here, as I just received a call with some news you'll be interested in."

Sherry reached for her pumpkin seeds and dropped the pouch in her basket. She hoped the news wasn't personal or negative in any way. After listening to word of Marla's marital difficulties, a second hit of sour relationship news in one morning might fully snuff out the competitive fire in Sherry's belly.

"Breaking news comes with the territory of running a newspaper. I'm being updated with good and bad news from multiple sources all the time. It's rare the police call, though."

"Have they found the prizes? I'd love to inform my neighbor, Eileen, if they have."

"Yes, the good news is the prizes have been found."

"That's great news. Or is it? Are they damaged?" Sherry hoped no bad news was to follow. "Where in the world were they?" She presented a smile in anticipation of the potentially amusing anecdote Warren was about to deliver.

"The prizes were found in a car at the Augustin Marina."

"The Augustin Marina? That makes no sense. Have the police figured out why they ended up there? And again, are they in rough shape?"

"They're all okay. The police are doing their best to fit together the puzzle pieces concerning how, why, and when. But that was only part of what the call was about." He paused and shifted his bag of walnuts. "One of the bakers from the contest was found dead on the Augustin Marina's property."

Sherry clutched the handle of her cart to steady herself. She shuddered. "Dead? Who? When?" After the words left her mouth, she silently chanted, "Not Eileen, not Eileen. Why weren't you in your front yard plucking weeds this morning where you always are, rain or shine?"

"I realize you were familiar with many of the contestants, so I hope the news isn't too much of a shock."

Sherry squeezed her eyes shut.

"Remember the man with the story about baking his cookies for a homeless shelter? His name is Crosby Currier. He went by the name Banks in the bake-off. Crosby Banks."

Sherry took a moment to process the name. "Oh, no. Crosby?"

"You did know him. I'm sorry."

"Barely, but yes. That's awful. What happened? When? Where?" The questions tumbled out of Sherry's mouth.

"I know you have a lot of questions, but I don't have all the answers. The police said his time of death was not long after the bake-off."

"I'm so sorry for the man and his family. Was there an accident or did he have a medical condition of some sort?"

"Neither. I'm afraid he died from neither of those. Police said they have every reason to believe he was murdered."

"Murdered?"

"He had blunt force trauma to his head, and he was tied to an anchor," Warren said. "Not in the water, but close to the pier. Behind the dockmaster's shed."

"Could have been an accident. Maybe he tried to move the anchor and took a fall? Sounds like he somehow got tangled in the anchor's ropes." The questioning tone of Sherry's voice did little to convince herself what she was saying was plausible.

"No question he was put in that awkward scenario against his will, the police said."

"And what about the prizes? Whose car were they found in?" Sherry asked.

"Crosby's."

"Crosby had the prizes in his car? That doesn't make sense."

"Unfortunately, yes. Another lost piece to the puzzle of why he would have stolen the entire prize package. Needless to say, the prizes are now being processed as evidence and won't be returned for some time."

Sherry winced. "Crosby, what have you done? He seemed like a nice man. What am I saying? I know he was a nice man." Sherry visualized Rachel's pinched expression when talking about her husband. "Obviously, not everyone thought so."

"Seems so."

"Did the dockmaster see anything? Maybe he's the murderer."

"No use guessing at this point. There's already a Detective Ray Bease on the case. He'll get to the bottom of it all. When I get back to the office, I'm going to do some research. I know the Curriers have been in our paper a few times, and I need to remind myself what for. Got to get going. My wife, Culli, has the flu, so I'm in charge of dinner. I came very close to not being able to judge the contest yesterday. I gave her a dose of nighttime flu medicine before I left for the bake-off, and she didn't even know I had been out when she woke up." He glanced at the piece of paper in his hand. "My to-do list. I now have a greater appreciation for all the errands my wife runs throughout the day. Next up is the cleaners."

"Good luck finishing your to-do list," Sherry said. "Hope your wife feels better soon."

"Thanks." Warren waved his bag of walnuts in Sherry's direction and turned to leave the aisle. He pivoted back. "If you see Eileen, tell her I'll be in touch about the prizes."

Sherry was so lost in thought she couldn't produce the words to bid Warren farewell.

"You look concerned. Is something wrong?" Marla emptied her armload of items into their cart.

Sherry pointed down the aisle. "That's Warren Yardsmith, editor of the *Nutmeg State of Mind*, walking away. Just got some shocking news from him."

"Wasn't he a judge with you yesterday?"

"That's right. He said Crosby Banks was found dead at the marina, not long after the bake-off, and it's looking like he was murdered." Sherry's voice trembled as she relayed the information.

"No. Way. We all ate dinner together two nights ago. And now he's dead? That's so bizarre." Marla shook her head.

"To say the least." Sherry stared at her cart. "I'm done, are you?" Without giving Marla a chance to respond, Sherry hurried the cart to the checkout line.

Chapter 7

"I'll take this call and be right in. Here you go. Take the key." Sherry handed Marla the house key. She reached for her ringing phone. "Can you stick the key on the front hall table when you get inside, please?"

"Will do." Marla scooped up two of the grocery bags and left the car.

Sherry punched the Accept Call key. At the same time, Sherry heard Eileen shout a greeting to Marla, loud enough to be heard through the car's closing door. Sherry twisted around to get a look at her neighbor. Eileen threw Sherry a wave from across the street. She was walking her cat, Elvis, on his leash. The relief that swept over Sherry when she saw her neighbor momentarily diverted her attention away from the caller.

The deep voice coming through the phone brought her back to the matter at hand. "Sherry? Are you there?"

"Sorry, yes. Hi, Don. How are you?"

"Great. Sounds like you're busy, so I'll be brief. Can I tempt you and your sister to take one of the final boat rides of the season with me? I was thinking of dinner at the Clam Shack. It's a bit chilly out on the water, but that just makes it all the more adventurous." Don's voice was dripping with enthusiasm. He clearly wasn't going to take no for an answer.

"You water lovers are a hearty bunch." Sherry considered how to say no without hurting the man's feelings. She had about as much desire to go boating in late November as she did to get a root canal. As she considered a "no thanks," the new relationship endorphins kicked in and "no" became "yes." She was reminded of how, in the relatively short time Sherry had known Don, his ability to mysteriously persuade her to participate in activities outside her comfort zone had become one of the traits she admired most about him. She liked to believe she was getting in the habit of letting whatever happened happen. Marla labeled the phenomenon, "giving up control," while Sherry labeled her newfound flexibility "maturation."

"Sure. Sounds nice. On the early side would be best. I have to work tomorrow."

"As do I," Don replied. "See you at the marina around six?"

"Perfect. See you at the marina. I'll be the one resembling the Michelin Man in my many layers." She laughed. She stuffed her phone in her purse, grabbed the remaining grocery bag from the back seat of the car, and made her way to the house.

When Sherry entered, she relayed the essence of Don's phone call to Marla. Initially, her sister, too was hesitant about Don's invitation, but for different reasons. She described herself as a third wheel. It wasn't long before Sherry convinced Marla that her presence wasn't only desired but mandatory.

"How long have you been dating Don?" Marla unpacked the butternut squash cubes from the reusable grocery bag.

"I wouldn't exactly label our relationship 'dating' at this point." Sherry paused and reassessed. "Actually, yes, when we get together, it is a date. There you go, I said it."

"Convenient he lives on Long Island. Not that far away. What a coincidence. Crosby lived one town away from Don at one point," Marla said.

"The two said they didn't know each other until they met here at dinner. Long Island's chock full of people. Chances they would know each other were slim to none."

"Remember, Crosby said he was only on Long Island for a few years. Not long after his short stint at Augustin High."

"Crosby said he lived most of his life around Augustin. His last job was teaching business courses. I have a feeling there's more to his story than he was willing to get into with an unfamiliar crowd." Sherry eyed the mismatched size butternut squash chunks on the cutting board. "The cubes need to be uniform dice cuts. Any volunteers?"

Marla raised her hand. One by one, she trimmed the cubes into equal-sized cubes as Sherry unpacked the remainder of the ingredients.

When she was done, Marla scraped the butternut squash cubes from the cutting board and spread them across an oiled baking dish. "I'm going to visit the ladies' room. Don't finish the dressing without me. I want to see how you make it."

Sherry sprinkled the squash with maple syrup, olive oil, garlic powder, chopped rosemary, sea salt, and pepper. She preheated the oven.

Marla's distinct heavy footsteps announced her arrival back in the kitchen. "Look what I picked up in the living room. The yearbook from your senior year. I want to take a look at Crosby's picture." Marla flipped through the pages, while Sherry wiped her hands clean. "Here we go. Mr. Crosby Currier, home economics. He looks like he's twenty here."

Sherry sat beside Marla for a closer look. "He couldn't have been much older than that. Wonder why the name change to Banks? And when? Maybe his move to Long Island had something to do with the name change? His wife uses the name Currier. She introduced herself to me at the bake-off. Rachel Currier. Doesn't make sense."

"You met his wife? The one he wooed into marriage with his cookie recipe? By the way, did the other judges like his story?"

"That's another mysterious thing. He didn't use the cookie recipe story he told us at dinner the night before the bake-off. He had a different story about baking the cookies for a homeless shelter, a story his wife hinted may not be accurate. She sought me out after the bake-off and told me both the cookie recipe and the story weren't his."

"It crossed my mind people might be tempted to embellish their cookie stories. But to have your own wife rat you out? That takes some guts."

"Who knows? Rachel, his wife, may have told him not

to use the original story. They didn't seem to be on the best of terms. Crosby said she was out of town when she wasn't, and she didn't have anything nice to say about him. Doesn't speak well for the status of their marriage."

"So, they're having some difficulties. I know what that's like." Marla cocked her head to the side and gave her full attention to the yearbook.

Sherry walked the seasoned squash over to the oven. She set the timer for twenty minutes.

"Do you think his wife killed him?" Marla asked.

"Knowing nothing more about the man than what I've learned in the past forty-eight hours, she would be at the top of my list. Can I see the yearbook?" Sherry wiped her hands on the kitchen towel.

Marla handed over the weighty book. Sherry examined the home economics class picture. Two rows of teenagers mugged for the camera with bowls, spatulas, whisks, and plates in their hands. Sherry, front and center, an apron across her lap. Her face was content and relaxed, while the boy next to her appeared to be elbowing her in the ribs. The memory of the shenanigans that boy engaged in during class produced an involuntary groan. Crosby put up with a lot during his one year at Augustin High. If more of the students took his class as seriously as Sherry had, she silently bet he'd have stayed longer. "Wonder why he only taught one year at Augustin High?"

"Hard to say. Let's get down to business and create your special dressing for the panzanella."

Sherry closed the yearbook. The oven timer beeped as she put the heavy book on the edge of the counter. As she glanced at the timer, the yearbook tumbled to the floor. Sherry reached down and righted the book. The pages that lay open in her hands captured her full attention.

"Right here. Crosby signed my yearbook. 'Sherry, you were the top student in my class and I nearly had to fail you. Years from now, you'll know I was only doing what was required of me. When you become rich and famous for your cooking exploits, think of me, your biggest fan.—Mr. Currier.'"

"That wasn't the nicest thing he did," Marla stated, with a matter-of-factness that stung Sherry.

"I know. He passed me so I could graduate, even though I failed the baking portion of the final exam. Everyone knew I was the best cook in the class. As for my baking skills, yikes. But he kept my baking disaster a secret until I was able to get the test passed on the third try. And that was with his assistance at every step. Probably why I still can't bake a decent cookie to this day. No one helps me."

"Your cookies are decent, they're just not great." Marla laughed. "You can't be great at everything."

"Baking is all about exactness. I prefer to fly by the seat of my pants when I cook. That's my culinary style. It's served me well in cooking competitions, and I'm not about to change so I can become a great baker. Let someone else have that title. Now, can we get back to the task at hand, please?" Sherry set the yearbook in a more secure location.

"Are you going to take the squash out of the oven or listen to that darn timer beep all day?"

Sherry donned her oven mitts and removed the butternut squash. The cubes were browned on the edges. The maple syrup and olive oil bubbled on the orange vegetable, while the rosemary released an earthy aroma. She then poured balsamic vinegar and a touch of maple syrup into a small saucepan and heated the tangy liquid to warm. After the vinegar simmered for a while, the liquid thickened. She whisked in a touch of Dijon mustard and olive oil. "Dressing's done, except the sea salt and pepper to taste."

"That's the easiest dressing ever." Marla sucked a drip of the dressing from a spoon she dipped in the saucepan. "Love that it's warm."

"Maybe too easy. I'll warm it again when I serve the complete recipe. The squash will cool while we take the dogs for a walk," Sherry suggested.

"Good plan. I'll hook them up to the leashes." Marla went to the front hall, followed by two excited Jack Russells. A moment later, the front door opened. Marla called out, "Sherry, there's some guy parked out front, staring at the house."

Sherry wasted no time wiping the last of the dressing from her hands and running to the front door.

"Anyone you know under that hat?" Marla asked. "Seems very interested in your house."

"I figured he'd be showing up eventually." Sherry left the house and walked to the gray sedan parked on the road.

Ray rolled down his window. "Sherry, how are you?"

Sherry opened her mouth to reply, but wasn't given the chance.

"I need to discuss something with you. Is this a good time?"

"Hi, Ray."

"Is that your sister?"

Sherry extended her arm in Marla's direction as she approached with Chutney and Bean. "Marla, you know Ray."

Marla waved her leashed hand. "Nice to see you, again. I think." Marla laughed. "Be back in a few." She continued down the sidewalk, led by two sniffing noses.

"What would you like to discuss, as if I didn't know?"

Ray exited his car and faced Sherry. She was reminded their relationship had inauspicious beginnings. Their first meeting was when he'd pegged her as the prime suspect in a murder investigation. There was something different about him since their last encounter, though she couldn't put her finger on it. That was until he moved to within arm's length. His signature well-worn tan hat was no more. He was wearing a fresh hat, devoid of frayed edges. His appearance could be described in one word—spiffy. He was as clean-shaven as Sherry had ever seen him. She also noted the laugh lines etched around his mouth had softened.

"How's your mother? Last time we spoke she wasn't feeling well but was accepting her move into the senior-care facility." Sherry took care to deliver the question with sensitivity.

"She passed away a few months ago." Ray removed his hat, squinted as the sun washed over his face, and immediately put the hat back on. "She had a good life."

Sherry studied the detective's expression. Despite the loss, he exuded contentment. "I'm so sorry for your loss."

"Appreciated." Ray shuffled his feet and firmed up his stance. "Back to business."

"Of course."

The man was never one to demonstrate vulnerable emotions. "I've been assigned a murder investigation. A man, aged forty-four, was murdered yesterday at the Augustin Marina. Uncovering the whereabouts of his last few days led me to the bake-off in which he was a contestant and you were a judge. I would like to ask you what you may have observed concerning Crosby Currier there."

Sherry took her eyes from Ray and located Marla in the distance. The two dogs were waiting at the bottom of a tree, and Sherry was willing to bet it was for a squirrel to reappear.

"He was like every other baker there. Excited, nervous, and I believe he came to win. Nothing out of the ordinary when it comes to cooking contests. Believe me, I've seen some weird stuff over the years. This bake-off ran very smoothly, except for the disappearance of the prizes."

"Okay, and that was your first time meeting Mr. Currier?"

"No. He was my teacher for a year when I was in high school."

"Your teacher?" Ray asked.

"Yes."

"Interesting. You knew he was in the bake-off prior to the day of the contest?"

"No, not until he stopped into the Ruggery the day before. He sought me out because he wanted my opinion on the story behind his cookie recipe. Big component of the bake-off. One thing led to another, and we had a nice dinner with Crosby, my family, and my boyfriend the night before the bake-off. Got rid of all my Thanksgiving leftovers."

"Dinner? And did you say 'boyfriend?'"

"Yes and yes."

"When Crosby was at your house or at the store, did he seem agitated, moody, depressed?" Ray asked.

"Neither of those times did I observe any unusual behavior." Sherry closed her eyes to visualize Crosby telling his recipe story, once at her house and the second time, an entirely different story, at the News Media building. When she was done, she opened her eyes. "At dinner, he seemed fine. Happy, though maybe a bit reserved. He knew some of us from long ago, but we're all different people now. The next day he seemed excited to be in the cookie bake-off."

"Okay."

"One thing I did find odd was his name change. When he taught in high school he was Mr. Currier. Somewhere along the line Crosby changed his last name to Banks."

"He may go by Banks, but his legal name remains Crosby Currier. Seems more trouble than it's worth, correcting people constantly when one wants to suddenly introduce oneself by a new name."

Behind Ray, Marla approached.

"Can you think of any unusual moods or mannerisms the man had? Anything he might have said that raised a red flag?" Ray asked.

Before Sherry could respond, Marla said, "Crosby was nice and polite as can be. He and Don got on especially well. He even sold Don his unloved boat."

"Don?" Ray asked with a nonchalance to match his body language.

"Sherry's boyfriend," Marla added.

"That's right," Sherry said. "Crosby and Don got on so well at dinner, they shook hands on the sale of Crosby's boat. Don is now the proud owner. Well, soon-to-be owner. After money has changed hands."

"Buying a used boat is buying someone else's troubles and making them your own. At least, that's what I've heard. I think Crosby was the smart one in that deal," Ray suggested. "Any mention of his wife? Crosby, that is, not your boyfriend."

"For your information, Don has never been married. Not unlike yourself, Detective. You'd like him, I bet."

Ray sighed. "You haven't changed a bit, Sherry. Still can't stay on one subject for any length of time."

Marla snickered.

"As for Crosby's wife, he said she was out of town. Beyond that, he didn't offer any information on his personal life, and I didn't go searching for any. I'm not good at getting too personal, too quickly. We kept the conversation mostly about cooking and high school," Sherry replied. "And boats."

Marla nodded in agreement.

"I met his wife, Rachel Currier, at the bake-off. I suppose she was there to cheer him on," Sherry said. "Have you spoken to her?"

"In a preliminary interview. Much like this one," Ray replied. "She wasn't forthcoming and wouldn't speak unless she had a lawyer present. I'm working around that for the time being. Let me ask you a question. Is it unusual for an ex-wife to attend her ex-husband's bake-off?"

"Ex? Now you're telling me they're divorced?" Sherry asked. "Crosby definitely wasn't forthcoming with us."

"Ten months, legally divorced. Legally separated a lot longer than that," Ray said.

Sherry decided against sharing the details of Rachel's negative comments concerning her ex-husband. If there was anything Sherry had learned from Detective Ray Bease, Hillsboro County investigator, after four murder investigations involving cook-offs, was never to assume. Assuming Crosby's marriage was a bad one and might have led to Rachel killing him was something to consider, but that was yet to be determined. Ray had a hard-and-fast dislike for speculation.

"What was your opinion of Rachel Currier?" Sherry asked.

"My opinion has zero to do with the case. But, off the record, she's the kind of lady who makes me glad I never married. Enough said."

"Wonder what kind of lady you've been looking for all this time?" Sherry knew the question would be ignored.

"The contest prizes were found in his car, which was parked in the visitors lot at the Augustin Marina," Ray stated. "Two trophies. Two checks. A plaque and a certificate to ride a float in a parade. The question is, why he would want the prizes without the actual win? The checks were the only things of monetary value, and they weren't filled out or signed, so they couldn't be cashed anyway."

"The editor of the sponsoring newspaper was planning on signing the checks when he presented them to the winners."

"Good move, if you ask me, not to presign the check. Otherwise, because the winner's name can't be filled in until the judges make their decision, the checks would be open to anyone filling in their name if they were to be stolen."

"I heard the prizes were found. My neighbor, Eileen, won the bake-off, and I have to tell her they'll be contacting her about the missing-then-found prize situation."

"She may not be so happy when you tell her the prizes are part of the evidence package and can't be given to her until the police are finished with them," Ray said.

"Just don't take her ride on the holiday parade float away from her or you'll really feel her wrath."

"If the prize was evidence, the department would need it, and your friend would have to understand."

"The question is, why was Crosby murdered? Why was an anchor tied to him?" Sherry shuddered.

"So, you do know that detail."

"Yes. Awful."

"His body was found by the Augustin Marina dockmaster. A man named Vitis Costa. He'd been dead for over an hour, although the time-of-death window may be widened for various reasons. The outdoor temperature was chilly. His body was in and out of the direct sun as a shadow moved across his torso. An exposed corpse warms and cools quickly with fluctuating air temps, making the time of death harder to pinpoint. Best early estimate is death occurred somewhere between one and four in the afternoon. The bake-off had been over for a few hours by then, correct?"

Sherry nodded. "That's right. It ended before noon." Sherry twisted her face into a grimace.

"Something you're remembering?" Ray asked.

"Crosby did have a rolling carryall at the contest. Good place to store prizes if one was to steal them. But most of the contestants had carryalls, too. I take one to every cook-off. It's how the contestants transport their cookies and platters unscathed."

"Did anyone serve the judges cookie crumbs because they had an accident on the way to the bake-off?" Marla asked with amusement in her voice.

"Only one casualty getting to the judges' table. Poor Tia, the secretary over at the mayor's office, tripped and went down hard. Her cookies and plate broke into a million bits. The contest was halted for about fifteen minutes while the cleanup crew worked their magic." Sherry visualized the downtrodden contestant as Hans helped the embarrassed woman clean up the mess."

Ray buttoned his oversized overcoat. "Getting cold out here."

Sherry and Marla exchanged glances. "I know, and we have a boat ride to take. Going to need lots of layers."

"Let me guess. With the boyfriend, the new boat owner?"

"Not sure why he needs a second boat, but yes. Soon-to-be new, second-boat owner if the deal is still on. He hasn't completed that transaction yet. Held up by Crosby's sudden passing. A bit of a stretch in terms of my interests, but the new, adaptable me is giving life on the water a try." Sherry laughed. "Actually, this is my first boat ride with him. He's taking us to the Clam Shack. You order ahead, pull your boat up, and eat out on the veranda. Hope it's heated."

"Have a good time. Stay warm and dry." Ray checked his phone. "You know how to reach me if any of your fellow cooks or judges has any information to share about Crosby Currier." He turned toward his car.

"Wait a second, Ray. I have a question."

He swung his head around toward Sherry.

"When I talked to Rachel Currier at the bake-off, she was anything but Crosby's biggest fan. I can't even imagine why she was there. She spoke so negatively of him."

"And your question is?"

Sherry glanced at her sister before returning her sights to Ray. "Never mind. No question. Bye, Ray."

Chapter 8

"I can't get involved," Sherry said with an air of certainty. "I've got too much on my plate, as usual. I made myself a promise to slow down the pace of my life and relax more. Don gave me some advice I'm trying to take to heart. He said, 'If, at the end of the day, your brain is more exhausted than your body, you aren't enjoying life to the max.' I didn't get it at first. Now I do, and he's right. How can I take on a murder investigation when I have a part-time job at the Ruggery, edit the town's newsletter, compete in cooking contests, and have a budding relationship with a man I probably don't deserve? Let alone a dog to care for, a community garden board to sit on, and a father, a sister, and a brother to keep an eye on. I hardly know Crosby Currier, or Banks, or whatever name he goes by."

"Don't need to convince me," Marla said. "I was merely confirming the obvious. You have too much on your plate to go looking for another murderer. I only mentioned it because you've seemed a bit distracted since we talked to the detective. You haven't even wanted to finish the panzanella recipe."

Sherry heard Marla's words and made up her mind to let her thoughts of Crosby and Rachel go. The investigators would unravel the murder. Ray was the best around.

"You're right. That's the last you'll hear about Crosby's murder from me," Sherry vowed. "What do you want to do this afternoon before we get back to the recipe? Don's picking us up at the marina later, so we have a few hours to goof off." Sherry winced. "If that's the new relaxed me talking, I'm not sure I can stand myself. I haven't goofed off in twenty years."

Marla burst into laughter. "Let the goofing off commence. I've booked us a tennis lesson and we have to be there in forty-five minutes, so let's go take a look at what workout clothes I can borrow from you. It's going to be a tight squeeze to get your tiny-sized clothes on this Oklahoma-sized body, but I'm up for the challenge."

Hours later, Sherry and Marla had their feet up on the living room ottoman. They were resting their showered and casually attired bodies on the couch after their tennis game.

"I'm vowing, here and now, to play more tennis in the new year." Sherry raised her phone to her face.

"I'm vowing to play more than once a year in the new year."

Sherry lowered the phone. "Change of plans. Don texted and wanted to move dinner up because the weather's taking a bad turn later. I was hoping we could finish the butternut squash recipe before dinner and taste test it, but no time now. He's already on his boat on his way to the marina." Sherry heaved her tired body from the couch. She reached for Marla's hand and yanked her upright. "Let's go bundle up."

Sherry checked her reflection in the front hall mirror. "Windbreaker, check. Fleece jacket, check. Hats, gloves, check, check."

"Are we going out on a boat or visiting the Arctic Circle?" Marla snickered. She stuffed a scarf in her coat pocket.

"Think it's too late to cancel? I may be setting a bad precedent with Don. He may get the idea I'm in some way adventurous. Who knows what he'll ask me to do next?"

"Yes, it's too late. It's good for you to get out of your cozy, small-town comfort zone." Marla opened the front door.

Chutney and Bean attentively watched their every move.

"See you soon, puppies. If we're not back in a few hours, send for the authorities."

"Don't even joke about that." Sherry followed her sister outside. "Nothing bad will happen."

The sisters stuffed their cold-weather supplies in the back seat of Sherry's car and set off for the marina.

"Augustin is such a pretty town." Marla gazed out the window. "Maybe I should move back."

An icy wave of emotions swept through Sherry's core.

Sadness combined with empathy for her sister's predica-
ment. She glanced at her hands clutching the steering
wheel. "You can't just pick up and leave your husband
without a fight."

"Aren't you the pot calling the kettle black, or whatever that saying is? Or does the saying 'don't throw
stones while living in a glass house' apply?" Marla laughed
softly. "You and Charlie split up after seven years of marriage and that's the mile marker Grant and I are at. At the
moment, I'm not serious about moving here, but no
telling what the future holds."

The rest of the drive was spent in silence. As the car
pulled into the marina's parking lot, the last of the day's
sunlight peeked out over the harbor. There was only one
other vehicle in the lot, a vintage pickup truck. Sherry
and Marla gathered their protection against the elements
from the back seat and went inside the harbormaster's
shed.

Before the screen door slammed, Sherry took an ad-
miring glance at the orange and yellow horizon. "I assume we'll be heading west if we're eating in Seaport.
The setting sun will be gorgeous. Marla, look at those
seabirds. They're so lovely." Sherry pointed out over to
the water behind the shed.

Marla faced the water. "Gorgeous."

"'If birds fly low, expect rain and a blow.' That's an
old sailor's adage." A weathered face that hadn't known
much if any sunscreen in its lifetime, greeted them inside
the small building. The man didn't smile. Instead, he surveyed Sherry and Marla from head to toe. "What can I do
you for?"

The shed was nearly filled to capacity with the three

adults. When the space heater hummed to life, it wasn't long before the temperature rose to an uncomfortable high in the confined area.

Sherry, in her many clothing layers, quickly began to overheat. "We're meeting a boat driven by Don Johnstone. He's taking us out to the Clam Shack before the restaurant closes for the season. Do we wait for him in here or outside on the dock somewhere?"

"And you two would be?" The man drew out the words, as if speaking to a lost child. He picked up a clipboard.

"Sherry Oliveri, and this is my sister, Marla." Sherry added, "And you are?"

"Vitis Costa. Dockmaster." The tone of his voice was a low rumble. "Yes, I see on the harbor log, Don Johnstone has reserved the visitor slip for his boat, *Buy-Lo Sell-Hi*, for the next half hour. Hope he's not late. I have another boat coming in for the evening. Only one slip available these days. And word to the wise, you best not be caught out on the water when the storm blows in."

"We trust Don knows what he's doing. He'll have us back before any bad weather," Sherry said with a slight break in her voice.

"We're counting on that," Marla added. "Is Don bringing the boat he bought from Crosby?"

"No. He doesn't own that boat yet. He's not quite a two-boat owner yet."

Sherry watched Vitis study his clipboard. "What do you do when there are lots of visiting boats?"

"They can anchor out at the buoys and radio in. I pick up the passengers in the dinghy, my fancy water taxi," Vitis replied.

Sherry peered through the wall-wide window behind

Vitis, overlooking the harbor. No sign of a boat arriving. "Vitis, how long have you worked here?" Sherry couldn't pinpoint his age. Her best estimate was early sixties, but he could be an excessively sun-kissed fifty-five.

"Twenty years."

"I see this framed article about the marina next to the clock." Sherry pointed to the yellowing newsprint enclosed in a decaying frame mounted on the wall.

Marla took a step closer to the framed article. She had to contort around the edge of a corner desk to get a better look. "This is an old article. I'm guessing before your time here, Vitis. Says there was a fire here?"

Vitis looked out the window behind him. He turned back with a deep scowl. "Wasn't here during the fire, though. You're young if you don't know anything about the fire. Or you're landlubbers."

"The second is the truth," Marla responded. "I wish the first was, too."

"I put the article up on the wall because the town's younger generation complains about the lack of facilities here. The kids want fancy and they're getting austere. What can I do about the past? Nothing. If they'd like to contribute to the rebuilding fund, they can put their money where their mouths are."

"We're not complaining." Sherry was eager to break Vitis's train of thought. "Just interested in the marina's history. Neither of us has much boating experience. Well, none really."

"The Augustin Marina was nearly totally destroyed by a fire around twenty years ago. It spelled the end of the Augustin Yacht Club and the prestige the club enjoyed up until that point. It's never been restored to its full potential, and now the big boats go elsewhere to dock. We don't even dredge the harbor anymore. Town says they can't afford it. We feel like second-class citizens when we used to be masters of the domain." Vitis's nostrils flared as he shook his head slowly.

Marla leaned in farther. "I'm having some trouble reading the faded type, but the article says a man named Lonnie Currier was the dockmaster at the time. Currier. Is that any relation to Crosby Currier?"

Sherry glared at Marla in hopes she'd discontinue the conversation fueling Vitis's irritation, but the subliminal message went unreceived.

"Yup. Crosby is his son. Imagine my shock when I was informed it was his body tied to the marina's anchor. Dead as that stuffed swordfish mounted on the wall." Vitis pointed to a huge fish arched across a mounting board, hanging on the wall by the door.

"Did you become dockmaster right after the fire?" Sherry asked. "Or did Lonnie Currier stay on?"

"Lonnie left his job soon after the fire. No sense sticking around when there were no boats coming and going. The marina wasn't functional for half a year. That's when I came on board. Plus, there was some debate about how the fire started and whether it was intentionally set. Personally, I think Lonnie wanted a career restart somewhere else."

"The fire wasn't an accident?" Marla asked.

"Never was resolved one way or another." Vitis shrugged. "Everyone's got a different theory."

"Sounds like the town decided rebuilding the marina wasn't a priority," Marla added.

"Yep. By the time I took over as dockmaster, the job was part-time. Summers and weekends only. That's it.

Depending on the weather, we may be open until mid-December or closed as early as December first. No longer year-round, like when Lonnie was here."

A boat's horn howled in the distance.

"This might be your ride."

"I'll go check. I can't get a good look through the window." Sherry rushed to open the shed door. She slowed her pace when she recognized the tall man at the helm of the approaching boat. His auburn curls protruded from under his knit cap. He waved and she made her way to the visitor's slip on the dock.

Additional overhead lights came on as the boat neared. Don threw Sherry a rope, which, to her surprise, she caught with one hand. He motioned for her to tie the rope around a dock cleat.

As Sherry considered the best way to keep the boat from drifting away, a voice startled her.

"I can help with that." Vitis collected the rope from her and spun a tight knot around the cleat, securing the boat. "Good afternoon, Mr. Johnstone." Vitis's baritone voice sliced through the low vibration of the boat's idling motor.

Don cut the boat's power. "Good afternoon, everyone. Hey, Vitis." His smile lingered in Sherry's direction. He secured a second line to the dock and leaped off the bow. "Brisk out there. But refreshing."

Sherry studied Don's rosy complexion.

"I'm dressed in layers." Blotches of white across his cheeks affirmed her suspicion the wind chill temperature was bone-chilling.

"Me, too." Marla cozied up to Sherry.

"Vitis, I'm gonna need another life jacket or two, if

you wouldn't mind me borrowing a couple." Don sported a reflective life jacket over his parka. "Need an extra-large to fit over all those layers."

"No problem. Let's go try a few on." Vitis extended a hand toward the shed. Sherry, Marla, and Don proceeded in that direction.

Outside the shed, Don dug through the bin of life jackets, handing his choices to Sherry and Marla to try on.

"Meet you all back at the boat," Vitis announced as he left the threesome sorting out sizes.

After a few minutes, Sherry was satisfied with their flotation fashion. They accompanied Don back down the dock, where they found Vitis talking on his cell phone.

"I always thought boat wear was so cute. I might have been mistaken. I feel like a stuffed turkey, and I'm sure I look like one." Sherry laughed.

Marla patted her sister's well-padded tummy area. "You kind of do, which means I do, too." Marla lifted her eyes from Sherry. "We're not the only turkeys on the sea tonight."

Sherry gazed beyond Marla to where another boat was idling within arm's length of Don's boat.

Vitis held his palm toward the boat, phone still at his ear. "Sorry I missed you. Come find me next time." Vitis put his phone in his pocket and cupped his hands around his mouth. "Hold your position. One minute. They are leaving." He turned back to Don. "They're early. Must have seen the forecast."

Sherry squinted at the woman standing on the neighboring boat's deck. "Who is that, Marla? I'm sure I know her."

Marla shook her head. "Couldn't tell you who either one of them is."

"That's Mrs. Currier. She's a fixture around here," Vitis said. "And the chef from Pinch and Dash Bakery is at the helm."

"Crosby's wife?" Marla asked Sherry in a soft whisper. "And Chef Buckman?"

"Ex-wife. Yes, that's her." Sherry didn't take her eyes off the boat. "And he goes by Barry."

"If you can pull over here, these fine folks will be heading out soon." Vitis positioned himself toward the elbow of the dock. The makeshift docking spot he pointed out would serve well temporarily, although Sherry calculated the boats to be only a wave's distance apart and vulnerable to possible collision.

"No rush." Barry adjusted his furry, mad bomber hat.

Vitis tied a line to a cleat and Barry cut his boat's motor. "Sherry Oliveri. What a pleasant surprise."

"Hi, Barry. Hi, Rachel." Sherry took a few steps closer to the boat. With a better view of the boat's stern, she made out the name of the vessel, *Sugar*. "Rachel, I'm so sorry for your loss. You must be beside yourself with grief." What kind of thing was that to say, when she obviously wasn't beside herself with grief at all? She was enjoying time out on the water with a friend. The same friend Rachel had had a close word with after the bake-off.

"Thank you, Sherry. Our family is devastated by Crosby's untimely death. You probably think I'm heartless, taking a boat ride the day after my ex-husband passed away, but each of us copes in our own way."

"I can't even imagine," Sherry replied. "This is my sister, Marla, and my friend Don, who both had dinner with Crosby before the bake-off." She vigorously waved Marla and Don over to Barry's boat.

Marla rushed over. "Nice to meet you. Sorry for your loss."

Don repeated the sentiment.

"How was it out there?" Sherry asked. "I'm a bit of a reluctant boater when it's not eighty degrees and sunny. I could use some encouragement."

"You sound like Crosby," Rachel scoffed. "He never wanted to go out on the water. That was the final deal-breaker for me. We ran out of commonalities."

Sherry cringed slightly before adding, "Crosby was once my teacher in high school. He encouraged me to pursue my love of cooking, which I came to appreciate many years later. I'm grateful to him for that."

Barry threw a tow line to Vitis, who guided the vessel farther forward, giving Don's boat ample clearance.

"You knew him at his peak," Rachel said. "He went downhill after his teaching career ended. I should never have married him. I thought I could change him, and that's an awful mistake to make."

Don cleared his throat. Sherry fought the urge to look his way because she knew he wanted no part of this awkward conversation. A number of questions for Rachel ran through Sherry's brain. Instead of asking any, Sherry bid Barry and Rachel farewell. The three returned to Don's boat. Vitis cast off the lines.

Buy-Lo Sell-Hi rumbled to life, smothering Sherry's attempt to pursue the previous conversation about Crosby.

Don backed the boat slowly away from the dock. Everyone waved and the marina grew smaller as they puttered away. "Take a seat, ladies."

Sherry and Marla nestled together in the cushioned seat next to the captain's chair.

"Why are you sharing a seat?" Don asked.

"We're cozy," Sherry replied. "Helping each other get our sea legs."

"Whatever makes you two sisters feel secure, but I'm a safe driver. I promise."

Once they passed the final buoy, marking low speed boating only, Don opened up the motor. Sherry's exposed hair, not saddled by her cap, whipped around her face. The cold wind iced her cheeks. She had to admit she was exhilarated by the speed, the darkening sky, and the salt spray curling away from the boat as it rode the waves.

A short time later, Don slowed the boat to a steady crawl as they approached a collection of lights. The boat entered an inlet where Sherry could make out a gray wood building. A porch, active with people and music, overhung a dock. The "Clam Shack" sign hung askew from the balcony, announcing the potential level of fun to be had by all patrons.

Don slid the boat into a slim slip and assigned Marla the task of hopping across the gap between the boat's deck and the dock cleat. He tossed her a rope. Sherry hoped he hadn't concluded Marla was the steadier hand to choose between the sisters. At the same time, she was glad she wasn't chosen. Creating the perfect Bolognese sauce was her thing, not securing a twenty-foot bobbing bathtub after leaping a watery gap. Marla was the right choice.

"Okay, Sherry, watch your step." Don crossed the gap and landed safely on the dock. He reached forward and pulled Sherry from the boat.

"I wore the wrong shoes. I didn't realize the boat's deck would get so wet," Sherry whispered to Marla. "Is that normal?"

Marla shrugged. "Not sure."

"What are you two whispering about?" Don asked.

"How hungry we are," Marla said.

After a dinner of fried clams, lobster salad, macaroni and cheese, and pinot grigio on the restaurant's space heater–warmed porch, the time came to head home. The effects of wine consumption made boarding the boat a bit precarious. Again, Don assigned rope duty to Marla. While casting off was taking place, Sherry noted the nighttime sky was moonless and starless. The clouds had moved in.

"I don't like this." Don shone a flashlight on the stern.

Sherry followed the beam of light to the glistening water, which was at least an inch deep.

Sherry's breath caught in her throat. "The storm coming in?"

"No. This water wasn't here when we left the marina."

She took a step closer to Marla. The warm glow of the pinot grigio disappeared and was replaced by turmoil in the pit of her stomach.

Sherry followed the flashlight's beam. "How worried should we be?"

"With just a flashlight, it's very hard to diagnose what's causing a leak, if that's what it is, let alone without lifting the boat out of the water. I'm fairly certain, if it is a leak, it's above the waterline, judging by the length of time the water took to flood the deck floor. So, if we travel back to the marina at slow speed, we shouldn't take on too much more water until we're docked. Fingers crossed the weather holds. We don't need a deluge from above on top of a leak from below."

After Don uttered the words "leak" and "flood," all Sherry heard of his explanation was "blah, blah, blah, blah." She tightened the strap on her life jacket.

"So, we're going to be safe?" Marla asked.

"Wet shoes will be the only casualties," Don said in a solemn, eerily calm voice. "Let's get a move on."

The return trip wore on Sherry's nerves to the point where every bump against a wave prompted a check of the vessel from stem to stern for enlarging cracks or deepening of deck water. When she wasn't looking at the deck, she was checking conditions overhead. She was beginning to relax when Don slowed the motor to a crawl. She raised her sights to the horizon. There were only dots of lights in the distance, a destination Sherry was sure they'd never reach.

"Why are we slowing down?" Sherry asked with as much positivity as she could muster.

When Don turned to face her, she saw the distress on his face.

"Take a look." Don inclined his head toward the sloshing water at their feet. "I don't feel safe anymore. I'm going to radio the Coast Guard for a rescue." He got on the radio and called for help. He stalled the motor. "Please stay seated so the boat is as steady as possible."

Sherry and Marla made light conversation as they drifted with the tide. For a few moments, Sherry did her best imitation of a coherent human, before she decided she needed to gather her racing thoughts with a moment of silence.

"Don, Sherry tells me you're a financial consultant on Long Island?" Marla's right-turn question lingered in the cold air while Don checked the boat's instruments.

He puffed out his cheeks. "That's right. I'll have to move closer to Augustin if Sherry and I want to see each other more often, though. Can't commute by boat all winter. After tonight, she may not want to see me ever again."

Sherry's mouth dropped open at Don's answer.

"Here's our ride," Don announced as a brilliantly lit boat motored toward them. "They'll tow us back to the marina, so if you two want to ride with the big dogs, that's the driest option."

The Coast Guard response boat pulled up alongside Don's boat. "Is everyone all right?"

"Yes, sir. We're taking on more water than I'm comfortable with and hoped to get a tow or escort back to the Augustin Marina to be on the safe side. These ladies don't want to experience a full-on water rescue on their first trip out with me."

Sherry and Marla were helped aboard the Coast Guard vessel, while tow lines were secured to Don's boat. The Coast Guard officer radioed Vitis that the two boats would be arriving at the dock within the half hour. Sherry's mind randomly wandered to Rachel and how, if she were to catch wind of the mishap, she would add Sherry to her deal-breaker list of those not loving the open water.

When the boats reached the dock, Sherry and Marla debarked and made their way to the shed to return the life jackets. Sherry kissed hers goodbye as she tossed it in the storage bin to join the pile of others. They remained in the warmth of Vitis's tiny enclosure while Don finished his business with the Coast Guard crew. When he finally appeared, his face broadcast bad news.

"The boat needs a full inspection and will be taken to dry dock early in the morning."

"How will you get home?" As Sherry asked, she realized there were other possibilities she wasn't prepared to offer, such as an overnight stay at her house.

"Already got that covered. I have some friends in

Hillsboro, and I texted them. They're on their way." Don shook out his foot. Water sprayed from his shoe.

"I'm sorry about your boat. At least you're not high and dry. You bought a boat from Crosby Banks, didn't you?" Marla asked. "Is the deal still on? Because he's, well, you know?"

"Coincidentally, I spoke to his lawyer this afternoon. The guy's already sorting out Crosby's possessions, but, yes, thankfully, the deal's still on. Already begun working out the transfer of ownership agreements. Boat's a beauty. If all goes well, I hope to get it in the water within the next week or so. When I heard about what happened to him, I considered canceling the deal, but reconsidered with the thought the boat still needs a good home."

"Wonder why he had a boat when his ex-wife said how much he disliked being out on the water?" Sherry questioned. "Glad you two got on so well at dinner. You don't have any clue as to who might have killed him, do you?"

Don folded his arms across his chest. "You go right to the point, don't you?" He winked at Sherry.

"Never know. Worth a try."

"He was a nice guy. We talked about finance, Long Island, and boats, obviously. Nothing about the guy stands out, except possibly a reference to animosity toward his ex, Rachel, and his father. In conversation, we glanced over his family, and mention of those two made his face pinch up like an old prune. Seeing her tonight, I can put a face to a name. Here's hoping she's not the guilty party."

"I second that." Sherry shivered and hugged her arms across her midsection.

The fact that Crosby and his father had a troubled relationship was news to Sherry.

"You two should get home and dry off so you don't catch cold. I saw that shiver. Hope you both had a good time tonight, despite the unscheduled excitement."

"We did. Thank you for the experience and the successful outcome to the adventure."

Marla backed away from Sherry. "I'll wait at the car."

Don hugged Sherry and gave her a kiss. As he released his embrace, she went back in for a lingering kiss. His resulting smile said he was thankful she had.

Don plunged his hand in his coat pocket. "Oh, and one of you dropped a glove on the boat. It's soaked, unfortunately. Hope the leather palm isn't ruined." He pulled out the damp glove.

"Not mine. Must be Marla's. I'll check with her." Sherry pinched one finger of the glove and let it dangle from her hand. "See you soon, I hope."

Chapter 9

Sherry was sorry the Thanksgiving weekend was over—
for about three seconds. While the cooking and eating
aspect of Thanksgiving was right up her alley, putting
aside her normal routine threw her off-balance. Monday
morning steamrolled in and she was excited to get back to
work at the Ruggery and her editing job for Augustin's
town newsletter, which had been on hiatus for the last
week. Marla wasn't thrilled about the early wake-up call,
but Sherry awoke with energy to spare, and her noisy tin-
kering throughout the house made for less than ideal
sleeping conditions. It wasn't long before Sherry suggested they go in to the Ruggery early.

A mug of coffee later, Sherry and Marla and the two
Jack Russells were on their way to the store.

"I'm running to the doughnut store." Marla shut the
passenger-side car door. "Any requests?"

"My request is no doughnuts." Sherry tossed a wave to her sister.

It wasn't long after she opened the store that the Ruggery's antique front door brushed against the bell, setting off a tinkle. Sherry emerged from the storage room to greet whoever had just walked in the store. Chutney and Bean trailed closely behind.

"It's me. I have returned," Amber said.

"Amber, I missed you so much. How was your Thanksgiving?"

"Hi, everyone. I missed you all, too. I had a very nice visit with my family."

Bean snuggled up against Amber's leg for a reunion with his owner. A moment later, he was off to play with Chutney elsewhere.

"Did I get the message wrong?" Amber asked. "Thought I was opening the store today. I'm surprised you're here so early."

It entered Sherry's mind that since Amber began working at the Ruggery, her friend had yet to take a sick day, show up late, or misread her schedule, so for her to ask about the possibility she'd misinterpreted the schedule was a rhetorical question. Sherry associated Amber's promptness and reliability with her training as a family therapist and marriage counselor in part, and in part because of the love she had for working at Erno Oliveri's store. When the two met at a cook-off, Sherry had no idea their fast friendship would blossom into a business partnership of sorts. The sight of Amber never ceased to remind Sherry of the wonderful people cooking competitions brought into her life.

"You got it right, as usual. I made a last-minute decision to come in early to make sure there were no Black

Friday remains. Dad's just not a fan, and I don't want him to be reminded the store held a sale. He'll be in after lunch, so let me know if you see something I missed. A sign, a sale tag in the waste bin, whatever."

"You can count on me. If I've learned one thing about your father, it's that he's a proud artisan. I'll do everything in my power to support him." Amber hung her coat on the rack by the store entrance. "Thank you so much for taking Bean over the weekend." Amber glanced at the dogs milling about the front door. "The pups find your shoes very appealing. Have you been somewhere new?"

Sherry glanced at the waterproof slip-ons she'd parked below the coat rack. Chutney and Bean were taking turns nosing around the rubber-soled shoes. "If you call the Long Island Sound new, then yes, I have. I was planning on not getting wet on a boat ride with Don and Marla, but you know what they say about the best-laid plans. I had those soaked shoes in the car, and they need to dry inside. By the end of the day, if the smell lingers, I'll have to go to plan B and disinfect them."

"Apparently, there's a juicy story to be told while we prepare for customers. Do tell."

"Good morning, people." Marla entered the store. "I brought doughnuts." She trotted over to Amber and gave her a bear hug. "So good to see you."

"I said, 'no doughnuts,'" Sherry scolded. "I ate way too much over the weekend."

Marla patted her stomach. "More for me. Amber, care to join me?"

"Don't ever change, Marla." Amber laughed. "By the way, I thought Sherry said you'd be back home in Oklahoma by the time I returned. I was sad I was going to miss you. Lucky me, you changed your plans."

Sherry attempted to intercept Amber's gaze, but she was unsuccessful. "Marla misses me and Dad too much."

"Nice try, Sher. You can't fool a therapist." Marla put her arm around Amber's shoulder. "I'll come clean. Truth is, Grant and I are on a downturn and we need a break. Not sure if it's life on a ranch, my restlessness, or just an early midlife crisis, but we need some space from each other."

"I won't pester you, but if you want to talk about anything marriage- and family-related, my office hours are wide open," Amber replied. "Even though I've retired my therapy practice in favor of retail, I have lots of past experience in almost any relationship dilemma to draw from."

"Or you could anonymously write to her online advice column. Not that I've ever done that," Sherry quickly added.

"Please do," Amber said. "In the meantime, a doughnut may be just what the doctor ordered. Can we get back to the story behind your smelly shoes? I'm intrigued Don was able to convince you to go out on his boat in the first place. I don't think it's your favorite activity, especially now it's almost December. Brrr."

Sherry related the story of last night's adventure on the water. As it progressed, Amber's brow knit tighter and tighter. Before she was able to conclude the story, Sherry's phone rang.

"Hi, Ray."

"Ray? As in Detective Ray Bease?" Amber asked. "Why am I getting the feeling you haven't gotten to the crucial details of last night's adventure?"

Sherry nodded, yes.

"How long were you going to take before you notified

me of your boat mishap?" Ray complained. "My department was contacted by the Augustin Marina dockmaster
and the Coast Guard regarding suspicious damage to a
boat you were listed as a passenger on. Do you realize the
police and EMTs were put on notice in case there were
injuries on your boat? Don't even try to convince me the
incident was no big deal."

Sherry's cheeks warmed. "Suspicious damage?"

"If the boat was deliberately tampered with and you're
looking into Crosby Currier's death, what does that suggest to you?"

Sherry glanced at the floor and back up again as she
considered her response. "I possibly have struck a nerve
with someone involved in the murder. On the other hand,
there's also the possibility my friend Don's boat just
needed some maintenance he wasn't aware of."

"That maintenance would include repairing the precise
knife cut of a hose attached to a pump that caused a slow
leak, perfectly timed to fill the deck with water after the
boat was well away from the dock."

"Ugh. So, the first possibility is more likely? Wonder
if the hose was cut on Long Island, before Don set off, or
in Augustin?"

"Keep me in the loop from now on. Your life might de-
pend on it." Ray hung up.

"Your frown tells me Ray had bad news," Amber said.

"Ray is seldom the bearer of good news," Marla said
before Sherry could reply.

"He wasn't happy. Don's boat was sabotaged, in all
likelihood."

"Does Don have enemies? I hope Ray wasn't suggesting someone knew you were going to be on that boat
and . . ." Amber said. "I can't even say the words."

Sherry had no time to answer before Amber answered her own question. "It is you, Sherry. Are you the one some-one was attempting to warn away? What is going on?"

"I may have struck something having to do with Crosby's murder. Although, I'm not exactly sure what that something is."

Amber groaned. "Murder? Who is Crosby? Can we start at the beginning? Please tell me this doesn't have anything to do with the cookie bake-off you judged on Saturday." When no one responded, Amber clutched her head in her hands.

"I'll set out the new shipment of winter colors while you fill Amber in on Crosby, his ex, and the missing prizes. And don't forget home ec and Augustin High." Marla carried her box of doughnuts toward the kitch-enette. "I'll be in the storage closet, organizing. After I eat a few doughnuts."

Sherry caught Amber up on what had happened be-tween the day after Thanksgiving through the previous night.

"I go away for five days and this is what I come back to?" Amber said. "This is a fine mess you gals have got-ten yourselves in to."

"You ladies gonna talk all morning?" Marla called out from the stockroom. "I could use some help."

"Marla's only been here for a few days and is already bossing us around." Sherry headed to the back of the store.

The early morning was slow in terms of sales. Sherry assumed patrons had overdone their shopping, motivated by sales, and were giving their wallets a rest. A few browsers came by to inquire about any sale item leftovers and left disappointed, though with the promise to return very soon. After one silver-haired couple spent nearly an hour scanning the lookbooks for an idea for their grandchild's bedroom before finally settling on a sea life and mermaid rug, Sherry was hit with a thought. She logged the thought away until after the couple completed their order. When they left the store, Sherry pulled the customer Rolodex from beneath the sales counter. She spun the card wheel until she reached the *B*s.

"What are you searching for? The couple that just left, the Kennans, have never been in before. I checked. They don't have a profile card yet," Amber said. "I'm about to pull a blank card for them."

"I'm searching the *B*s and the *C*s for Banks and Currier." Sherry twirled the knob of the filing device her father had maintained for decades. Every single sale was transcribed on an alphabetized card, with preferences, inquiries, and any other pertinent information Erno felt applicable to his customers. Whenever she used the Rolodex, Sherry was reminded of all the times she'd urged her father to go digital and he'd resisted. Now, she couldn't imagine the Ruggery without the charm of the antiquated Rolodex system. While no Banks had placed an order, she found a completed sale to Alonzo and Ivy Currier. The card described a rug portraying a boat on the ocean with clouds and blue sky. The rug was entitled *Perfect Honeymoon*. She wondered if that was a reference to the name of the boat or to the subject of the rug itself.

"Here's something I've never seen before." Sherry removed the card and held it up.

"What's that?" Amber asked.

"The back of the card has a note about an inquiry into

replacing the rug. Says 'damaged beyond repair.' I don't
see any further purchases, though. As if the inquiry never
proceeded to any further action."

"Is that important?" Amber found an empty card in the
drawer under the sales desk. She didn't wait for an answer. "I'll start a customer card for the Kennans and let
Erno fill in the details when he gets here later."

"I don't know if it's important or not whether the couple were customers here." Sherry glanced at the Rolodex.
"That's not true. It's very important." Sherry pushed the
Rolodex toward Amber. "Thank goodness for Dad's system."

The volume of shoppers was low throughout the
morning. Given the extra time, Sherry decided to change
the display rack from an autumnal motif to a winter one.
The area rugs, sized from small ovals to five-foot, scenic
rectangles depicting autumn scenes, were transferred to
labeled bins. Winter-themed rugs took their place on the
wooden display rack. When the swap-out was complete,
Sherry stepped back to absorb the store's transformation
into a winter wonderland. While she reveled in her handi-
work, the front door opened. A quick glance back toward
the door developed into a double take.

Marla welcomed the incoming couple before Sherry
had a chance to make her way across the store. The woman,
protected from the outside chill by a windbreaker and a
scarf, greeted Sherry with a nod. The bearded man by her
side simply said, "Hello, Sherry."

Sherry caught Marla's puzzled expression. "Marla, do
you remember Rachel Currier? She and I met at the bake-
off. We saw her at the marina briefly when we went out
with Don last night. And this is Chef Buckman, who
judged the cookie bake-off with me. You met him briefly,

also. He's the owner of the bakery Eileen will have her cookie featured in."

Barry nodded. "Please, call me Barry. Today is the first day Eileen's cookies are available at the bakery. I'm sure they're selling like hotcakes. I'll be heading back there soon and I'll see for myself."

"Eileen is beyond thrilled. I'll have to stop over and buy a dozen of her winning cookies," Sherry said. "Thank you for coming in to the Ruggery. What can I show you both?"

Chapter 10

"We came in for two things," Rachel said. "One, Barry is interested in perking up his apartment. I thought one of your gorgeous rugs would do the trick. And two, I'd like to talk to you about Crosby."

"Marla, would you like to work with Barry while Rachel and I have a chat?" Sherry forced a grin while considering the uncertainties of what was to come.

"Right this way, Barry. I'll show you the lookbook to get you started." Marla led Barry to the demonstration table before pulling up two stools and locating one of many product books.

Sherry kept her sights on the two until they appeared settled. "I didn't know Crosby well, I have to say right off the bat. Again, I'm so sorry for his passing."

"Thank you. Even though we were divorced, his death is an awful tragedy. I'm now all his father, Lonnie, has left in terms of family. I believe I'm a beneficiary in Lonnie's will. He jokes that unless I change my last name from Currier, I stand to become a mildly rich woman. As long as I'm a Currier, I'm obligated to see he's never neglected. And I'm happy to fulfill that obligation. Maybe that's why Crosby chose to change his name to his mother's maiden name. Freed him from family duty." Rachel took a deep breath. "I'm rambling."

"This must be a rough time for you." Sherry cringed at her trite choice of words. She glanced over to Marla, who seemed to be involved in banter with Barry. *Please get to your point*, she willed Rachel.

"What's difficult is, Crosby is haunting me from the great beyond. A Detective Bease has tried a number of times to contact me, and I'm pretty sure he thinks I killed my ex-husband. I didn't." Rachel's voice had a hint of desperation.

"I know the detective. He does a thorough investigation. He would never rush to judgment. He's probably gathering information." Sherry searched Rachel's eyes for signs she had soothed the woman's anxiety.

"Why wouldn't he suspect me? I'm the evil ex-wife."

"Again, I know the man. He never goes into an investigation with preconceived notions, such as every ex-wife is a vindictive murderer." Sherry wondered if her choice of words was too strong.

"There's more to consider. When he starts sniffing around, I'm going to come off in a poor light. Truth is, ever since Ivy Banks Currier died, Crosby has been spiraling out of control. The two had a strong mother-son bond that only deepened as she grew sicker. When she died, I think he lost all purpose in life. I tried my best to reunite him with his father, but he fought me at every turn. Crosby and I had split by then, but I still cared about the guy. I even brought Lonnie to the cookie bake-off, knowing Crosby was baking his mother's cookies. My hope was they could bond over the competition, especially if he won. Lonnie was all for the idea, even though his own marriage had been less than perfect. Unfortunately, Saturday, Lonnie was suffering stomach issues and spent most of the time in the men's room."

"What a mess. Wonder why Crosby and his father had a falling out." Sherry said.

"Goes way back. The fact they barely spoke definitely played a part in the estrangement of Ivy from Lonnie. Or it could be the other way around. Not a subject we touched on often during our marriage, for the sake of keeping the peace. He and I eloped, rather than force the family to come together for our sake. It just wouldn't have been possible."

"Wow, that does sound like a family torn apart." Sherry's gaze drifted back to Marla and Barry.

"I know you'd like to get over there and help your sister, so I'll get to the point." Rachel was clearly struggling for the right words. "Can you find Crosby's killer? Lonnie lives in Sunset Village, the Augustin senior community, and I'm the only family he has. He'll have no one to visit him if I'm arrested." Rachel's calm voice morphed into a plea.

"Hey, Sher. We could use your expertise over here," Marla called from across the room. "Amber ducked out to go to the bank."

"Thank you," Sherry mouthed to her sister when Rachel turned her head toward Marla. "I can't make any promises, Rachel." She took a step away.

The smile on the face of a woman she barely knew descended into a frown. "Crosby told me you were his favorite student in high school."

"Let's go see what those two have come up with." Sherry chose not to respond to Rachel's comment, which hit her like a hammer.

Sherry answered Barry's questions about customizing a rug for his bakery, rather than his apartment. The large rug would take two months to complete and would serve as a focal point for the corner of his shop where people congregated to drink coffee and share sweet and savory baked goods. At the sales counter, Barry signed the receipt for a deposit to begin work immediately.

"There's a nip in the air today." Rachel zipped up her puffy down coat. "Winter's on the way."

"You dropped your glove." Barry bent down to pick it up. "It's early in the season to lose one."

"Too late. This is an orphan." Rachel held up the gray wool glove with the leather palm.

Sherry's breath caught in her throat and she choked on her attempt to swallow a gasp.

"You okay?" Marla asked.

"Some dust in the air." Sherry voice became strangled. She tilted her head in Marla's direction. "Do you have any gloves like Rachel's single?"

"I don't. Only gloves I have are work ones, and I left those in Oklahoma." Marla turned to face Rachel. "It's an early season loss. Maybe you'll get lucky and find the missing match."

"Hope so." Rachel stuffed the glove in her coat pocket. "Thanks for everything. Have a good evening."

"Thank you," Barry said. "I'll have to pick another rug for my apartment on the next visit."

As soon as the pair left the store, Marla approached

Sherry. When they locked gazes in a sisterly, intuitive exchange, Sherry confessed the reason behind her astonished expression. "That's the matching glove to the one Don found on the deck of his boat. I brought it home to see if it belonged to you. It's still in the car. I confess, I forgot all about it after the boat mishap."

"What are you saying? That Rachel was on Don's boat?"

"That's exactly what I'm saying."

"I'm back." The voice came from the direction of the opening door. Erno entered the store. "What's that collective look on your faces? Did I scare you?"

"No, Dad, we were discussing something." She didn't even have to ask where his attention had wandered off to. Sherry saw her father checking the store for the aftermath of the Black Friday sale.

"Place looks great," Erno remarked. "No damage done selling a few items at a discount after all."

"You need a different perspective on the sale," Marla told her father. "Yes, your rugs are lovingly designed by you and can easily be considered works of art. Making a small number accessible to a wise consumer, once a year, is a nice gesture."

"The rugs are all my children. I want to make sure each goes to an appreciative home. I'd feel the same way if I had to sell you or Sherry."

"Thanks for that sentiment, Dad," Sherry said. "I can confirm, the customers who bought the rugs were beyond appreciative."

"That's all I ask," Erno said. "Now that I'm here, why don't you gals go find something fun to do?"

"Marla, that's code for 'Dad needs some Ruggery-time,'" Sherry explained. "When we're not here to eyeball him, he changes the display, reorganizes the yarn storage area, and generally has quality alone time with his rugs."

"The bad news is, you won't be alone long. Amber's at the bank and soon to return. She took the pups with her," Marla said. "Better get going on your solo rug time."

Sherry and Marla shared a laugh as they headed out the door. "We'll call you later."

In the car, Sherry read a text she'd received from Tia, the mayor's secretary. "Do you mind if we head over to the library? Tia from Town Hall would like me to cover a Christmas tree safety demo the Augustin Fire Department has set up over there. The mayor wants a blurb and a photo in next week's newsletter."

"As long as we can grab something to eat soon. I'm starving."

"Deal." Sherry checked the back seat for her notebook. Sitting on top of the notebook was the mirror image of Rachel's glove. Sherry switched on the car while giving the situation more thought. "Even if Rachel was on Don's boat while we were in Vitis's shed trying on life jackets, it doesn't mean she was involved in causing the leak."

"You read my mind, except for the part where I believe she was the cause."

"Rachel said she didn't want Lonnie to be alone, so why would she kill his son? That would remove Crosby, and her, from Lonnie's life." Before Marla could comment, Sherry added, "Although it's noteworthy she mentioned she's in Lonnie's will until she changes her last name. Unless she was kidding. Is Crosby in the will? Not necessarily, given the family's fractured history. More for her if he isn't. It's a moot point now he's dead."

"What's the story with Crosby's mother? He told us

she died within this past year, but why did she and Lonnie never get a divorce, living apart as Rachel said they had. Families are nuts sometimes."

"Seems the more we learn, the less we know," Sherry replied.

Arriving at the library, Sherry found a parking spot next to an Augustin fire truck. "The demo's inside, which is kind of scary, but apparently they have a fireproof capsule for the holiday tree they're going to ignite."

The automatic doors opened into the library's lobby. A crowd had gathered around a clear enclosure that housed a three-foot tall, lit and decorated tree. Sherry spotted two firemen. The demo appeared to be getting underway, as a firefighter donned an oxygen mask and tipped the tree from its perch. Not long after, an overturned lit candle ignited the tree's dry needles and the fire was off to the races. The glass tomb contained the fire, but viewing the firefighters in action was difficult under the smoky conditions.

"Those guys do amazing work." Sherry admired the precision it took to douse the flames with an extinguisher in a short amount of time. "Fires are an awful tragedy under any circumstances, let alone a controlled environment like this."

When the demonstration was over, the crowd applauded, especially when one firefighter removed the protective gear to reveal a woman acknowledging the admiration sent her way.

"Augustin's first firewoman. I've read about her. I'm so excited she's here today. A great angle for my story." Sherry was giddy with excitement. "I'll be back in a few." She made her way to the front of the dispersing crowd. "Your demonstration was a real eye-opener. I'm writing an article about what I learned for the town newsletter. Hope it saves people from holiday tragedy."

"A little knowledge goes a long way," the woman said. "We appreciate you getting the word out."

"Can I ask you a fire-related question?" A nod from the uniformed woman gave Sherry the green light. "Years ago, there was a fire at the Augustin Marina. Do you know any details about the fire, such as how it may have begun?"

"It was before my time, but yes, we use the story of that day as a training exercise every six months. That fire took four neighboring companies, besides us, to tame. It was the worst fire in over one hundred years for Augustin. Back then, nearly all the structures were wood, basically with a match waiting to be struck, so that's saying something."

"Wow" was all Sherry could lend to the conversation.

"The docks were old wood as well. Giant matches for the inferno. Boat fuel fed the flames and the combination was the worst-case scenario to try to get under control in a timely fashion."

The woman's attention drifted away as she raised her line of sight above Sherry's shoulder. Sherry imagined the woman was visualizing herself on the front line of the fire battle.

"Was the cause ever pinpointed?" Sherry hoped to get a short answer, as Marla must be wondering where she was.

"Arson was highly suspected. Charred rags, saturated with flammable liquid acetone, were discovered in what used to be the yacht club's clubhouse. Nail polish remover. Acetone, the main ingredient, is highly flammable. Once they were ignited, the wood structures went up and the boat fuel exploded. What a mess. Hard to believe no one was seriously injured. You can understand why the only good to come out of the disaster was the opportunity for furthering firefighting education."

"No one was ever charged. Isn't that correct?" Sherry asked.

"That's right. Suspicion lay heavily on the head of the dockmaster's son. He was in his early twenties and didn't approve of his father's philandering ways. The Augustin firehouse aided as best they could in the investigation, but the police lacked one or two crucial pieces of evidence to lock in his guilt. In the end, it was a he-said, she-said standoff. The father said his son did it and the mother said he didn't. The old-timers at the firehouse, who still talk about the twelve hours spent fighting the fire, say it was a shame no one was ever punished for the act. Why all the interest?"

"The facts seemed incomplete when I read an article about the fire. Thank you very much for your time." Sherry backed away from the woman.

"You're very welcome. Stay safe during this holiday season."

Sherry returned to Marla, who was helping a young boy insert his foot into a sneaker.

Beside them, a woman juggled a baby in a carrier, a diaper bag, and a juice box. "Thank you," she managed to say to Marla before she began a chase after the escaping little boy.

"You're welcome," Marla called after the woman.

"Make you want a few of your own?" Sherry asked.

"A few little ranch hands would be useful." Marla laughed.

"While we're here, let's take a look at a back issue of the *Nutmeg State of Mind*."

"What are you up to, Sher?" Marla asked as Sherry led her to the reference desk.

"Curiosity is getting the best of me."

A heavyset woman with a chestnut-brown, bobbed hairdo pushed a book cart up to the copy machine and turned her attention to her patrons.

"Hi, Ethel. We'd love to take a look at a back issue of the newspaper if that's okay."

"Sherry, hello. This must be your sister. I haven't laid eyes on her in years." Ethel, Augustin's longtime head librarian, lowered her brows. "As I recall, you were late returning nearly every book you ever borrowed, young lady. Have you mended your ways?"

"I had to move out of town to escape the shame. I do think if you gave me another chance, I'd pull through."

"Glad to hear it. You know, we librarians get an undeserved reputation for enforcing rules, but we just want everyone to enjoy the books we offer, and if they aren't returned on time, the domino effect takes over and no one is happy."

"Yes, ma'am." Marla bowed her head.

Sherry was directed by Ethel to take a seat at the microfilm projector to view back issues of the newspaper, while Marla checked out a laptop. Ethel gave Sherry a brief lesson in the machine's use.

"You gals could do this at home if you had an online subscription to the newspaper, you know. Depending on how far back you need to go. But I'm happy you're here in person. Not often do I get to help one of the town's tastiest celebrities. Now, what time period are you looking for?"

Sherry didn't want to admit she didn't subscribe to the paper that often featured her wins. Buying a copy on the newsstand worked well enough for her needs. "Let's start with Ivy Banks Currier's obituary. Then we'll see where that leads us," Sherry replied. "Marla, can you get the date?"

Ethel excused herself while Marla pulled up a chair next to Sherry and opened the laptop. "I'll be over at the circulation desk if you need me."

After a few clicks, Marla said, "Looks like we can get the full obit right here because it's so recent." Marla read the half-page obituary out loud.

"Lists Lonnie Currier as a surviving family member. Refers to Crosby as Crosby Currier. Maybe Crosby uses the Banks name now as a tribute to his mother," Sherry suggested.

"Maybe if Rachel wouldn't change the Currier last name after they split, he changed his?" Marla countersuggested.

"Hard to speculate. The obit mentions the family's connection to the Augustin Marina. 'In lieu of flowers, please make a donation to the Augustin Marina Restoration Project.' Ironic that's where Crosby's body was found not long after the bake-off. What was he doing there? Rachel said he didn't like to be on boats."

"Ladies." Ethel came up alongside Sherry's chair. "Is there anything else you need from me?"

Sherry checked the wall clock. "Thank you, Ethel.

We're all done. We didn't use the projector after all. We really appreciate your help."

Smile lines formed as Ethel's mouth drew up into a bright grin.

Marla lifted the laptop. "I'll meet you outside. I have to return the laptop. On time."

Chapter 11

"What did you talk to the firefighter about?" Marla asked when she joined Sherry outside the library.

"She was telling me about the Augustin Marina fire." Sherry made her way to the car with Marla at her side. Once inside the car, she continued, "Seems Crosby was the prime suspect in the arson investigation."

"Why would Crosby burn down the marina?"

"His father may have been the cause of his parents' separation. Speculation was, he had a wandering eye that threatened to break up the family, and Crosby may have wanted to hit his father where it hurt. I gather the evidence couldn't conclusively prove his guilt, or his mother, Ivy, may have talked her son's way out of prosecution."

"Is the latter even possible?"

"Lonnie was the dockmaster. If charges weren't pressed, or maybe evidence was lost somehow, the case couldn't move forward. Leads me to believe the fire may have had a lot to do with the family split, Crosby's relocation, and maybe even his eventual name change, if he and his father were estranged over the incident."

"Maybe a visit to see Lonnie Currier would enlighten us?" Marla suggested.

"I shouldn't get any more involved." Sherry steered the car down her street. "But, for the sake of a former teacher . . . I owe it to him to at least sniff around until this thread goes nowhere. Do we have time to stop at Sunset Village before we go home to finish the recipe?"

"I don't think it matters whether we have time or not. The tone of your voice says it's going to happen. Sounds like we're heading to Sunset Village. What about something to eat first?" Marla asked.

"I'll buy you a treat on the way. How about we take out from the Soulful Sandwich? I'm in the mood for a New England po'boy. A bit of the north and a bit of the south all in one bite. Now that's a perfect recipe."

"Great accompaniment to my breakfast of doughnuts." Marla grinned broadly.

Parking at Sunset Village was restrictive. So many spots were reserved for the handicapped. Sherry had to circle the lot twice until one of the few undesignated spots became available. Once the car was parked, the sisters followed the brick path up to the sprawling, one-level complex. The landscaping around the building was abundant and varied and led to a welcoming sight. Even the chilled air of late autumn didn't dim the warmth of the colorful plantings.

Sherry breathed in the earthy, dry-leaf fragrance the

trees put off during their last gasp before snow arrived. "Such a pretty garden. That's another thing I love about Augustin. Attention to detail. Everyone is so proud of their spot on the map. Come to think of it, maintaining this garden might be a nice project for some of the Augustin Community Garden interns to take on if the facility needs help."

"Is this a glimpse into our future?" Marla asked as she and Sherry navigated past a couple holding hands between their wheelchairs.

The gray-haired woman and the bald man seemed to be sharing a moment of garden appreciation. Not long after, the couple was on the move toward the building.

"Could Grant and I ever make it to that stage?"

"That's up to you both," Sherry said in a near whisper. "Sunset Village is a lovely facility. I don't think any of us are quite ready to move in yet, though. When we do, I hope we're as happy as those two lovebirds." She stopped in front of a posted map of the Augustin Meadows Senior Living Community. She pointed to the building on the map with the "You are here" labeled red star. "Sunset Village is the facility that houses seniors without major medical issues, it says. Check-in is this way."

Sherry and Marla followed the wheelchairs inside and veered to the right to stand in line at the reception desk. When their turn came, they were called forward to sign in and specify their reason for visiting. The woman behind the desk lowered her reading glasses down the bridge of her nose and glared at Sherry.

"We're here to visit Lonnie Currier. We were in the area and decided to drop in unannounced," Sherry explained.

"Mr. Currier doesn't know you're visiting? He's in the

middle of teaching a class." The woman checked the clock. "For the next twenty minutes. You're welcome to attend. He's a very good cook and you could learn a thing or two from him."

Sherry side-eyed her sister. "Perfect. I could use some cooking tips. We'd love to attend."

The woman behind the desk stood with the help of a cane she retrieved from under her desk. She pointed to a set of double doors at the end of the wide hallway. "The kitchen is through those doors. Please shut the door behind you to keep out the lobby noise. You'll find chairs in the back of the room. Feel free to move them forward to get a good view of Lonnie's demonstration." She sat back down. "Bon appétit."

The hallway was littered with wheelchairs, both occupied and empty, an ominous gurney, and a cart bulging with medicine bottles. The smell of rubbing alcohol, elderly human existence, and cafeteria food permeated Sherry's nose, and she quickened her pace toward the kitchen to shorten the amount of time she had to endure it all as her stomach began to feel queasy. When she yanked open the double doors, the doorjamb screeched across the linoleum, announcing their arrival.

Heads rotated in Sherry's direction. The man at the front of the room, in a white chef's coat, was huddled over a baking pan. He straightened up and stopped talking in midsentence. He made a point of glaring at the clock on the side wall. "You two ladies have missed half the class." His tone was less than welcoming.

"Sorry." Sherry located an empty chair, dragged it forward, and sat, as did Marla.

"Good afternoon to you, too. Geesh, what a grouch," Marla hissed.

A silver-haired woman, seated beside Sherry, lifted her cupped hand to her mouth and directed a comment the sisters' way. "His recipes are worth tolerating his crankiness for. Beware of asking questions. He might bite your head off. Consider yourself warned." The woman did a double take when she finished her warning. "Lord have mercy. You're Sherry Oliveri. What in tarnation are you doing at a cooking class? You should be the teacher. By the way, my good friend, Eileen Weisberger, is over the moon she was chosen the winner of the Story For Glory Cookie Bake-off. She said she wasn't your first choice as the winner. Luckily, the other judges had the good sense to choose her Pawprints.

"I was in the audience with my daughter. Next year we'll definitely enter. She makes the yummiest Butterscotch Lace Cookies. She has to work on her backstory, though. She leads such a boring life."

"Thank you." Sherry wasn't interested in another scolding by Lonnie. She did her best to redirect the woman's attention back to the demonstration by staring straight ahead.

Marla elbowed Sherry. "What kind of cookie is that?" She made a subtle gesture toward the pan of bar cookies by the oven.

"Those are definitely the cookies Crosby baked for Saturday's contest. Tropical Dream Bars," Sherry replied.

"The same cookies? Are you sure? Why would . . ."

"Something you two would like to share with the rest of the class? You've been chatting the entire time you've been here. Not only have you missed the first half of the recipe, you're on your way to missing the second." The man's level of exasperation made Sherry wince. He placed his hand on his hip and stared down Marla before shifting his attention to Sherry.

The woman next to Sherry leaned in closer. "He has no idea who you are."

"I can call you Lonnie? Or Chef Lonnie?" Sherry pointed to the name tag on the chef's coat.

He nodded and raised his glasses above his eyes. "Lonnie is fine. Do I know you?"

"I was a judge in the Story For Glory Cookie Bake-off last Saturday and had the pleasure of tasting the best cookies Augustin has to offer. My name is Sherry Oliveri."

Lonnie gripped a spatula in his hand. His knuckles grew white. "Ah, yes. Sherry Oliveri. I didn't recognize you with my reading glasses on. Pressure's on to impress you. You've obviously tasted the cookies I'm preparing because my son entered them in the bake-off. As I recall, you liked them very much. I saw your look of satisfaction up there on the judging panel."

"They were better than Eileen's?" the woman next to Sherry whispered.

"No," Sherry whispered back.

"His cookies didn't win because I believe he made a technical error in their preparation. He left out a crucial ingredient." Lonnie cracked a grin. "Please enjoy the class. Questions are welcome, but not encouraged." Lonnie produced a gruff laugh.

"You made him laugh," the woman beside Sherry whispered. "That's a first."

The class continued without interruption and, in the final minutes, Lonnie beckoned the students forward for a sample cookie. *Oohhs* and *aahs* filled the room.

"See you all next week, when we'll make curried butternut squash soup," Lonnie announced when the front-desk receptionist appeared inside the double doors.

She tapped her cane on the floor. "Time's up, people. Thank you, Chef Lonnie. Water yoga starts in fifteen minutes."

The crowd dispersed with the exception of one man, who joined Lonnie. Sherry assumed he was there to help clean up, but it wasn't long before she was proven incorrect.

"That recipe's getting long in the tooth, don't you think?" The man with a thick tuft of salt-and-pepper hair held a cookie in the air.

"You don't seem to have much trouble wolfing them down. Maybe it's you who's long in the tooth." Lonnie's quick retort prompted a humph from the recipient.

Lonnie turned his attention to Sherry. "It's Sherry's opinion that holds weight. What did you think of the cookie? I followed the recipe to a T, unlike Crosby."

Sherry felt all eyes on her. "Very good."

"Why are you here? Certainly not for the master class in baking."

The other man backed away from the table. "I'll see you at dinner." He turned and left the room.

Lonnie acknowledged the comment with a grumble. "Sick of sitting in the mess hall with the same old geezers."

"The reason we're here is that we'd like to talk to you about Crosby if that's okay. We'd also like to help you clean up." Sherry tore some sheets of paper towel from a roll sitting on the counter. She began corralling the cookie crumbs that were scattered across the counter. She tossed a loaded paper towel in the garbage and ripped off another sheet.

"You're a cook-off judge *and* a detective? A full résumé." Lonnie collected his bowls and utensils and walked them to the expansive stainless-steel sink.

Sherry edged closer to the sink. "One and done for the first label, never have been or want to be for the second. I like cooking in cook-offs much more than I like judging other cooks."

Marla cleared her throat. "We had dinner with Crosby the night before the bake-off. He taught both of us a class in high school. Such a nice man. Not much older than Sherry, too."

"Crosby had his attributes, along with his vices."

Sherry considered the delicacy of her next question. Had she won Lonnie's trust in the very limited time she'd known him? More to the point, had she lost any chance of gaining his trust somehow?

"Crosby's wife, Rachel, introduced herself to me at the bake-off. I was surprised to learn she was actually his *ex*-wife. He told us she was out of town. I was quite surprised when she introduced herself to me. Seems she wasn't out of town after all."

Lonnie lay the cookie pan down in the sink, producing a metal-to-metal clang. He turned slowly to face Sherry. The sternness of his expression chilled the skin on her arms.

"I never could understand why the boy said the things he did. Listen closely to me. Rachel didn't do it. I had many more reasons to want Crosby to disappear than her. He's been a thorn in my side his entire adult life. I'm not perfect, but I was a darn good role model. Gave him everything he needed to be a successful adult and he flopped. Couldn't even come up with an original cookie recipe for the bake-off. Had to take his mother's recipe and call it his own. The detective who asked me questions was concerned about Rachel's relationship with Crosby. She's a good girl. She visits me often and makes sure I don't feel too neglected."

"Rachel told me she brought you to the bake-off. You must have gone to cheer your son on, even if you didn't approve of his recipe." Her statement was more of a question than a comment. She paused.

Lonnie stayed silent for a moment. "I'm sure the cookie was a nod to his late mother. When Rachel told me he had entered the recipe in the contest, I had to see for myself."

Sherry forced a smile in hopes of thawing Lonnie's icy glare. "Were you and Crosby's mother divorced?"

"Young lady, you must take me for a fool if you think I don't realize you know the answer to that question." He held an unwavering glare on Sherry. "I didn't cheat on my wife as is widely rumored. Crosby may have even been the perpetrator of that rumor. He had his reasons for seeing me take a fall. To answer your question, no, we never divorced."

Sherry peered over at Marla, who returned the look with a subtle nod.

"The detective said if Rachel can't provide a verifiable alibi, he is going to have to arrest her." Lonnie dropped his voice to a near whisper. "I wasn't with her the entire time at the bake-off. I was having some stomach problems. You won't want me to get too graphic, but I made multiple trips to the men's room."

With the impression she had softened Lonnie, Sherry sucked in a deep breath and plunged in. "You can't deny you had a contentious relationship with your son. You said as much right here. What would make me believe you weren't somehow involved in his murder if Rachel wasn't?"

Marla dropped the handful of forks she was holding, and they scattered across the floor. "Oops."

"You're right. That detective fellow's making a mistake not putting me at the top of the suspect list. I'll tell you a secret. If I was going to kill Crosby, I would have done it long ago, when he deserved it. He wasn't very nice to his mother and me on occasion. You'll have to take me at my word; I couldn't be bothered doing time for the deed these days. Not worth the effort. I've moved on."

Sherry glared at Marla in hopes her sister would enter the conversation. Marla was busy corralling the scattered forks. Sherry was at a loss as to which direction to proceed.

When she added the final fork to her collection, Marla took a step closer to Lonnie. "The other night, Sherry and I were waiting to be picked up for a boat ride, and I read an article about your career as dockmaster for the Augustin Yacht Club."

Lonnie's eyes brightened. "If it's the framed article on the wall of the sad excuse for the current Marina headquarters, you got an idea of how prestigious the position was in those days when you read it. The yachts—and I mean yachts, not boats—had to check in with me, attain my permission to dock, and radio me to get passengers ferried to shore. I ran a tight ship. Nonmembers constantly approached me with interesting requests. I could have gotten rich from the bribes I refused to accept. Not that I wasn't tempted, mind you. I was offered so much money for the preferred slip and the longest dock time allowance, I couldn't even tally the amount. Sadly, the place is now a shell of its former self. I feel bad for Vitis

Costa. He stepped into a minefield when he took over my role. In more ways than one. But, yes, I loved my career."

"How did the fire start?"

"Crosby. He wanted to punish me for separating from his mother. Taking away my livelihood was his idea of hitting me where it hurt the most. And he was right."

"But why wasn't he ever convicted of arson? If you don't mind me asking."

"His mother. She made sure the case never went to trial and he got off scot-free." Lonnie shook his head. "I let it go. That was a battle I wasn't willing to undertake. Even if it meant ending my career."

"And he moved away after that?" Marla asked.

"That's right. Not long after the fire, there was a very damaging article in the local paper by a vindictive writer that strongly suggested Crosby was guilty of setting the fire. The article spelled the end of his short-lived Augustin High teaching career. Worked out okay for him. He moved to Long Island. He eventually returned and met Rachel."

"Do you have any idea who may have taken your son's life?" Sherry asked.

"I just know who didn't take his life. Let me ask you something. Would you be able to prove my daughter-in-law innocent by finding the killer? It's no secret you're a pretty good sleuth. I have a sneaking suspicion that's why you're here today. To get to the bottom of his murder."

"I'm here out of respect for your son. He did something nice for me when I was in high school, and it had some continued significance in my life. I wanted to meet you and tell you that."

"I appreciate that. Crosby and I had issues, as I told the detective. It probably put me on the suspect list right behind Rachel. Can't turn back time and undo what's been done." Lonnie shrugged his shoulders. "What do you say? Will you have a look around and find Crosby's killer so his long-suffering wife can have some peace?"

Sherry lifted her head. "I'll see what I can do. In the meantime, thank you for letting us sit in on your cooking class." Sherry's sweet tone may have come on strong, but she wanted to leave Lonnie on an upbeat note.

Chapter 12

The next morning, when she opened her eyes, Sherry's phone glowed in her peripheral vision. *Who would be texting so early?*

She reached over to her bedside table and grabbed the phone. *Not a text. A voice mail. Probably Dad. Hope he's okay.* Before she could listen to the message, something crashed to the floor below her bedroom. She hauled herself out of bed.

"Sorry, did I wake you?" Marla asked as Sherry entered the kitchen. "I was trying to empty the dishwasher quietly, but no good deed goes unpunished. I dropped the cutlery caddy."

Sherry didn't reply. Marla had talked over a sentence of the phone message she was listening to, but the gist came through loud and clear. Sherry lowered the phone from her ear.

"Sher? Hope you're not hearing bad news. The look on your face says you are."

"Don left a late night or rather an early morning message—actually, three messages—saying Rachel and her lawyer say the boat belongs to her. He couldn't take delivery of it and the check was going to be ripped up."

"Interesting." Marla shut the dishwasher door. "Must have been a piece of property in the divorce that didn't get divided properly. Was he upset?"

"Well, yes, because his boat is being assessed for seaworthiness, and if it's too expensive to salvage, he wasn't going to bother with the repairs if he was taking ownership of Crosby's boat. He said Rachel has no desire for negotiation and the deal is off."

"Maybe it's for the best," Marla said. "Crosby's boat might have some bad karma attached to it."

Sherry set down her phone on the counter. "So does Don's."

"It does have one strike against it, but I'm willing to give his captaining skills one more try."

"I was thinking. Rachel would like me to find Crosby's killer. But her glove was found on Don's boat the night it nearly sank. How can I believe in her innocence? How can I believe anything she's telling me?"

"I have a feeling you won't be happy until you discover the truth, one way or another. By the way, if Don doesn't have a working boat, will that make seeing him difficult?"

"I'm worried about that. The drive from Long Island is a tough one just for a date." Sherry sighed. "Let's cross that bridge when we have to." Sherry gazed around the kitchen. "Thanks for cleaning up. I never leave a mess unattended overnight, but we ate so late last night, I ran out of energy."

Sherry's phone alerted her to an incoming text. She collected her phone from the counter. "Amber's texting. Wants to know if we can spot her at the store for a bit this morning. I'd better get to work on my fire safety article for the newsletter if we're spending the morning at the Ruggery." Sherry punched in a few words and hit the Send key. "The answer is yes." Sherry poured herself some coffee and went upstairs to shower and get dressed for the day ahead.

"Put me to work, Dad." Marla hung up her fleece vest. "Sherry and I are pinch-hitting for Amber for a few hours until she settles some personal issues."

"Everything okay with her?" Erno asked.

"She's making some Black Friday returns, and because she bought them out of town, she has to drive a long way to find stores that'll take the merchandise back," Sherry explained.

"Another reason I hate Black Friday sales. People buy too much prompted by saving money, when, in reality, they're wasting money on discounted excess," Erno said. "If someone comes in this afternoon and tries to return one of my rugs they bought on a whim, put them on the Black Friday blacklist."

"Dad, we don't have such a list and never will. People change their minds. It's a fact of life," Marla scolded. "When is the last time someone returned one of your hand-loomed, hand-designed rugs?"

Erno's gaze lifted toward the ceiling and returned to Marla. "Only one attempt I can recall. An engaged couple who placed an order and broke up before the rug was completed. The husband tried to return it for full price—thousands, as I recall. It was huge, but the wife already had the rug listed in the prenup as her possession, so he was out of luck."

"Pretty good track record," Sherry added.

"We do get plenty of repair requests. As a matter of fact, the Currier man who died at the bake-off—" Erno began.

"Hold on," Sherry interrupted. "No one died at the bake-off. Crosby died a few hours afterward. But thanks for reminding me. I've been meaning to ask you about the Curriers and Bankses as customers. What can you tell me about them?"

"As I was about to say, Crosby's father and mother had a rug made here. A beautiful sailboat scene on the water for the dockmaster building. They never tried to return it, but it was destroyed in the awful Augustin Marina fire, and Ivy Currier was desperate to have it remade. Insurance didn't cover the cost, so the plan fizzled when she couldn't afford the price. She was on her own at that point, and her husband wasn't keen on the idea of spending money for a rug replacement for her."

"We saw an article about the marina and the fire when we were waiting to get on Don's boat to the Clam Shack," Sherry said.

Erno shook his head. "Changed the landscape of the harbor. Put Lonnie out of work and he never went back, even after the marina reopened in its new, reduced form."

Sherry followed her father to the hooked-rug demonstration table. Even after years of working at the Ruggery, she continued to admire the area in the store where customers were introduced to the art of rug hooking. In front of her, a canvas lay blocked on a wooden frame stand. A punch needle threaded with a vibrant green stood upright, partially punched in the canvas, ready for a willing customer to be educated. She remembered how, as a child, she was in the store after school. Her favorite activity was spelling out her name on canvas in wool, punching loops of colorful yarn in script, block letters, and illegible abstract designs only she could decipher.

"Have you ever heard of a local journalist named Cap Diminsky? He wrote the article about the marina," Marla asked her father.

Erno retacked the canvas to the frame, where customers had pushed too hard with the punch tool and loosened the contact point. "Sure. I've read his articles for years. He's a very good writer. Local fellow. Older than me. Must be retired by now. Maybe even, you know, dead."

"You might be right. I hope not, though." A note of dismay lingered in Sherry's voice. "I'd like to find him."

"Wouldn't your co-judge from the bake-off be able to help you with the man's whereabouts if he's still in the area? The editor of Diminsky's paper might have his email address." Erno tested the tautness of the cotton canvas by pushing the needle through the material. The yarn formed a loop when he gently retracted the needle from the underside of the canvas. "Perfect."

"Good idea. If I need to, I'll ask Warren. He may not know either, if their careers didn't overlap."

Marla assisted Erno with bundles of yarn.

"Dad, we can take over from here. Why don't you take Ruth out for a morning coffee?"

"My daughter is a mind reader. I was just thinking about my sassy lassie." Erno laughed.

Sherry shook her head. "You two kids go and have some fun."

"Marla, I haven't even asked you why you're still here. Grant's gone back to Oklahoma. Why aren't you with him?" Erno asked.

Marla side-eyed Sherry, who lowered her gaze. Marla was going to have to handle this topic all on her own. "Things are a little rocky between Grant and me at the moment."

"Say no more. That sounds like Amber's field of expertise, not mine. I don't need details, but you do need to know you have my full support. As your father, my job is to be here for you in your time of need. Let me know when that time is and I'll jump into action." Erno gave Marla a kiss on the cheek before handing her the bundles of yarn. "Best remedy for family troubles is more family. I'll be back in an hour." Erno headed toward the front door. He took his jacket from the wall hook and was gone in the blink of an eye.

"Bye, Dad," Sherry and Marla said in unison.

"I knew he'd have trouble handling my marital problems." Marla placed the colorful yarn in the proper bins. "I'm having trouble, too."

Sherry and Marla spent the next hour with a customer, designing a raw canvas to be made into a rug. The scene depicted on the rug's canvas would be a rolling meadow, outlined by Erno's expert hand. He would be drawing from a photo the woman brought in. As the process developed, the customer grew unconvinced Sherry and Marla would properly relay her color palate and design details to Erno and was about to reschedule her visit when he returned with Ruth.

"Just in the nick of time," Sherry joked as her father

entered the store. "Victoria Templeton is asking for the boss. Would you mind helping her with her rug specifications?" Sherry pointed in the direction of Marla and Victoria, gathered around a large lookbook.

"That's what I was born to do." Erno hung up his coat. "I'm on my way."

"Hi, Ruth. Come talk to me while Dad finishes with Victoria." Sherry led Ruth to the customer counter, where she pulled up a stool for his father's friend.

"How are you doing, dear? I hear you're struggling with one of your contest recipes. The butternut squash whatchamacallit. It really wasn't terrible, just not your best effort."

"I strive for the best, I'm afraid. This recipe's giving me agita. Something's missing."

Ruth leaned in. "Maybe it's time for a new hobby? Have you considered taking up poker or bunco? My best friend, Frances, and I host a group of parlor game players every Tuesday evening. I'm sure we could squeeze out Kirk Loveland and shoehorn you in. Works out perfectly. We think he's a cheater and have been devising his exit for months."

"I would love to join you all on Tuesday nights, down the road. You know me, I'm like a dog with a bone when it comes to my recipe contests. I can't let go very easily."

"The offer stands for the future. Erno was telling me you had questions about Cap Diminsky, the journalist. You know, he lives over at Sunset Village."

"Really? I was over there recently. Wish I'd known."

"He's lived there for about three years. I know, because, as a member of the Augustin Historical Society board, I presented him with a lifetime achievement award for his contribution to the betterment of our town's communications. As the editor of the Town Hall newsletter, one day you may get one, dear, for keeping Augustin in the paper with your contest wins."

"I'm sure there will be much more deserving citizens than myself, but thank you for the thought." Sherry considered the information Ruth had shared. "Cap is healthy? I'd be interested in speaking to him about the marina fire. He wrote at least two articles about the event. I've read one and have some questions."

Ruth unbuttoned her cardigan. The collar of the sweater was decorated with feathers, giving her long, sinewy neck a birdlike resemblance. "He was healthy about a year ago. That's when he was presented the award. Haven't heard otherwise. We had to move up the ceremony when our astute intern, at the time, realized this coming year was the twentieth anniversary of the marina fire. The timing worked out quite well. He received his award last year and his work is on exhibit this year. His articles will be featured as well. The Historical Society will be presenting an exhibit featuring artifacts and photographs from the marina disaster in honor of the firefighters, Coast Guard, police, and the Augustin maritime community in the new year. The hope is to raise money to refurbish the marina area as best as can be afforded. The history of Augustin is deeply rooted in the mariner community of yesteryear."

"I sure would love a look at that exhibit. I'm writing an article for the newsletter about fire safety and I might be able to gather some more material. Unfortunately, you say it's not running until January?" Sherry asked.

"I think I know someone who can get you a sneak preview." Ruth straightened her posture. "The items are currently laid out in the holding room. I can take you over there and let you look. How's this afternoon?"

Sherry took a look at her father and sister guiding Victoria Templeton through the rug design process. At the same time, her phone vibrated. She held up one finger to indicate her answer was on its way. "Hi, Eileen. Is everything all right?" Sherry gripped the phone with extra intensity, anticipating her neighbor may have had an accident, because she rarely called. The last time the woman had called her, she had sliced open her shin falling on her garden sprinkler.

"Very much so."

Sherry blew out a sigh of relief.

"Can you please take me to Pinch and Dash Bakery this afternoon? I'm obligated to make an appearance there to promote my cookie win and, without consulting me, they've advertised today as the day. I'm too nervous to drive myself. I've never done anything like this before. I'll pay you for your time."

Sherry smiled at her phone. "Of course, Eileen. And you certainly don't have to pay me. One cookie is all I ask for in return." She laughed. "Would you be put out if we made a stop at the Historical Society? They're very close to each other, and I have an errand to run there. Won't take too long."

"We can stop anywhere you want. I'm supposed to be there around three. Maybe for an hour, they say. No one's interested in meeting me anyway, but I may never be asked again, so I should go."

Sherry lowered the phone to her side and faced Ruth. "Would it work for you if we visited the Historical Society around two fifteen today? Eileen will be with me, if that works. We will then continue on to the Pinch and Dash Bakery, where she's making an appearance."

"Perfect." Ruth shifted her attention to the approaching male. "Just like you."

Erno hugged Ruth as she remained seated on her stool. "You're perfect too, cutie pie."

"I'll pick you up at two. See you then." Sherry ended the phone call.

"I was hoping I had a chance with your father." Victoria positioned herself next to Erno at the sales counter. "Now I see the competition is too strong. Ruth, you're a lucky lady."

"I certainly am," Ruth said. "But I can be bought."

"Ruth!" Erno wagged his finger at his girlfriend.

"We will treasure the rug when it arrives." Victoria paid the deposit. "I guess that's the most Erno I can hope for."

"Don't let this go to your head, sweetie." Ruth wagged her finger at Erno.

"Have a good afternoon, everyone." Victoria tossed a wave in everyone's direction and let herself out.

"That was interesting," Marla said. "My dad, the sex symbol."

"Can we get back to work, please? Enough of this nonsense." Erno pulled a card from the Rolodex. "She's been a good customer for years. Lost her husband about five years ago. Probably lonely."

"Don't go getting any ideas of filling her empty hours, young fellow," Ruth said.

"Not in a million years. I wouldn't have the energy for two of you gals."

"Okay, that's enough," Sherry said. "Dad, around one thirty, Ruth and I are going to run a few errands, if you don't mind. Marla can stay with you at the store, and Amber should be back by then." Sherry made eye contact with Marla. "Can't you? Unless you want to come with us, or I can drop you at home to hang out with Chutney. I have to pick up Eileen, so I can easily drop you at home."

"What do you say, Marla? Stay here with your old man?" Erno asked. "We can have a chat, if we get the chance."

"Can't pass up that opportunity. I'll stay here with Dad." Marla tilted her head in the direction of the Rolodex. "In the meantime, don't forget to fill out that card for Mrs. Templeton while the information's fresh in your mind."

"And I'm off to meet Frances for an early lunch. Sherry, I'll be back by one thirty." Ruth rose from her stool, gave Erno a peck on the cheek, and headed out the door.

Chapter 13

Walking from her car to the museum, Sherry recalled the last time she'd visited the Augustin Historical Society. Last year, during the holiday season, a model train exhibit featuring miniature replicas of every aspect of Augustin landscape was the hottest ticket in town. She'd joined Erno for some father-daughter time to get a bird's-eye view of their hometown. Erno was beyond proud when he located the Ruggery in all its tiny glory. He was so familiar with the history of the town's commerce, he could have led the tour himself.

The building that housed the rotating collection of Augustin memorabilia was itself a tribute to fine New England craftsmanship. Even before she entered the building, the colonial wooden house, built in the 1700s and in various stages thereafter, filled her with awe as she stepped up on the massive marble block leading to the front door.

Sherry stood in front of the carved wooden doors with antique brass hardware until Ruth poked her from behind.

"Are you going to open the door, dear? We don't have all day."

"This door is so beautiful. I'm imagining the skilled hands that did the carving." Sherry held the door open for the other two ladies.

"Follow me." Ruth bypassed the ticket desk and walked into the "please touch" colonial kitchen. Stationed by the water pump next to the kitchen sink was a woman outfitted in a period dress and apron. Her bonnet was secured on her head with a giant bow under her chin. Sherry sympathized with the women of the day when she spotted the rigid leather shoes the woman wore. She silently thanked her lucky stars to have been born in the era of memory foam shoe inserts.

The woman greeted Sherry, Eileen, and Ruth. Ruth and she clearly needed no introduction. They embraced and shared a whisper. The woman appeared conflicted as to whether to break character or maintain her role as an eighteenth-century homemaker.

"Nice to meet you, too, Dolly," Sherry said after hearing the woman's period-correct name. "Is that your real name?"

"It was a choice between Dolly or Deliverance, so I chose Dolly. It's my real name when I step through the doors of the Historical Society." Dolly didn't offer any other name she went by outside of work.

After a brief conversation with Ruth, Dolly plunged her hand in her apron pocket and retrieved a ring of keys. She unlocked a door in the darkest corner of the kitchen.

Ruth led the ladies up a steep set of rickety stairs. Sherry was last in line, with the pretense that she wanted to tie her shoe before climbing the narrow steps. In reality, her intention was to ensure Eileen and Ruth journeyed upstairs without incident. Sherry intended to save them from toppling down the staircase, illuminated by only one bulb, at the top of the staircase, leaving the bottom a dark, risky venture. Somehow, being below the others seemed to make the most logistical sense to stop them from somersaulting down too many risers. Falling down these stairs might have been a contributing factor to the early mortality rate hundreds of years ago.

Surviving the climb to the second floor, Sherry was faced with a low-ceilinged room with wood as the primary décor. Heavy beams supported the ceiling, wood paneling lined the walls, and wide planks comprised the floor. Again, the room was underlit. The idea of whacking her head on one of the beams was foremost on Sherry's mind as she followed the ladies.

"This is the holding room for our next exhibit." Ruth pointed out a collection of framed photographs propped up against the wall, single file. "Photographs over here. Artifacts and articles over there." Ruth pointed to the opposite wall.

Sherry carefully crossed the room. She kneeled in front of the framed articles. "Is there an article by Cap Diminsky?"

Ruth joined her. "More than one. We haven't put them in any sensible order yet. Let me hunt his down." She tipped back each frame to better see what was behind the glass.

"I'll take a look at the photos." Sherry crossed the room and squatted in front of the first photograph. It was an eerie sepia panorama of the aftermath of the marina fire. Smoldering debris, damaged boats, and a roofless shell of a clubhouse, shot from an overhead vantage point. The next frame displayed two photos, a before and an after of the Augustin Harbor vista. The fire had transformed an idyllic coastal landscape into a charred eyesore. Sherry sat on the floor. "These are amazing."

Eileen joined Sherry on the floor. "Take a look at this photo. A beautiful boat laid waste to. I bet the owner was devastated by the loss."

Sherry scooted backward on the floor to take another look at the first photograph. Her sights locked on the largest boat, remaining somewhat intact. The hull was crumbled and blackened, while the stern appeared to have escaped severe disfigurement.

"The firefighters did their best, but fire is such a force," Eileen said. "I remember hearing the sirens that day. The responding trucks came from all directions. You couldn't get through town because the roads leading to the shoreline were all blocked off."

Ruth approached, announced by the creaky floor. "That's one of our most dramatic photos. It was taken by a photographer who climbed into a crane that was moved in to remove the damage."

"Quite an amazing photo."

"Did you find what you're looking for?" Ruth asked.

"That's a good question. Not quite sure what I'm looking for, to be honest. I've heard so much about the fire recently, but until you see these photos, you can't imagine what the event entailed," Sherry said. "Brings a lot of emotions to the forefront."

"Funny thing is, half of those who lived through it don't ever want to talk about it again and the other half can't let it die. A very black-and-white topic, especially for the fact that no one was ever charged with the crime of arson, even though all evidence indicated the fire was set intentionally."

"Ladies, I found an interesting article by Cap Diminsky on the fire," Eileen called out. "I skimmed it and came away with one major theme. He wasn't shy about suggesting Crosby Currier set the fire to punish his father for letting his marriage dissolve without a fight."

"How would Cap know such an intimate detail about the Curriers' marriage?" Sherry questioned.

"Let me rephrase that," Eileen said. "Says in the margin that this article ran in the Op-Ed section of the paper. You know, the section where opinions don't necessarily have to be fact-driven or fact-checked. The piece was written by Diminsky for the purpose of questioning why Crosby never had to go to trial when so much evidence pointed to his guilt."

"Can't imagine the Currier family was happy about the defaming of the family name when this was published," Eileen added.

"Good reason why Crosby left town. And Lonnie never returned to what was left of his dockmaster job," Sherry said.

"This other story relays straightforward facts about the fire. You might be interested in this one, Sherry," Eileen said.

Sherry hoisted herself from the floor and crossed the room. "This is the one Vitis has framed in the dockmaster shed at the marina. Would you mind if I snap a photo of it? I'm writing about holiday fire safety awareness and a reference to how devastating fire can be, citing an actual case, is priceless. I want to get the facts straight."

Ruth trailed Sherry to the article. "This is the first article visitors will see when they enter the exhibit hall."

Ruth held up a framed newspaper front page, featuring the headline Augustin Marina incinerated.

"A little higher, please." Sherry captured the image on her phone. "Got it. Thanks."

"You're welcome to photograph anything here." Ruth positioned herself at the top of the stairs while Sherry clicked a few more photos.

"Thank you." Sherry tucked her phone in her pocket. "I'm all set. I really appreciate your time, Ruth."

"My pleasure, dear."

Sherry let out a hearty chuckle.

"Sounds like you all are having a fun time up there," a voice called up the stairs. "Is there anything you need?"

"That's her way of saying our time is up," Ruth whispered. She raised her voice. "No thanks. We're on our way down."

After spending a few bonus minutes hearing about the activities of women in the 1700s, Sherry drove Eileen and Ruth to Pinch and Dash. She had to circle the block once when she couldn't find a parking spot within reasonable proximity to the bakery, which was unusual, because the store sat beside empty lots on either side.

"Now I see why we're having trouble finding a parking spot. Take a look at that." Sherry pointed toward the store after exiting the car. "There's a line out the door."

"Hurry, I think we're late." Eileen trotted down the sidewalk.

"Guess she's not nervous anymore." Sherry laughed.

Her neighbor shouldered her way through the line, igniting a round of applause as she led with the comment, "I'm Eileen Weisberger. I've come to talk about my winning cookie."

As Sherry neared the bakery, she heard her name called.

"Sherry, over here." Barry was at the side door, waving her in closer. "Come in this way."

Sherry linked arms with Ruth. They bypassed the customer line snaking out the front entrance.

"All the bake-off judges are here. This is amazing." Barry put his arm on Warren's shoulder. "When Eileen told me you were bringing her today, I contacted Warren, who generously moved an appointment around to be here. That's why we have such a huge response from customers. Thank goodness for social media. A few posts and the word spread like wildfire." Barry grinned from ear to ear. "I've set up a table specifically for Eileen. If you guys wouldn't mind, we'll sit alongside her and answer any questions customers might have."

"Oh my gosh," Sherry said. "I would have spruced up if I'd known. Barry, can we have an extra chair for Ruth, please. She didn't have any idea she'd be sucked into the cookie madness."

"Of course," said Barry. "The more the merrier. Ruth, just have a few recipes in mind when a customer talks to you. It's all about trading baking secrets."

After an hour of chatting with cookie connoisseurs and watching the delighted response to their first bite of Eileen's cookie, the crowd dwindled to only a few patrons.

Barry thanked each contributor, with special exuberance expressed to Eileen, who captivated the crowd with her tales of baking, gardening, and teaching her cat to walk on a leash.

"Thank you, Sherry, for chauffeuring the ladies here.

The bakery appreciates the effort," Barry said. "And Warren, special thanks for spending an hour of your valuable time amusing my customers with your journalism stories. And Ruth, what can I say? You delighted the cookie lovers with your recipes handed down through generations. That's what cooking and baking is all about." Barry's voice wobbled.

"Our pleasure," Eileen replied.

While Sherry waited for Eileen and Ruth to freshen up in the ladies' room, the opportunity for Sherry to speak one-on-one to Warren, without interruption, arose.

"You shared so many interesting stories of your days as a journalist, and now as the newspaper's editor." Sherry paused to assess Warren's facial expression. He seemed receptive of her comment, so she plunged on. "Do you have any recollection of a journalist named Cap Diminsky? He wrote for the *Nutmeg State of Mind* many years ago. Maybe twenty. I believe your father was the editor at that time."

Warren nodded. His eyes drifted upward before returning to Sherry, as if temporarily lost in thought.

"Cap Diminsky was a wonderful writer. You're absolutely correct. He was at the newspaper during my father's time as editor-in-chief. I overlapped him a bit when I came on as a staff writer. I considered him a mentor. I read any article he wrote. His style was so unique. He had a way of submerging himself in his stories, as if he were a witness to whatever the subject covered. From biographical interviews to breaking news, he was engaging and nonjudgmental."

Not always. Maybe Warren hadn't read every one of his pieces. "You're speaking about him in the past tense. Is he still alive?" Sherry asked with a note of caution.

"I'm happy to report I believe he's still alive and kicking in Sunset Village. Probably runs the show over there. You've reminded me, I should visit him one day soon. He and my father were quite close. My father's memory isn't what it used to be, so I'm quite certain he wouldn't recognize anyone from his working days, which is sad." Warren pushed back his chair and rose to his feet. He extended his hand to Sherry, who accepted the assistance to rise from her chair. "Did I answer your question sufficiently?"

"Yes. Thank you. Oh, and sorry about your father."

"He had such a remarkable life. It's okay." Warren's lower lip protruded slightly. "Have a great afternoon."

"We're back," Ruth said.

"Eileen, again, great job. Everyone loves your cookies. We may have to negotiate a deal to put them on the menu permanently." Barry took Eileen's hand. "I'd like to offer each of you a dozen cookies of your choosing to take home."

"How generous. Thank you. Warren just left. Should I try to get him back inside?" Sherry asked.

"That's okay. He comes in often. His wife has a sugar addiction, he claims, although I'd say he does, too, judging by how many sweets he buys a week. I'll give him his dozen next time he comes in."

"Come on, ladies, let's go choose." Sherry surveyed the offerings in the glass case at the front of the store. "I'll take six of Eileen's and six of the Tropical Aloha Bars, please."

"Same for me," Ruth said.

"I'd love a variety of sandwich cookies, please. I don't need any more of mine for a while," Eileen said.

Behind the counter, Barry held open a take-home box one at a time and filled it with sweet treats.

"Thank you so much," Sherry said.

Barry handed the boxes over the counter.

"Are these bars the ones you said are similar to Crosby's? I barely see any difference at all, unless there's a secret ingredient in them I can't identify."

"You have a good eye," Barry said. "Yes. In the name of transparency, my friend Rachel shared the original recipe with me. Did you know the recipe was the winner of the last and only other Story For Glory Cookie Bakeoff, held about twenty years ago?"

Sherry took a lingering look at the remaining bars in the display case in front of her. Her gaze lifted back to Barry's face. "I didn't know that. That's amazing. Who entered the recipe?"

"Rachel's mother-in-law, Ivy Banks Currier. I even know the story behind the recipe. Rachel said the recipe was invented to win over Lonnie. The couple went on a picnic and Ivy baked the bars and brought them along. Lonnie proposed on the spot. May be somewhat embellished, but kind of a cute story."

Sherry opened her mouth to comment, but the words didn't come.

"You look stunned," Barry said.

"I am. Did you recognize the bars at the bake-off as the previous winner right away? You didn't say a word."

"The cookie bars are one of the most popular items on my inventory here at the bakery, so yes. I've been offering them for sale throughout the year. Rachel gave me a copy of the recipe after her mother-in-law passed away. She said she thought it was a fitting tribute to the woman who was 'a wonderful force of nature,' as she put it. That being said, I couldn't have chosen Crosby's cookie bars as the winner of the bake-off for a number of reasons."

"Sherry, I need to get back to the Ruggery to meet up with Erno," Ruth said.

Eileen nodded in agreement.

"Yes. We'll be on our way. Thanks again for the cookies. We didn't know we'd be part of the event, but we were glad we were. Right, Ruth?" Sherry asked.

"I had so much fun. I was able to share my recipe for Double Chocolate Brownie Cake Cookies. I think I'll enter them in next year's cookie contest." Ruth wrinkled her brow. "Now I regret sharing the recipe. What if someone replicates it and it shows up at the bake-off? I always thought you were a bit selfish, not sharing your recipes, Sherry, but now I'm beginning to understand your motivation. You don't want them appearing at the next recipe contest under someone else's name."

"Glad you don't think I'm selfish anymore, Ruth," Sherry said with a defensive intonation.

Ruth showered Sherry with a smile that cleared the air of any hard feelings.

"Nice seeing you again, Barry." Sherry took a step toward the front door.

Barry made his way around the back of the display case and opened the door for the ladies.

"I'm curious," Sherry said in a quiet tone. "How long have you and Rachel been dating?"

Sherry was startled by the intensity of Barry's laughter. When he regained his composure, he answered, "Rachel is my sister from another mister. That's all. I've been with the dearest boyfriend for six years. I thought that was common knowledge."

Sherry's hands covered her face for a few seconds. "I'm always the last to know."

"Rachel's a wonderful friend, but we could never make it as a couple. For obvious reasons," Barry joked. "See you pretty ladies soon, I hope."

Chapter 14

Sherry led Eileen and Ruth into the Ruggery, where they were met with cheers. Erno, Marla, and Amber congratulated Eileen on her bakery appearance, following up with a plea for a sample.

"We have treats for everyone." Sherry set her box of cookies on the sales counter and stepped aside. "Ruth and I ended up participating as well."

"Are you serious?" Erno asked. "Ruth, that's amazing. Did you talk about our favorite raspberry chocolate kisses? Ruth makes them for me on special occasions. I may be jealous if you gave away our treasured shared recipe."

"Don't worry. Our recipe is safe with me. Now that you mention it, I may have to enter it in next year's cookie bake-off. I'll have to clean up the story behind the recipe, though." Ruth blew a kiss in Erno's direction.

"Anyway," Sherry sighed, "a fun hour was had by all."

"Sure sounds like it," Marla said.

"Unless you need me, Dad, I'll drop Eileen at her house. And I have to finish my fire safety article for the newsletter. I got some fascinating material about the marina fire from the Historical Society exhibit we were honored to have a sneak peek of. All the articles are due today. Seeing that I know the editor, it's okay if mine is the last to meet the deadline." Sherry checked her phone. "Maybe it's not the last. Still haven't received Patti's blurb. I need to shoot her a reminder for her bake-off recap."

"Mind if I join you?" Marla asked.

"We'd better ask the boss." Sherry directed her question to her father. "What do you say—can Marla join me at home?"

"Sure. Don't need you or Marla for the rest of the day. She's been a fantastic help. I drew out Victoria Templeton's canvas design while Amber and Marla attended to the customers, so I'm one step ahead of the game. Just have to order some wool and dye and we're on our way."

"In that case, I won't even unzip my coat." Sherry lifted Marla's coat from the hook by the door. "Let's hit the road, Marla and Eileen. Bye."

"The only problem with you and me doing something together is there's no one home to walk Chutney," Eileen pointed out as they left the store. "I'm your go-to dog walker when you're busy, and if we're busy together, the poor dog is out of luck."

"You're right," Sherry said. "This is the exception rather than the rule. He certainly will be happy to see us when we get home."

"It might be good for him to have some me time," Marla suggested. "Worked for me. It's knocked some sense into me to have some time to myself."

Sherry side-eyed her sister, who returned the glance with a kind smile.

"Why didn't you park next to Dad's car behind the Ruggery? I'm not complaining about this walk to the municipal lot, but, in the winter, trudging through the snow is going to be tiresome," Marla said.

They stepped off the curb to cross another street.

"I usually would, but there's been a problem lately. Won't be for much longer. The store next to ours was vacant for most of October, and the parking back then was so spacious. Now the lingerie store has moved in. While they're sprucing the place up, trucks are always knocking around back there. Plus, they've temporarily relocated our shared dumpster, so poor Dad has to squeeze his beloved wagon into what used to be a roomy spot. I don't want my car to get nicked, so I'm staying far away until the construction's done."

"Aren't these emerging Christmas decorations lovely?" Eileen slowed.

The group gathered around her as she studied a nativity scene in the window of the local watering hole, Wine One One.

After a short while, Sherry edged forward, as did Marla, but Eileen stayed still. "You okay, Eileen?"

"I'm a bit exhausted from all of today's activities. My day is usually weeding, lunch, reading, dinner. The added excitement of a public spectacle has suddenly drained me. I just need a minute."

Sherry glanced down the row of stores. "Let's go into Sal and Effi's cleaners. It's only two stores down. I know they'll let you have a seat. We'll pick you up in the car in a few minutes."

"I wouldn't mind. It's been a long day. I'm in a full sugar low right now," Eileen said.

"That's exactly what's going on. I feel the same dip in energy," Sherry said.

Sherry and Marla sandwiched Eileen for the next two blocks. They stopped in the doorway of the Shore Cleaners.

"Let's go inside and explain ourselves. They'll understand." Sherry held the door open.

Marla hooked her arm around Eileen's elbow and steered her inside.

"Good afternoon, ladies," Sal announced from behind the cash register.

The noise of the conveyor mechanism transporting clean clothes to the sales counter nearly drowned out the owner's welcome.

"Who's picking up today? Did you bring your ticket?"

"I'm afraid we're dropping off Eileen, if that's all right. I parked so far from the Ruggery, it's a challenge to drum up the energy to get to the town lot. We've already had an exhausting day. Marla and I will be back in a few minutes with the car to pick her up."

"Now that's a unique drop-off if I've ever heard one," Sal said.

"Good day, ladies," Effi sang out as she appeared from the depths of the laundry-filled room. "Sherry, my favorite cookie judge. So nice to see you."

Sherry was happy Effi garnered no ill will against her for not choosing her cookie as the winner.

"Hello, Effi. I was explaining to Sal why Eileen would love to have a seat here while I run to get the car."

"Anything for Augustin's best cookie baker," Effi said.

"Did you hear that? I'm Augustin's best cookie baker." Eileen's eyes twinkled as her smile lines framed her grin.

"Yes, you are," Sherry confirmed. "At least for one year."

"Too bad about that young man, Crosby Currier. Sounds like he met a grim end down at the marina," Sal said.

"The family has been one of our longest-running customers, although I hadn't laid eyes on any of them for months until the bake-off," Effi said.

Sherry was struck with a thought. "Effi, you've reminded me of something. Sal, when you and Effi were approaching the judge's table with Effi's cookies, you said a word to Crosby."

Sal furrowed his brow. "Yes, come to think of it, you're correct."

Sherry hesitated before continuing. She summoned her gentlest tone. "He must have been wishing you both good luck in the bake-off?"

"Sherry, dear. You're not fooling anyone," Effi said in her singsong voice.

Sherry's eyebrows lifted as her gaze darted in Effi's direction.

"Why don't you come right out and ask Sal what he and Crosby said to each other? I did."

Sherry's cheeks warmed. "Okay. What did you two say to each other?"

"I'll tell you, like I told Effi," Sal said. "It's no big secret. Rachel Currier dropped off a coat a long time ago, end of last winter, I believe. I'd have to check the ticket at this point for the exact date. The store's policy is, if no one picks up an item after an extended length of time, we donate the piece. We're not a storage facility. Rachel said it was Ivy's. She said her mother-in-law lent her the coat, and it was soiled. Then she wouldn't pick it up, even after multiple reminders." Sal raised both hands high. "What am I supposed to do about an unclaimed coat when I know who it belongs to? But I would like to get paid."

"Don't leave us hanging," Marla said. "What was Crosby's reply?"

"He said Rachel wasn't his wife anymore. He also said his mother had passed away. He said I could do what I wanted with the coat. I told him the pockets weren't empty when I received the coat. After cleaning, I returned the item to the pocket. He didn't show any interest in finding out what that item was."

Sherry wondered if Marla had the same thought as she. When she saw her sister open her mouth, she was certain she did.

"Is the coat here? May we see it?" Marla asked. "I mean, technically, the coat no longer has an owner, so you wouldn't be violating anyone's privacy."

Effi stepped forward. "Eileen, please have a seat." She pointed to two chairs outside the tiny fitting and alterations changing room.

"Thank you, I thought you all forgot about me. What's all this fuss over a coat?" Eileen took a seat. "I will admit, this is getting interesting."

"Yes, the coat is in-house. I just moved it to the room for unloved garments downstairs. I'll be right back." Sal shuffled away on his short legs dressed in baggy, cuffed dress slacks.

When Sal was out of sight, Effi motioned Sherry

closer. "I want to show you something. Sal would never mention it because he thinks business will suffer, but I'm scared to death."

"What is it?" The concern Sherry had for Effi caused her voice to crack.

Effi lifted the well-worn cash register to reveal a sheet of paper. She wriggled the paper out from under the machine and handed it to Sherry. Marla peered over her sister's shoulder.

"I can't see from here. Can you tell me what's going on?" Eileen called out.

Sherry put up her index finger to indicate she would advise Eileen as soon as she herself knew what was going on. Sherry read the words printed in a large, blocky font. "Mind Your Own Business Or Else!" She handed the paper back to Effi, who received it with a shaky hand.

"We don't even know what business we're supposed to be minding, or not minding."

"Not the best print job." Marla pulled away from Sherry's shoulder. "Mystery threatening person could have sprung for a cleaner sheet of paper."

"Would you mind if I snap a picture?" Sherry pulled out her phone.

"No, but please hurry. Sal doesn't want anyone to know we received this. It was slipped under the door, and we found it on Monday when we came in to work. He's not telling the police and won't allow me to even bring up the notion. Says we'll lose too much business."

Sherry clicked a photo and Effi returned the paper to its hiding place. Sherry tucked away her phone.

"Maybe we shouldn't be showing you Ivy's coat. Maybe that's the business we shouldn't be minding."

"That doesn't make sense. Why would someone threaten you about a coat? I wouldn't worry too much." As Sherry spoke the words, she realized she didn't believe what she was saying.

"Sorry for the wait. Here's the coat. Looks like it's your size, if you want it. Try it on. Its next stop is the thrift store." Sal pulled the plastic bag over the baby-blue wool coat and passed the garment to Sherry. "Mirror's behind Eileen in the fitting room."

Sherry handed her jacket to Marla. In the fitting room, she slipped on the timeless duffel coat.

"Do you like it? It's such a beauty. I'm sure it was very expensive," Effi said.

Sherry admired the coat's fit as she gazed at her reflection in the full-length mirror. The color was the only sticking point. Baby blue might have been popular years ago, but it was impractical with Sherry's active lifestyle.

"Very nice, dear," Eileen said. "Reminds me of the style my mother used to wear before she passed away. Bless her heart. Has a bit of an odor, though, wouldn't you agree?"

Sherry used a more critical eye assessing the A-line drape of the coat. Nice for hiding figure flaws. She plunged her hands in the spacious pockets and struck a pose. Her admiration was interrupted by the sharp edge of something in the pocket jabbing her palm. She withdrew her hand with the something clutched tight. She inspected the greeting card, adorned with a colorful beach scene. She opened it and read the simple note. *"Aloha, my love."*

"Sherry, this isn't a Paris fashion show. What's taking you so long? Let's see how it fits," Marla called out.

"Coming." Sherry stepped out of the fitting room and gave her best imitation of a fashion runway twirl.

Her sister's expression drooped.

"The color, right? A little too last decade."

"Might come back in style. Fashionistas always say, 'what's old will soon be new,'" Marla said. "Could use a day to air out." She waved her hand across her nose.

"I love it. I always admired my mother's fashion choices. If I weren't smaller than you, I'd take it. Might need a touch more alteration. Old clothes have that distinctive, musty smell. This coat is more pungent than usual," Eileen said.

The thought of styling herself after Eileen or her mother helped seal the deal.

"Not for me," Sherry said. "I'm sure it'll find the right owner. You say it was Rachel who dropped it off?"

"Yes," said Sal. "She did mention it was her mother-in-law's, though. She was only borrowing it. Now none of the Curriers want it. Can't figure people out."

"We don't have to. As long as they need dry cleaning, that's all that matters," Effi added.

"And pay us for our service," Sal added. "That matters, too."

"Thank you for showing me the coat. You're right. It will find a nice home. It's lovely." Sherry handed Sal the coat and the hanger.

"I'll put it back under the Currier name and give them a longer grace period. Maybe Rachel will change her mind when she sees it next to her other cleaning."

"Hope so." Sherry envisioned the card inside the pocket. "But I doubt it. We'll be back in a few minutes with the car, Eileen."

"No need. I'm all rested." Eileen stood. "I can make the walk back to the car."

"Thank you, Sal. Thank you, Effi." Sherry held the door open. "Oh, and Effi, I'll be in touch soon about that little matter."

"I look forward to hearing from you," Effi said.

Chapter 15

In the parking lot, the car next to Sherry's began to back out as she crossed behind it. She held up her hand to ensure the driver saw her. The brake lights went on and the car jerked to a stop.

The driver rolled down the window. "I'm so sorry." Patti leaned her head partially out of the car. "Sherry. Just the person I was going to email. Hold on one sec."

"The doors are unlocked. I'll be right there," Sherry said to Eileen and Marla, who got inside Sherry's car.

Patti opened her car door and waved a sheet of paper in front of Sherry's face. "I was on my way home to type up the article and email it to you. The newsroom's network is down while the tech team does mysterious, and probably unnecessary, upgrades. We all have to work offline. Only one printer is working in the whole building and it isn't wireless."

Sherry shook her head. "So old-fashioned." She laughed.

"Yes! I got your article done at least. The queue was so long, this took an hour to print. I could have read the whole thing over the phone to you faster than waiting for my turn. Trying to send it to the printer using the one available cable was a feat of magic all in itself. No email in the office, nothing. No one uses a cable anymore. Silly me. I didn't bother bringing in my laptop today, which I fully regret. That wouldn't have worked anyway if the network was down." Patti groaned.

"No worries. I'll retype it for you on my laptop. I'm on my way home to pull the newsletter together. You need a break."

"Thank you. I'm so spoiled, having the latest and greatest technology available at my fingertips that when it's not available, I become a big baby." She handed Sherry her printout.

"I'm going to keep moving. My poor neighbor, Eileen, is exhausted." Sherry gestured toward her car. The passenger doors were open. "We attended a cookie meet and greet after I dragged her to the Historical Society to gather information for my article."

"Anyone trying to keep up with your activities is a superhero. She'll love the bake-off recap. Her cookies were so good. I snuck a few from her tray before she left. See you soon."

"Bye-bye." Sherry made her way around Patti's car and joined Marla and Eileen. "We're finally on the way home."

After Sherry dropped off Eileen, she turned to Marla. "I'd like to go to Sunset Village, but I have to get the newsletter together now. Would you mind if we went there first thing in the morning?"

Marla kept her sights out the windshield. "Sure. Any time, as long as it's before dinner. I've changed my plans once again. While you were out with Eileen and Ruth this afternoon, I had a long conversation with Amber and Dad. I bought a return plane ticket back home and I'm leaving tomorrow night."

Instead of backing the car out of Eileen's driveway, Sherry waited for Marla to meet her gaze. She studied her younger sister for signs of whether the trip home was something she was happy about or the contrary. Marla's stoic expression offered no clues.

"Are you okay with going home a few days early?" Sherry asked. "You're welcome to stay with me as long as you want or need to."

"It's the right thing to do," Marla said simply. There was a moment of silence. "So, what did you guys learn at the Historical Society?"

Sherry backed up her car. One more turn of the wheel and it was in her own driveway. "Let's get inside and I'll fill you in. I'm really going to need your help sorting through fire photos and articles."

Chutney greeted his owner at the door with all the enthusiasm of a dog who's aware his afternoon meal is late. After he was fed, Sherry and Marla took a seat at the kitchen table.

They spent time looking at the Augustin Marina fire photos and related articles. "The marina fire was devastating and spelled the end of the Augustin Yacht Club. Lonnie's job ended the day of the fire. Cap Diminsky clearly felt Crosby set the fire in retaliation for what he believed was his father's mistreatment of his mother. Pointing a finger at someone without one hundred percent proof positive is risky business."

"Risky because of what the person under suspicion is put through?"

"Yes, and what if Crosby decided he needed payback for all he was put through being a suspect."

"But as far as we know, the case was dropped and that was that. Crosby's death probably had nothing to do with the fire. How could it? The fire was so long ago. Wouldn't you agree?" Marla asked.

"So far, like the fire, the evidence in the murder investigation isn't pointing one hundred percent in any certain direction. Twenty years ago, Crosby was never charged with a crime because the evidence hit a dead end at some point."

"It's a stretch that there's a connection."

"Consider this. Crosby's body was found at the marina. Tied to an anchor. Has to be significant. A parting shot at Crosby. A calling card, in a sense. Some sort of satisfaction received for the trouble of setting up the crime scene in such a way."

"Or a diversion?" Marla asked.

"Possibly."

"Let's put the diversion theory on ice for the time being. Back up a minute. If Crosby was guilty of arson, everyone with a boat damaged or destroyed in the fire would be his enemy. But why wait so many years after the fire for retaliation?"

"Exactly."

"Exactly what?" Marla asked.

"I think the field of suspects is a lot slimmer than meets the eye. The list includes his father, Lonnie, who lost his livelihood in the fire; Vitis, who seems to hold a powerful grudge against Crosby for destroying the Augustin landmark; Rachel, who is Lonnie's close ally and Crosby's biggest critic."

"That's a crowded field, not a slim one," Marla said.

"My feeling is, the fire might be related, but I'm not so sure it's the motivating factor behind the murder."

"Your phone is buzzing." Marla pointed toward the front door. "It's on the hall table."

Sherry scooted back her chair and raced to the phone. Under the table, Chutney stirred from a nap and began barking.

"Hi, Ray." Sherry walked back into the kitchen. "Shhh."

"Shhh?"

"Chutney. Not *you*, Ray. I startled the dog. What can I do for you?"

"A search of Crosby's car has yielded an interesting item. A document from the Connecticut Department of Motor Vehicles filled out with a request to change the name of his boat."

"Is that unusual?" Sherry asked.

"The boat in question is currently named *Rachel's Way*. The application was a request to change the name to *Sweet Revenge*."

Sherry's gaze met Marla's, and she raised her palms in question.

"What's he saying?" Marla asked.

"Crosby wanted his boat to be renamed *Sweet Revenge*. The current name is *Rachel's Way*," Sherry whispered as an aside to Marla. Sherry clicked on her phone's Speaker button. "Sounds like he's not over her. Unless the revenge is aimed toward someone else?" She knew Ray wasn't going to answer her speculative question. "If this is the boat my friend Don was purchasing from Crosby, why the last-minute name change?"

"What was the date on the application?" Marla whispered.

"What was the date on the name change application?" Sherry relayed Marla's question to Ray.

Sherry heard paper rustling through the phone.

"I can hear we're on Speaker. No need to whisper," Ray said.

Sherry winced.

"Dated a week ago. Just needed to be submitted, and obviously it wasn't."

"That was prior to our dinner and the gentlemen's handshake between Crosby and Don on the boat sale," Sherry said.

"That's right. Makes sense," Ray said.

"Don would say the boat was his, because they shook hands, but no money had been transferred at the time of Crosby's death. Don had every intention of paying Crosby right after the bake-off. Even after Crosby's death, the sale was moving forward. Crosby's lawyer contacted Don to ask if he was still interested in the sale and Don said he was. That was, until Rachel stopped the deal," Sherry said. "She told her lawyer to contact Don and relay the message that the boat was hers after the divorce. Crosby had no right to sell it out from under her."

"Sounds like you're as up-to-date on the boat situation as I am. Here's a tidbit you may not be aware of and the reason for my call. The search of Crosby's car produced two other items of note." Ray paused.

"And they would be?"

"A cookie recipe for Tropical Aloha Bars. Interesting detail: The recipe was typed by a typewriter, not printed from a computer. I'd like to send you a snapshot of the recipe and have you confirm whether it's the one from the cookie bake-off."

"Of course, but what if it is? Why is that important?" Sherry realized it would be unusual for Ray to give a straight-up, detailed response to her probing questions, but it was worth a try.

"The recipe was tucked under the prizes in the back seat of his car. Also, the other item of interest found in the car among the prizes was a handgun. What could have gone down at the bake-off might have been awfully messy."

Sherry shuddered and Marla gasped.

Sherry's phone buzzed. "I got your text and I'm looking at the recipe." She examined the words in the photo Ray had snapped. Sections were difficult to decipher because the paper he'd photographed had fold seams in thirds from end to end.

Coconut, white and dark chocolate chips, brown sugar, vanilla, macadamia nuts, oatmeal, lime, and guava jam were all among the ingredients. "Does look like Crosby's entry for the contest. We docked him for what wasn't an outstandingly different take on a somewhat generic recipe. He didn't use guava jam, which the recipe I'm looking at calls for. That would have been a twist the judges would have given him points for."

"I don't need to know the ins and outs of your judging techniques. Simple question is, is this the recipe he entered in the contest, because you can see his name isn't on the recipe, his mother's is."

"It is the recipe. Using a variation on the name. His mother won the only other cookie bake-off the newspaper held many years ago. With the same recipe, apparently.

Her daughter-in-law has granted the rights to that recipe to her friend, Chef Buckman, for use in his bakery. It's a best seller."

"You cooking contestants are a tight-knit group, aren't you? How could the same recipe even be considered to win two separate times in the same contest? Isn't there a rule against that?" A note of confusion entered Ray's voice. "I don't get it."

"In a smaller contest, like Story For Glory, the organizers may not have the resources or desire to check the authenticity of every recipe. If they get duped, it's more of a shame than anything else. The truth does eventually come out, so if the baker is willing to risk the backlash when the older win resurfaces, I suppose he'll take his chances. Next time, the contest organizers need to do their homework. Chef Buckman became aware of the recipe when he tasted Crosby's cookie, and he later told me he could never have chosen him as the winner for that reason. The previous contest was so long ago, it seems no one bothered to check what the winning recipe was."

"Cook-offs have given my department trouble in the last few years. They need a deeper level of monitoring. They're serious business."

"I always say, competition can bring out the best and the worst in people." Sherry paused. "What was Crosby doing carrying around his mother's original recipe if he wasn't going to give her credit for the recipe in the bake-off? He claimed it as his own."

Sherry waited for Ray to add his opinion, but she should have known better. He used any pause in a conversation to plan his next question rather than his reply.

She decided to turn the tables on her friend. "I have another question for you. You spoke to Lonnie. I'm sure you asked him about his relationships with Crosby and with his wife, Ivy. Did he give any reason why he and his wife split up, but never went the extra step to divorce?"

"He said they stayed together for Crosby's sake. He said Ivy wanted it that way."

Sherry glanced at her sister, who appeared deep in thought.

"Why the gun?" Marla asked.

"What did she say?" Ray asked.

"That was Marla. She heard you mention the gun. So, I'll repeat her question. Why the gun?"

"Didn't you just say competition can bring out the worst in people? Something for you two to mull over. Thanks for your time." Ray's end of the phone went silent.

"As annoying as ever," Sherry said. "We answer all his questions and he ignores ours."

Chapter 16

"Ray doesn't seem any closer to solving the murder than you are," Marla said.

"Don't count him out. He holds his cards close to the vest. I need an hour to work on my newsletter article. Would you be interested in walking Chutney while I write? And when you do, think about what you'd like for dinner."

"Yes to all the above. Take your time." Marla headed to the front hall.

A moment later, Sherry heard the front door open and shut. Sherry set up her laptop on her corner work desk and signed in. Faced with a blank document, she opened her phone's photo library for inspiration. She scrolled to the video she captured of the library's fire safety demo. The ten seconds the fire took to go from spark to smoky inferno impressed and frightened her yet again.

Writing about avoiding such a disaster would be one of her easier assignments. The piece would write itself. The overall message would be to keep the holiday tree hydrated, unplug the string of lights each night, and keep any open flame far from the tree. Her final point would be to make sure a fire extinguisher is in working order and within easy reach. All straightforward stuff that could be embellished nicely with a reference to the Augustin Marina fire. The destruction of that fire would drive home the point better than a mere list of safety precautions. A photo of the fire would punctuate the article as well as any exclamation point.

Sherry scrolled farther on her phone to a photo from the Historical Society exhibit. As she studied the snapshot of the aftermath of the fire, Sherry became momentarily overwhelmed. Thus far, she'd had an easy time removing herself from what the emotions of that day might have been like, but this time a different perspective washed over her. Instead of fighting the feelings, Sherry tried her best to walk in the shoes of Lonnie, the boat owners, and the fire personnel, working their hardest to save what they could of one of Augustin's most treasured landmarks.

The photograph must have been taken from what was now the parking lot behind the dockmaster's shed, which was a supply hut in those days. The dock configuration appeared to be the same as she knew it, despite the burned debris scattered across the planks of wood. Sherry widened sections of the photograph piece by piece. The small phone screen proved frustrating when Sherry attempted to zoom in on the most minute portions of the scene.

Sherry emailed the marina photo to herself and brought

it up on her laptop. With the intention of cropping the picture, she enlarged the area of the marina that had suffered the most damage. When she zoomed in, sections began to blur, so she reduced the size just enough to include the partially submerged boat, the blackened pier, and a man inspecting the boat. Another figure was looming in the background, resisting Sherry's efforts to identify gender. The camera images of yesteryear weren't nearly as sharp as her phone's camera and that was taking some getting used to.

"We're back," Marla announced from the front hall.

Footsteps and canine toenails tapped across the wooden floor until Sherry could see the enthusiasm on her dog's face. "Of course you deserve a treat, Chutney." Sherry left her laptop and rummaged through the cookie jar she had converted into a dog treat container that stored Chutney's crunchy nuggets.

"How far have you gotten on the newsletter?" Marla asked.

"I'm getting a bit distracted by the material I brought home from the Historical Society." Sherry sat back down in front of her laptop. "Pull up a chair and join me."

Marla dragged a chair from the other side of the kitchen table and parked it next to Sherry's.

"What do you notice about this photo? Take a long, hard look."

"First thing I notice is the quality of cameras has drastically improved over the years." Marla was quiet for a time. "Right there is the part of the dock Don's boat pulled up to. Right?" She pointed to a section of the screen.

"I'm very sure it is, yes."

"The upper dock closest to land appears to have survived the inferno. Really no damage at all. The fire must have started farther out, toward a cluster of boats. There's almost a line halfway down the dock where the fire appears to have been contained. The fire definitely started on a boat or in what was the elevated clubhouse." She went silent again. "More likely a boat, because the clubhouse is a charred shell, but there appears to be more damage to the boats. With all that boat fuel around, it's a miracle anything can be identified."

Sherry adjusted the zoom for a closer inspection of the boats.

"Who's that man?" Marla pointed to the image of a male in rain gear who appeared to be surveying the remains of a large sailboat.

"Probably the owner of that sailing yacht."

"There's someone else in the distance. Did you see that? Looks like a woman."

Sherry squinted and leaned in. The image was fuzzy, but the details of the figure were clearer. "You're right. I'm sure it is a woman."

"You can certainly tell by the style of her coat what decade it was."

Marla gasped. Then Sherry did as well.

"Ivy and her infamous baby-blue coat. This is a black-and-white photo with minimal pixels, but I'd still wager the house that's the same baby-blue coat I tried on."

"Has to be," Marla agreed.

"She must have been helping out the day after the fire. Although I wouldn't wear such a fancy coat to check on fire devastation." Sherry leaned back. "I don't believe that's Lonnie in the rain gear."

"I can almost make out the name of the partially submerged boat. Seems as if a few letters are missing. Can you zoom in to the butt end of the boat?" Marla asked.

"That end of the boat would be called the stern in sailor terminology."

"In Oklahoma terminology, it's the butt end. As in, the butt end of a steer is where it's branded," Marla pointed out.

"Classic landlubber." Sherry zeroed in on the back of the boat. "Can't make out the name. Maybe the paint melted away during the height of the fire. I don't think I'll be using this photo in the newsletter anyway. I have enough of what I need."

Sherry stood and retrieved a paper from the front hall table and returned to her seat. "I'm going to type up Patti's submission, then we're set. I'll insert the Christmas tree fire photo, and if it makes sense, I'll insert a small photo of the marina fire. I'm beginning to think the newsletter is getting too grim for the holiday season, so I may leave it out."

"While you do that, I'm going to raid the refrigerator." Marla stood. "I need sustenance to tide me over until dinner."

Sherry propped up Patti's essay against a book for better viewing. "Wonder how long the newspaper newsroom network is down for? Patti was a little distraught at the inconvenience." She began to type. When she reached the end of the paragraph, she studied the paper itself.

"I'm making us a turkey salad with ranch dressing and toasted tortilla strips. You can steal the recipe for your next contest if you like the end result," Marla called out.

"I appreciate that. I'll be right in." Sherry picked up

the paper and her laptop and carried both into the kitchen. "Let me read you my article."

Marla nodded because her mouth was full of turkey bits.

When Sherry reached the conclusion of her article, she spoke the closing words with extra enthusiasm. "'In summary, be vigilant about the location of your holiday tree display, water the tree regularly, keep open candle or fireplace flames a safe distance away, and unplug the decorations when you leave home or retire for the evening. Have a safe and wonderful holiday season.'" She shifted her eyes from the computer screen to her sister's face.

"Informative and nicely written. The blurb about the Augustin Marina fire was chilling. Of course, the fire didn't start with a Christmas tree, but the destruction a fire can cause is relatable. Wonder how it did start."

Sherry set her computer to the side.

"You have a theory about the murder, don't you? Does that theory lend itself to twenty years later, when the dockmaster's son is found dead at the very same dock that burned?" Marla brought over two plates to the table. "Bon appétit."

"I had a theory, but that went out the window when I saw Ivy in the fire-aftermath photograph. Before that, I had another theory, and that went out the window when Effi and Sal received a threatening letter. By the way, I will be stealing this turkey salad recipe. It's so yummy," Sherry said after one bite. "The crispy tortilla strips have a sprinkle of olive oil and powdered ranch dressing mix? That really puts the salad over the top." Sherry fed her hungry stomach until her plate held nothing but a smear of dressing.

"Gee, thanks. If you've finished your newsletter, do you want to work on your contest recipe dilemma? I hate to return home to Oklahoma without knowing whether you've solved your problem."

"Can we? What I really need to fine-tune is the dressing for the panzanella. The contents of the salad works well, but the flavor of the dressing lacks pizzazz and drags down the whole recipe."

Chutney took up a ready stance under the table in case one of the diners dropped a turkey chunk.

"Pizzazz. Is that a culinary term?" Marla snickered. She carried her empty plate to the sink. She rotated and found a measuring cup in the cupboard. She put it on the counter, along with a whisk and a spoon. "I have a suggestion for you to take to heart or completely ignore; you're the expert."

Sherry brought her empty plate to the sink. She found the best olive oil she had in the cupboard, along with balsamic vinegar, and lined up the bottles next to each other. "What's the suggestion?"

"You say the flavor lacks pizzazz. Well, I think the recipe name lacks pizzazz as well. You always say the recipe title is very important because, let's face it, people judge a book by its cover. If the name is exciting, the judges will look forward to reading the recipe with great anticipation."

"You're saying Roasted Butternut Squash Panzanella with Balsamic Dressing isn't exciting enough?" Sherry took a long look at Marla.

Her sister's eyes were shut, her head was cocked to the side, and she was snoring.

"Okay, okay. I get your point. I rushed the name due to feeling the pressure of the looming deadline." Sherry spun the oil and vinegar bottles until both labels faced her. She took a moment to study the words on the labels.

"Want me to get the Dijon?" Marla asked.

Sherry nodded, and Marla removed the condiment from the refrigerator.

"And while you're in the refrigerator, can you grab the mango chutney? It's on the door shelf."

"You didn't use chutney in the last version. Has something changed?"

"I think that's what the dressing has been missing. Adding one missing ingredient will make all the difference. The chutney was there right in front of my face the whole time, and I should have recognized that." Sherry pulled a small bowl from a cabinet under the counter. "Now we're making progress. Marla, you're a genius."

"Why do I get the feeling you're not talking about your recipe anymore? Here you go." Marla handed Sherry the mustard and the chutney.

Sherry whisked together the oil, vinegar, chutney, and mustard. She sprinkled in rosemary and sea salt. She dipped the end of her pinkie in the dressing and swiped the finger across her tongue. "The chutney adds a fruity, gingery kick to the dressing. The flavor was one-dimensional and dull before. I think this will be the perfect pairing for the roasted squash cubes."

"Are we going to make a new batch of squash?" Marla asked. "I don't think we have any more leftovers."

"Nope. The dressing's perfect. I've got that winning feeling. The one I get when I've hit the mark. All I have to do is type up the recipe and email it to the contest." Sherry wiped her pinkie finger on a sheet of paper towel. "Actually, we're not done. I need to change the recipe title, as you suggested. A proper name is very important.

When you name something and take the time to really give the name meaning, a story has been told."

"Again, why do I get the impression you aren't only talking about your recipe? Do you like the name Happy Holiday Butternut Squash Bread Salad?" Marla asked.

"Not quite." Sherry pondered the name. "How about we change 'happy' to 'snappy' to celebrate the zippy flavor chutney adds to the dish? Snappy Holiday Butternut Squash Panzanella?"

"Cute, festive, fun. I like it."

Chapter 17

"I've hit the Send button. The newsletter's in Tia's hands at Town Hall now. I think it's my best work yet. Holiday safety, Augustin's cookie bake-off recap, the mayor's letter of plans for the new year, photos of historical events, all great reading for the locals." Sherry closed the lid of her laptop.

"I have to give you credit. You pack more into a day than most people pack into a week. Great job. You need a raise." Marla let out a hearty laugh.

"Your mouth to the mayor's ears." Sherry stood and stretched her arms over her head. "Feels good to complete a task. I don't like the feeling of an incomplete job hovering over me."

"What are you looking at?" Marla asked.

"Patti's printout." Sherry sat back down. She reached

for her phone beside her laptop. She clicked on her photo library.

"Was the article that good that you want a picture of it? Isn't it in your computer, all typed up?" Marla asked.

"A picture's worth a thousand words. The important issue at hand is, what should we do for dinner on your last night here?"

"I'm taking you out to dinner. You've been so kind to host me, I want to treat you to a seafood extravaganza. Lobster, shrimp, scallops, you name it, I'll foot the bill. As long as you promise me one thing," Marla said.

"Wow, that's quite an offer. What's the catch? Besides the fish, ha, ha."

"Promise me you'll find Crosby's killer. It's important to you, his ex-wife, his father, so, by association, it's important to me."

"You know I can't promise I'll find him or her." Sherry's voice softened. Her gaze shifted to her kitchen. Crosby had played a role in Sherry's commitment to her time spent in that room. His encouragement at the inception of her interest in cooking held a special place in her heart. "I'll try."

"Now, how about we go find some dinner?"

"I'm going to spend the morning with Dad at the Ruggery. He's picking me up any minute." Marla threaded her arm through her jacket sleeve. "I'm all packed. I'll call for a ride to the airport around four. Want to meet up at the store at noon for lunch? Want me to bring Chutney in with me?"

"Chutney can stay home. Eileen said she'd walk him

this morning. I like your plan to meet up at noon. Don texted. He wants to come to your farewell lunch."

Marla checked her hair in the front-hall mirror.

"Says he's in town on business, but I suspect otherwise."

"How sweet of him. He's really trying to get on your good side." Marla turned and faced her sister.

"Are you looking forward to going home?"

Marla lowered her gaze. "I'm ready to face our problems head-on, instead of avoiding them, yes. I'm looking forward to going home. If I keep repeating that phrase and visualizing contentment, good times lie ahead. That's Amber's advice."

"Leave it to Amber to give sage advice. Hope she's right." Sherry picked up her phone and car keys.

"Where are you off to? Sunset Village?"

"Yes. A quick visit to have a word with Cap Diminsky, the writer of the marina fire articles."

"What if you run into Lonnie? Won't he be upset you're visiting the person who may be one of his worst enemies?"

"They live in the same facility. I'm not responsible for that choice. If I see Lonnie, I'll say a cordial hello and tell him the truth: that I'm there to see how the Community Garden board can be of assistance to the seniors. Not exactly the whole truth, but good enough to keep me honest."

"Good luck and see you around lunchtime."

On cue, a horn honked.

"Here's Dad." Marla patted Chutney on the head and let herself out.

Following her sister's lead, Sherry added a second pat

to Chutney's head and made her way to her car, sending her father a wave as he pulled out of her driveway.

Sunset Village parking didn't disappoint in terms of limited availability for visitors without handicap designation. On her way from her car to the main lobby, Sherry was slowed by a mini bus maneuvering close to the building entrance, which involved reversing, then inching forward, multiple times.

Once inside the building, Sherry had instant regret that she hadn't called ahead to check the Sunset Village's daily schedule. A cluster of seniors was gathered around a woman holding a clipboard. Sherry glanced over at the reception desk. The woman with the cane, who previously sat behind it, was putting on a puffy jacket.

"Are you here for the field trip?" she called to Sherry. "Please come sign a waiver."

Sherry glanced around the room, hoping she could get some clarification of what was going on.

A man broke away from the gaggle of seniors and approached. "Sherry Oliveri. Are you moving in? You're becoming a regular."

"Hi, Lonnie. I think I picked a bad time to see about talking to the Village residents concerning their spring gardens. I should have called ahead."

"Lonnie, they need your snack preference." A man wearing a plaid, newsboy cap put his hand on Lonnie's shoulder.

Sherry noted it was the same man who'd aggravated Lonnie during his cooking class.

"I know what you like, but I also know you'll blame me if they get it wrong," the man said.

"Excuse me, Sherry. I need to take care of this earth-shattering matter. Snack preferences." Lonnie backed away, leaving Sherry and Plaid-Hat Man facing each other.

"You're the woman from Lonnie's cooking demonstration who said she judged the recent cookie bake-off."

"And you're the man who has a continuing running banter with Lonnie Currier."

The man let loose a chuckle that knocked his cap askew. "That describes our relationship to perfection. The young people might label us frenemies."

"Cap, I'm here. I was delayed driving behind a funeral procession. I never thought I'd get here on time. Where's Lonnie?" Rachel's gaze passed over Sherry. "Sherry? Surprised to see you here."

"Uh, hi, Rachel." Sherry turned her attention back to the man next to her. "Are you Cap Diminsky?"

"One and the same. I know you're Sherry Oliveri, cook extraordinaire. You prickled Lonnie's hide the other day at his cooking class, and I am forever grateful for the entertainment that provided me."

"Ma'am, I need you to sign a waiver. The bus leaves in three minutes. Your help is fully appreciated, but we have to file the paperwork in case of emergency." A clipboard was waved in Sherry's face. "The Augustin Earthspace and Rescue Center doesn't provide food to anyone besides the residents at this time of year, so I hope you brought a midmorning snack. If not, I should be able to beg one from Betsey." The woman with the cane tipped her head in the direction of a rotund woman in a tent dress. "She could use to lose a few pounds, her doctor told me. We'll only be gone two hours, so you probably won't need a snack anyway. I just have to be mindful of our residents' requirements. Many need to eat five small meals a day."

"See what we're put through here? They do all our thinking for us. We just have to show up." Cap sighed.

"Looking out for your best interests is what we do best, Cap. You know you love us." The woman blew an air kiss with her free hand.

Sherry's head swiveled from person to person as the conversation progressed. She realized, all at once, that she had found Cap by happenstance, she unexpectantly was going on a field trip, she was standing next to the ex-wife of a murdered man, and she was being forced to sign away any right to sue if a mishap occurred on the trip. Sherry put her autograph on the waiver and handed the clipboard back to the woman in charge.

Cap extended his hand. "Sherry, let me formally introduce myself. Cap Diminsky. Nice to meet you. We'll be spending the next two hours together, it appears."

"Nice to meet you, Cap. I haven't been to the Augustin Rescue Center in years."

"It's remarkable. You'll love it. I've been numerous times."

"Have you lived at Sunset Village long?" Sherry asked.

"This is my third year. At first, I thought I was being put here to wither away but have come to realize it's not a bad place after all. Three square meals a day and lots of activities, and I have made plenty of lifelong friends. Not sure they could get rid of me even if they wanted to."

"All aboard, folks," the driver bellowed from outside the double doors.

"I told Lonnie I'd sit with him, but you're much easier on the eyes, so let's continue this conversation on the bus. We can be seat neighbors. Besides, he has Rachel. She comes on all our field trips."

"Okay. Looks like I'm going on a field trip." Sherry tucked her purse under her arm and followed Cap to the bus. Once aboard, she settled in next to the man.

"Do you volunteer at the Village much?" Cap asked. "I've only seen you once, besides today: at Lonnie's cooking class, which was odd in itself, because you're such an accomplished cook. Why would you be taking one of his classes?"

"Testing the waters. On volunteering here, I mean. Not on cooking. My time is somewhat limited right now, but in the future, I'd love to. I had an idea about using some of my Community Garden interns to teach gardening classes in the meantime."

"Not teach cooking?" Cap asked.

He and Sherry adjusted their seat belts as the bus lurched forward.

"I can't teach cooking because it puts my amateur status for cooking competitions in jeopardy. Rules say I can't receive pay for any cooking-related activity. I could volunteer in the kitchen, of course."

Lonnie, in the seat in front of Sherry, tilted back his head and rocked the rest.

"Not eavesdropping, are you, old boy?" Cap leaned forward and tapped the top of Lonnie's head.

"Nothing you could say would interest me. Except if you said you were moving out of Sunset. Sherry, on the other hand, is quite an interesting person," Lonnie replied.

"Oh, please. You'd be lost without me," Cap said.

Sherry cringed. She lowered her voice. "I have to say, I read an article or two you wrote about the marina fire and the Currier family. Must be awkward now, living in such close proximity to someone about whom you penned an inflammatory article. Am I speaking out of turn? There does seem to be a certain amount of animosity between you two."

"Lonnie's a feisty old sea dog," Cap said. "I was a journalist whose job it was to write about current events. His family happened to be in the eye of the storm during the period after the big fire. How do you know Lonnie and his family?"

Before Sherry could respond, the loudspeaker over the windshield blared out a crackle and a screech. "Good morning, everyone who signed up to visit the Augustin Earthspace and Rescue Center."

"And one who didn't," Sherry whispered.

A man in the front row of seats raised a mic over his head. "As usual, I'm your tour guide."

"Who's that?" Sherry asked Cap.

"Tommy. Even though his father, a former resident here, passed away last year, he's grown attached to the rest of us. He leads most of our field trips," Lonnie explained.

"We'll be arriving at the Rescue Center in a few minutes. If the driver wouldn't mind slowing the bus down, I want to point out the beautiful Augustin Harbor on your left. The two scenic properties, the marina and the wildlife center, are neighbors. Not such a terrible detour that the bus must circumnavigate the marina property due to improvements being made to the roads approaching the harbor. I'll use this time to point out a few of the historical facts about the marina, as we'll be offering a field trip to the Historical Society next month to see their upcoming Marina fire exhibit. I hope to pique your interest in attending."

"Oh no, is this a setup? Are you behind this, Cap?" Lonnie craned his neck backward to look at him.

"As much as you'd like to believe you were responsible, it wasn't you who put the marina on the map. The place existed long before you were dockmaster," Cap said.

Lonnie lowered himself into his seat a little.

"Take a look at the view, folks. Another reason why Augustin is an extraordinary place to live. Am I right?"

Clapping resounded throughout the small bus. The bus slowed to a crawl.

"See that man walking out of the dockmaster shed? That's Vitis Costa, the marina dockmaster." Tommy pointed out the window. "Interesting fact: Vitis eats his lunch every day in the neighboring Earthspace courtyard. On rainy days, he eats inside the animal enclosure wing while watching the rescued raptors get fed. A bit early for lunch now, so I don't think we'll see him at Earthspace." Tommy chuckled.

"I never took my lunch hour anywhere but the clubhouse, with my walkie-talkie in hand," Lonnie said.

"Vitis is out of his office during his lunch hour," Sherry said to herself. "Interesting. Crosby was killed sometime around that time of day." She put up her hand.

"I guess we're taking questions. Yes, ma'am?" Tommy asked.

"How do boats come and go if the dockmaster is out?" Sherry asked.

Lonnie raised his hand. "I'll tell you. There's a way to schedule the boat traffic to provide gaps in the activity. Isn't always popular with the boaters, but the dockmaster needs a moment off every now and then."

"Thank you for that insight, Mr. Currier. I don't want to burden you with questions about your past, but I appreciate anything you wouldn't mind discussing."

"That's it." Lonnie's tone shut down the possibility of further sharing.

Vitis waved to the onlookers, as if he were a feature on a celebrity tour. He walked down the dock to the location where Don's boat had been docked.

"Is that Crosby's boat?" Lonnie asked.

In the seat next to Lonnie, Rachel tipped forward with her finger up to her lips.

Sherry squinted, which helped bring the boat's stern into focus. *Rachel's Way.*

"So embarrassing," Rachel said in a loud whisper. "He said he'd change the name before I took possession. Guess he didn't get around to it, or didn't care to."

Sherry bent forward and wedged her head between the seats in front of her row. "I couldn't help overhearing Lonnie say that's your boat, Rachel." She sensed Cap's glare in her peripheral vision. She glanced at him and he gave her a mild headshake.

"Yes, you heard correctly. It's getting winterized for storage. Before we separated, he bought me the boat, which I enjoyed for years. It was registered in his name. When it came time to divide our possessions, I thought he'd be nice and give it to me, no strings attached. That wasn't the case. Turned out he was selling the boat right out from under me. To your friend Don Johnstone."

"Excuse me, would you mind keeping your voices down? They don't pay me enough for a doctor's visit to treat a case of laryngitis I might get from trying to speak over you." Tommy let loose a hearty laugh.

"Sorry," Rachel called out.

Sherry sat back and pondered the name of the boat Crosby was in the midst of changing to *Sweet Revenge*. Was that Rachel's idea or Crosby's? And who was the owner seeking revenge against?

"The spit of land the marina is located on was an Indian settlement up until the late sixteen hundreds," Tommy continued. "Oysters, clams, mussels, and many varieties of fish were abundant in the shallow waters that edge up to the wetlands, once dominant in the area. Along came European settlers and out went the Native American way of life. The wetlands eventually succumbed to development, before the discovery of how vital their health was to the success of every local and migratory species of flora and fauna was made. The Augustin Marina was born in the nineteen twenties, and the area became a haven for the wealthy sportsmen and -women who summered in the area."

Through the partition between the seats, Sherry heard Lonnie humming. He must know every aspect of the marina's story.

Sherry positioned her hand alongside her mouth to steer her comment in Cap's direction. "Is the fire going to be mentioned?" Sherry whispered.

"I asked that it not be brought up. I found out what the narrative would be today and made sure no mention would be made," Cap said. "Took me by surprise when the old guy jumped in to comment on an aspect of the dockmaster job. That's a first. He doesn't talk much about those days."

"Seems like there's admiration between you two—delivered in a backhanded fashion, but still admiration. So, you two do like each other after all. At least, you're looking out for his feelings."

"We have a million reasons not to want to spend a minute together. In the end, we have more in common than we have differences. He's a cranky old son of a gun, but, after his wife passed away, we nearly lost him. He spiraled so low, he was almost impossible to revive. But he's back, as ornery as ever, and that's how I like him. You know, I even wrote his wife's obituary for him."

"But they didn't even live together. Why would he be so broken up by her passing?" Sherry asked.

"It wasn't his choice to live apart. Ivy said that was the only way she'd remain married to him. He had no choice."

"And Crosby's death? How did that impact Lonnie?"

Cap opened his mouth to respond.

"Folks, we're here. Please don't leave any belongings on the bus."

Cap closed his mouth. The passengers stood. Rachel took Lonnie's arm and guided him to the aisle, followed by Sherry and Cap. Once off the bus, the group proceeded to the small theater inside the educational building.

An hour and a half later, the group had learned how to care for an injured red-tailed Hawk and start tomato plants from last year's crop. The demonstrations were fast-paced and comprehensive, designed to keep minds active and engaged. And designed to keep conversation to a minimum. Throughout the trip, Sherry observed Rachel never leaving Lonnie's side. Cap made an effort to check in with his Village mate a few times, only to have their interaction interrupted by the lecturer.

"Double-check that you have everything you brought with you before we board the bus," Tommy said as the Villagers formed a line to exit the building.

"They treat us like we're in elementary school," Lonnie complained.

"Sometimes you act like you are," Cap replied.

After the last passenger took his seat, the door shut and the bus rolled away.

"Mind if I ask you a personal question?" Sherry asked Cap.

"Depends. Give it a try."

"How did you and Lonnie become friends after you wrote an article basically accusing his son of arson?" Sherry followed up her question with a glance in his eyes.

His gaze shifted from Sherry to the back of Lonnie's head in the row of seats in front of them. "Old age comes with a certain amount of acceptance. Every year since we've lived at the Village, we've celebrated his wedding anniversary together. No Ivy, no Rachel, no Crosby. Just him and me. It all came about when I found him sobbing one day and asked him what the matter was. He said the day was his wedding anniversary, the day he'd made the best and worst decision of his life."

Sherry lowered her voice and leaned into Cap's ear. "Did either Ivy or Lonnie have a connection to Hawaii you're aware of?"

Cap's head snapped in Sherry's direction, almost colliding his nose with hers. "They went there on their honeymoon. Why are you asking? And please don't ever ask Lonnie about that. He's just beginning to return to some level of emotional normalcy." His words were delivered with such force, Sherry recoiled.

"Hawaiian honeymoon. I see. Makes sense, with his love of boating. Was Ivy a sailor?"

Cap fiddled with a fingernail before returning his attention back to Sherry. "She was learning."

"That's romantic, that Hawaii was their honeymoon spot."

"Let's change the subject before Lonnie's ears start to burn." Cap glanced out the window, ending the conversation.

Sunset Village came into view as the bus took the turn at the complex's sign.

"Thank you all for making this field trip a success. I hope we won't need to put our newfound knowledge into use, saving a raptor's life, but we certainly will be starting plants from seeds in our greenhouse next month. I hope you all were paying close attention to the process. And please, sign up for the trip to the Historical Society to learn more about the fascinating history of the Augustin Marina, which is marking a milestone this coming year. Thank you all."

The passengers spilled out onto the driveway and made their way into the lobby. Sherry found herself next to Rachel as they awaited further instruction.

"That was very enjoyable," Rachel said. "I didn't get a chance to speak with you all morning. How nice of you to come. Outside help is always welcome."

Sherry noted the cautious tone of Rachel's voice. She was aware Rachel had had many chances to strike up a conversation with her during the field trip yet had kept her attention solely on her father-in-law. Whenever Sherry opened her mouth to speak to her, Rachel turned away and busied herself with a pressing matter concerning Lonnie.

"My pleasure. I came to Sunset Village this morning to meet with Cap Diminsky, and next thing I knew, I was swept onto the bus for a whirlwind trip to the Rescue Center."

"Seems as if you had a nice chance to meet with Cap, because you were seatmates. You know, I heard you talking about Lonnie, Ivy, and Hawaii. If I were you, I would take Cap's advice and stay away from that subject."

"Cap and Lonnie seem to be in a good place. Considering their past history, that's quite a feat." Sherry tried her hardest to sound convincing when she herself could hardly believe the two could tolerate each other's presence.

"I want to tell you something before I leave." Rachel's tone was rigid. "When I spoke to you about being a suspect in my ex-husband's death, I didn't understand where you would take the mission of proving me innocent for the sake of Lonnie. I'm beginning to regret our conversation. If Lonnie suffers further in any way, I couldn't live with myself."

"I think I'm making some progress. The Currier waters are muddier than meets the eye, though, and clearing them is taking some doing."

Rachel squared her body up to Sherry's. She didn't even blink. "I'm going to say something I hope you take to heart. I think you're sticking your nose somewhere it doesn't belong." She paused and tightened her lips. "Do you understand me?"

Sherry scanned the room. Out of the corner of her eye, she saw Lonnie and Cap approaching behind Rachel. "I'm sorry. What is it I'm supposed to understand?" Sherry enunciated each word so anyone within a few feet could hear her clearly.

"I've changed my mind. Stay out of our business. Do I make myself clear?"

Lonnie placed his hand on Rachel's shoulder. "Thank you for coming today, Sherry." He steered Rachel toward the front entrance.

Chapter 18

Sherry located Cap exiting the restroom. She beelined over to him. "Glad we had a chance to talk today."

"Me, too. I hope you volunteer here more often."

"I was thinking, would you be interested in writing a follow-up article about the marina fire?"

"Would a twenty-year gap between articles still qualify for a follow-up?" Cap smiled.

"Sure. An article that could be included in the Historical Society's exhibit? People would be very interested in learning the results of the fire investigation. I admit, I've tried to get some answers myself, but after such a gap in time, those closest to the event are hard to locate. And here you are, right in front of me. How can I pass up the opportunity of asking you?"

"Might be nice to dip my toe back in the journalism pool. The only writing I've been doing lately has been

obituaries. I've even written my own for someone to submit after I pass on. I want full control on what's put out
there about me."

"That's a good idea. Speaking of obituaries, you said
you wrote Ivy's?"

Cap nodded. His eyes shifted in the direction of Lonnie and Rachel. "That's right. Lonnie said he didn't think
Crosby was up to the task."

"Lonnie must trust you. I mean you of all people might
put something in the obit that could damage the family."

Cap shrugged his shoulders. "Never. I didn't write
those articles to damage anyone, by the way. I wrote what
was news at the time. After all we've been through, I can
say in all sincerity, Lonnie and I trust each other. As a
matter of fact, you're giving me an opportunity to share
that fact when I write the article."

"Do you have any idea what may have happened to
Lonnie's son?"

Cap turned again toward Lonnie. He held his gaze
until Sherry repeated the question.

"Cap? Do you have any idea?"

"I wish I could be certain, but I'm not. I've learned my
lesson to stick to the facts at hand. So, the answer is no."

"Hey, old man. Lunchtime." Lonnie neared. "Sherry,
are you sticking around? How much can you take of this
place? Rachel's gone. She knows when she's had enough."

"No, I'm on my way out. Just saying goodbye to my
new friend," Sherry said.

"I can't understand your attraction to this guy. He may
be a good writer, but that's about all there is to him." Lonnie shifted his attention to Cap. "I'll save you a seat. No
one else will." Lonnie chuckled as he walked away.

"That's what I call tough love," Cap said. "He's a

lonely character who likes to portray a crusty outer shell. Defense mechanism, I'd say."

"Would you mind emailing your article to me? Within the next week? I'll run it by Ruth Gadabee, who's on the Historical Society's exhibit board. I know she'll be thrilled with your additional contribution."

Sherry fished in her purse and brought out a small card. "Here's my business card. It's actually less of a business card than it is a bookmark. Comes in handy, because it has my email address on it."

Cap tucked the card in his pants pocket. "Thanks. I'll get right on it. Say hi to Ruth for me. She was nice enough to present me with a lifetime achievement award I didn't deserve. And Sherry . . ."

"Yes?"

"I think you're trying to help, but you're treading on thin ice. Friendly warning, because I like you, be careful." Cap turned and ambled down the hall.

Sherry took one last look around the lobby. Only the woman with the cane remained, and she was hobbling back to her seat at the reception desk. Head full of vague suggestions of what to beware of, Sherry left the facility. On her way to her car, she created mental bullet points for what she'd learned from Cap. When she got home, she'd sort out the details and assign importance to what was fact and discard what was opinion. At the moment, her list of facts seemed sparse in comparison to the opinions.

Deep in thought, Sherry was slow to realize something was different about her car, but when she did, she uttered a curse word she didn't know was so close to the tip of her tongue. She stared at her car in hopes she wasn't seeing what she thought she was. Her two front tires were flat.

I think I would have noticed if I had run over an object big enough to pop two tires. This reeks of the same bad odor of the words on the note Effi and Sal received— Mind Your Own Business Or Else. Why does someone always have to pick on my poor old car? Wasn't too long ago I paid to have a headlight-to-taillight scratch repaired, thanks to someone warning me to stay out of a murder investigation.

"Looks like you could use a hand, young lady."

Sherry, in the midst of searching her purse for her phone, lifted her eyes in the direction of the voice. When she saw the familiar face, Sherry sighed with relief. "Hi, Vitis. Are you offering?"

"Getting two flat tires at the same time is a hard trick to pull off. How did you manage it?" Vitis shifted a brown paper bag from one hand to the other.

"I don't think it was my fault." Sherry eyed what she suspected was his lunch sack. "You're on your way to eat. I can call my father or sister. I don't want to inconvenience you. I should've joined a roadside assistance service. You never know you need them until you do."

"Bringing doughnuts to my dad." Vitis walked around the front of Sherry's car. "I don't see any other damage, but these tires are as flat as my singing voice." He looked back over his shoulder at the Sunset Village building. "Do you have a relative living here?"

"No, at least not yet. I came by to talk to a resident and suddenly found myself joining a field trip. By the way, on our way to the nature and Rescue Center next to the marina this morning, we spotted you outside the dockmaster shed. That led to a discussion of the history of the Augustin Marina, which was quite fascinating."

"Hope I wasn't the highlight of the trip. That would

make for a very disappointing outing. Let me run back to my truck and grab my tools. We can change one tire and put on your spare. I have a can of Inflate A Flat, sealant plus inflator, for the other that could get you as far as the overpriced tire store, where you'll be at the mercy of whatever they're able to sell you. Beggars can't be choosers in this case."

"Uh. I find myself in this situation a bit too often. Thank you." Sherry watched Vitis traverse the parking lot until he let himself into a vintage pickup truck.

The truck chugged to life and cruised over to the empty parking space next to Sherry's injured car. "Hate to have you give up such a coveted parking spot," Sherry said when Vitis exited the truck.

"No worries. I have a handicap badge I hang on the mirror when I come. My dad's here. I bring him his favorite doughnuts once a week. He's called this place home since he was eighty-one. He'll be eighty-five next year. I try to get over here a couple of times a week, and boat traffic is certainly slow this time of year, so I'm able to sneak in a visit before my lunch. He loves to hear about the birds and animals I saw at the Rescue Center, which is where I eat my lunch." Vitis rolled up his sleeves and placed the tire jack under the car's front end. "Shouldn't take too long."

While Vitis was repairing the tire damage, Sherry texted Marla, then Don, to say she'd be late for the farewell lunch. Marla texted back that she was going to be late because she was running some errands with Amber while Erno manned the store. Don texted to say he'd see her soon.

When the miniature spare tire was secured, Vitis lowered the car's front end and relocated the jack to the other side. Sherry stepped closer to Vitis as he squatted down to check the car's underside.

"Lonnie and Rachel Currier were on the field trip today."

"That's nice. I run into Lonnie a few times a month on my visits. He's always quick to ask me how everything's going. This truck was courtesy of him. He sold it to me when I took over his job. I admired it one day when he was showing me the ropes, and he made me an offer I couldn't refuse."

"I was curious how long you've known Rachel Currier. I've gotten acquainted with her recently, but I'm finding her quite guarded beyond a certain level of familiarity."

Vitis raised himself up and traced his finger across the exposed tire tread. "Here's the puncture. Neat, clean cut. Should hold the air and take the sealant well. Inflate A Flat is magic in a can." He stood and located the can of tire sealant next to his tools. "Rachel Currier has taken sailing lessons at the marina for years. Her mother-in-law raced sailboats for the Augustin Yacht Club until her husband left his position as dockmaster, so, before my time. Rachel began sailing after she married Crosby, despite the fact he had no ambition for spending any time on the water. I never saw them sail together. I barely saw him, come to think of it—only her. She had plenty of company other than him. Especially her chef friend."

Vitis settled back down beside the tire. From her vantage point, she couldn't see what he was doing, but she heard the hiss of the canned repair product. He stood and crossed in front of Sherry's car.

"This was under your car." Vitis handed Sherry a receipt from Pinch and Dash. "Love that place."

"Thanks. We got cookies from there yesterday. Hopefully, it says we don't owe anything. They were supposed to be on the house."

"Lucky you."

"Why do you have all this equipment?" Sherry asked.

"Look at my truck. If I didn't fix it myself, I'd have a devil of a time paying the repair bills. Tough enough as it is. I want to keep the old girl going for another ten years."

"Vitis, let me pay you for your time. This repair would have cost a fortune if I hired a tow truck." Sherry handed Vitis two twenty-dollar bills. "Buy your father a nice dinner, or more doughnuts."

"Thank you, Sherry. You're very kind," Vitis said in a soft voice. The lines around his eyes deepened as he smiled. His scruffy facial hair was flecked with gray, yet his energy was youthful as he kept the task moving along at a fast pace. "He'll like that. You should be fine to drive home or to the tire store. I wouldn't go much farther than that. And maybe find out who's trying to send you a message in such a destructive way. Hope to see you under more pleasant circumstances next time."

"Thank you again," Sherry called after him. "I'm pretty sure I know who sent me this message. If I could send her the bill, I would."

"Her?" Vitis asked.

"I mean him or her."

"Be careful, then. It appears someone's not happy with you."

"Will do, and thanks again."

Vitis sauntered toward Sunset Village.

* * *

"If you can meet me at the Augustin Garage and Tire Center, I'll drop my car off. I called ahead and they said it would be done in an hour. Two new tires plus labor I wasn't budgeting for. It's sure to be a wallop of an expense, and right before the holidays." Sherry closed her eyes and rubbed her temple. "I'm getting a headache."

Sherry's drive to the tire store was harrowing. Every bump and pothole in the road begged a mental check of how the car was riding and an assessment as to whether one of the two front tires had survived the jarring. When she arrived, her palms were damp and she breathed a sigh of relief.

When she spoke to the tire center manager, she pointed out that she had no idea how the tires had been compromised. "The second tire is in the back seat. I'm very interested to learn what you think punctured both tires."

"Yes, ma'am. It's not always possible, but we'll do our best. Give us an hour and your car will be good as can be. Will you be waiting?"

"No, I'm going to get some lunch. I have a ride. I'll be back in an hour, give or take a few minutes. Thank you."

Sherry left the tire store and located Erno's car. Sherry squeezed into the back seat of the subcompact station wagon. She was forced to contort her legs at an angle to get comfortable in the limited space available. "It's been a long time since I've sat in this back seat, Dad. I must have grown taller in the ten years you've had this car."

"Or you're not as flexible as you were ten years ago," Marla said.

"No doubt," Sherry replied. "Easy for you to say from your luxurious perch in the front seat."

"Hey, it's not my fault your car keeps getting picked on," Erno said with an air of defensiveness.

Marla cleared her throat. "It's kind of her fault. She was on the trail of a murderer last time her car was purposely scratched from end to end, and there's a good chance the flat tires today come from someone who doesn't appreciate her sniffing around their business."

"In that case," Erno said as he waited for a red light to turn green, "I retract my statement. The fault may lie with you."

"I have to admit I have a growing interest in who killed Crosby, but I certainly wasn't counting on being targeted by a lunatic. I'm ninety-nine percent positive Rachel Currier's behind my tire slashing," Sherry stated with no uncertainty.

"If that's the case, why didn't you call the police?" Marla asked.

"I took pictures of the damaged tires. I'm considering my next step. My insurance deductible doesn't cover the cost of new tires. When I called ahead, the man at the tire store said I have some time to think about filing a report."

"You just don't want Detective Bease on your back, do you? You'll get that with a police report," Marla said. "If he gets wind of this incident, you'll have some explaining to do."

"That may be part of it. I need to summon the courage to listen to an earful of Ray's good advice."

"If you say you're sure it was Rachel, that's a good place to start," Marla suggested.

"She was at Sunset Village at the same time as me. She may have overheard Cap Diminsky and me discussing the Currier family. She delivered a stern warning to me to stay out of the family's business. She left the facility before I did, giving her ample time to do the deed. The one percent of uncertainty I have that she wasn't the slasher is enough to give me pause, though. Unless she left her business card on the hood of my car, I'm missing the smoking gun. And I'm sure she didn't leave me one."

"Didn't Rachel ask you to find the killer? Are you saying she's having you run circles around her to clear her name while, in reality, she's the guilty party? Sherry, I think you're in over your head this time."

"I may just be, but now I'm in so deep there's no turning back. What I learned today is that Cap and Lonnie aren't the enemies we thought them to be. Quite the contrary. They celebrate anniversaries together. Lonnie had Cap write Ivy's obit, giving Crosby no chance to. More friends than frenemies."

"What is it between Lonnie and Crosby?" Marla asked. "Did you get that detail ironed out?"

"Every time I closed in on the topic, a wet blanket was thrown over the subject. I've broached the subject so many times, with so many people, I'm not sure where else to turn. By the way, with all this commotion going on, I almost forgot to ask what restaurant you guys picked. I need to text Don the address. He's been window-shopping for the last hour, biding his time, I think."

Marla turned to face Sherry from the front passenger seat. "We've talked so much about tropical cookie bars lately, I thought we should go to the Big Island. I want to see what the attraction is."

"Poke bowls are all the rage for lunch," Sherry said. "I'm not a raw fish eater, so I'll pass on that. The fried rice is supposed to be fantastic. Will Ruth be joining us?"

"Ruth and Frances will meet us at the restaurant. The ladies wanted to say goodbye to Marla. Frances has been out of town, visiting her son for Thanksgiving. I haven't seen her in over a week. Ruth is very out of sorts when her best friend isn't by her side for days on end."

Sherry smiled at her father's observation. His women friends kept him young and entertained, and that was priceless.

Erno backed the car into a curbside parking spot. Everyone climbed out. "Who do we have here? Two lovely ladies in need of company."

Ruth and Frances were seated on a bench outside the restaurant. Each was wrapped in a colorful scarf, a coat that hung down below their knees, and black gloves, giving each the appearance they shared the same fashion stylist.

"We would love the company of the Oliveri family." Frances stood and embraced each member. "Thank you for including me in Marla's farewell lunch."

"You all are making it sound as if I'm never returning." Marla laughed. "I have every intention of visiting more often. It's good for me to reconnect with my roots."

"Let's get inside. I'm not as well dressed as these ladies, and it's chilly out here." Erno wrapped an arm around Ruth and guided her inside the Big Island.

Sherry noted the tropical-themed décor was colorful and bright. Predictably, the hostess was adorned in a lei and a grass skirt apron. She led the party to a large, round table with room for expansion.

After they were all seated, the hostess passed out menus. "Can I get you a pitcher of piña coladas to start you off?"

"That certainly would start me off to an afternoon nap," Erno said. "No thanks."

"Your waitress will be right over." The hostess walked away.

"Is that Rachel?" Marla pointed across the room from behind the shield of her propped-up menu.

Sherry turned her head. She was stunned at the sight of the woman who might have slashed her tires only a few hours earlier. "Sure is. And that's Chef Buckman with her."

"Look over there. Don made it." Erno tilted his head toward the door.

Chapter 19

Across the spacious dining room, Don was chatting with the hostess. Sherry raised her hand and fluttered it in his direction. She couldn't catch his eye, so she pushed back her chair, stood, and crossed the restaurant to the hostess stand. Leading Don back to the table, rather than avoiding Rachel and Barry's table, she diverted Don as close by the duo as possible.

"Rachel. Barry. What a surprise to see you here," Sherry said.

Rachel raised her eyes from her bowl of greens. "Hello again, Sherry. We must be on the same schedule."

"Right." Sherry forced a smile. She put out her hand in the direction of Don. "This is my friend Don Johnstone. He was driving the boat we were on the night we saw you both at the marina." Sherry avoided eye contact with Don.

"Don Johnstone. Yes, hi," Rachel said. "You're the unfortunate person stuck in the middle of a divorce settlement. I assume you got word from Crosby's lawyer concerning my boat?"

Don took a step forward. "Yes. I was sorry to lose out on the purchase of Crosby's boat. It's a beauty."

"It's all really too bad. At the time Crosby and Don made an agreement on the sale of the boat, there was no way to know what would happen to Don's current boat soon after. Now he's left with no boat at all," Sherry added.

"What do you mean?" Barry spread some butter on a roll.

Sherry's attention shifted from Barry to the roll before settling on Rachel. Hoping to detect any sign of Rachel already knowing what had happened to Don's boat and, beyond that, having caused the damage, she held her gaze on the woman. If Rachel was holding the winning poker hand, she never let on.

"Don's boat was sabotaged the night we saw you two at the Augustin Marina. We made it as far as dinner in Seaport. On the return trip, we started taking on water and had to be rescued by the Coast Guard. Further inspection of the boat revealed essential pump lines were cut. Cut by someone who knew exactly how to time the damage so we were pretty far from land before the boat took on dangerous amounts of water."

Rachel and Barry exchanged looks.

"Which one of you two has an enemy?" Rachel's coolness gave Sherry pause.

"I'm beginning to think I have an albatross around my neck because today, when I came out of Sunset Village, I was greeted by two slashed tires on my car. Vitis helped me change one tire and do a temp fix on the other. And when I say he helped me, I mean he did the whole job himself. Such a nice fellow."

"Have you considered the possibility he's the culprit? Sounds like Vitis was at both places where you ran into bad luck," Rachel said with an air of casualness.

Barry turned to his dinner partner. "Weren't you at the Village today, too? That would mean you were at both places Sherry's run into bad luck, too."

"Sherry and I aren't enemies. We're working together to find out who killed Crosby."

"You are?" Don and Barry said simultaneously.

"Not exactly together. As a matter of fact, Rachel says she's no longer interested in me finding Crosby's killer. Isn't that right?" The intensity of the glances exchanged between the two women gave Sherry the motivation to add a decisive nod. Her version of getting in the last word on the subject.

"You misunderstood me. I'm grateful for any information on Crosby's killer. Letting long-retired skeletons out of the family closet is what I'd like to avoid."

"Crosby was one of the better influences on my young life. He understood me. I'd like to find who killed Crosby so no one else gets hurt. I feel a sense of responsibility toward a man who aimed me in the right direction in high school. Despite the restrictions you're putting on me, I'll forge ahead. If I can't get beyond the shallow surface of the Currier family, there's not much chance I'll get to the muck. Do you understand me, Rachel?"

Rachel dropped her fork with a clatter. "Yes, I understand."

"We've never been here before. Is there a dish either of you would recommend?" Sherry matched Rachel's frosty tone.

"One of our favorite places to eat," Barry said.

"I always get a poke bowl." Rachel's voice was barely audible. She kept her gaze down on her bowl of greens. "If you want to try something else, the special of the day never disappoints."

"I go for the Kahlua Shredded Pork Buns. I recommend you try anything on the menu. Hawaiian cuisine is a bit of an unknown in Augustin, but I think you'll be pleasantly surprised by how good it is," Barry said. "Save room for the chocolate lava cake. Not Hawaiian, but delicious."

"Cap mentioned the Curriers spent time in Hawaii." Sherry kept her voice as steady as possible.

"Not all of us," Rachel said. "I've never been."

"Maybe your in-laws?" Sherry asked.

"Yes, they went there on their honeymoon. Ivy constantly talked about returning because the sailing was so challenging there, but Lonnie never took her back. She would have loved this restaurant."

"You never told me that," Barry said. "Maybe we should bring Lonnie here."

"He would hate it." Rachel's tone put a period on the subject. "Enjoy your meal." Rachel picked up her fork.

"Thank you." Sherry backed away from their table.

On their way across the dining room, Don came to a halt. "What have you got up your sleeve, young lady? The way you talked to Rachel wasn't like two people working together toward the same goal. Is there something you haven't told me?"

By the time they reached the table, Sherry had filled Don in on the morning's car mishap. They took their seats next to each other. Sherry noticed the others had their menus facedown in front of them, as if they'd made their meal selections. She scooped hers up and read the choices. She side-eyed Don and saw him set down his menu.

"Are you done already?" Sherry peered over the top of her menu.

"I've been to Hawaii. I know what the specialties are," Don said. "I bet everything is tasty."

"So, I didn't have to ask Barry and Rachel what to order?" Sherry asked.

"You didn't have to, but you were going to anyway. I wasn't born yesterday." Don smiled. "You were asking them because you, for some reason, needed to know whether they were connoisseurs of Hawaiian cuisine. Am I right?"

"I see amateur sleuthing in your future, Don," Marla teased.

"I was asking their opinion because I've never been to the Big Island, the restaurant or the Hawaiian island, and I assume Barry eats all sorts of cuisines and knows what to order."

"If you say so," Don said.

"Okay, I'm all set. Ruth and Frances, are you set with your orders?" Sherry asked.

"Yes, dear," Frances said.

"May I take your orders?" The waitress held a pen to a pad of paper.

"Guest of honor goes first," Erno said.

Everyone turned to Marla.

"I'll have the fish special of the day," Marla said.

Each diner placed their order, and the waitress walked away with a pad full of tropical dishes.

"Don, did Sherry tell you about her latest run-in with someone trying to send her a nasty message?" Frances asked.

"I just told him the abbreviated version of the story. And speaking of sending a message, we ran into Rachel Currier and one of the other judges from the cookie bake-off, Chef Buckman, over there." Sherry tilted her head in the direction of the table at which the two were seated. "Rachel was at the marina the night Don's boat ran into trouble and she was at Sunset Village today when my car's front tires were slashed."

"Do you think Rachel was behind those warnings?" Ruth asked.

Before Sherry could respond, Don commented, "Wouldn't make sense. She asks you for help, then she turns around and threatens you? She tells you to your face not to ask the family too many questions? And add to that, she sabotages my boat and slashes your tires?"

"Let me tell you something, Don," Erno said. "When Sherry gets herself involved in one of these murder investigations, anything goes. Just keep your head down and hope for the best."

"Dad, that's not what's happening. Rachel asked me to help find the killer to ensure she isn't the one pegged for her ex-husband's murder."

"Why do you care about whether she is or isn't the murderer, dear?" Ruth asked.

"Rachel's afraid Crosby's father, Lonnie, will have no

one to care for him if she goes to jail. There isn't any family left," Sherry explained. "I would hate to see that happen. Crosby was a nice man and his father seems just as nice, only he has a rough exterior."

"What if she's guilty?" Marla asked. "From all indications, her hands aren't clean."

Don nodded in agreement.

"Then I've found the person who killed a teacher who did me a nice favor and gave me positive support when I was younger," Sherry said. "Excuse me, I'm going to visit the ladies' room." She stood.

"I'll join you," Marla added.

Sherry avoided Rachel's table in favor of crossing the path of the constantly opening and closing kitchen doors. On the return trip from the bathroom, rather than dance around the swinging door as she had been forced to do before, she edged close to a table with two diners appearing to be enjoying a shared appetizer plate.

"Hi, Patti. That looks delicious," Sherry commented. "I thought Hawaiian cuisine was all fish all the time, but today I'm learning otherwise."

Patti looked up from her plate of food. "It's so fresh and delicious. We should all eat this way all the time, fish or otherwise. I'm reviewing the restaurant, so I have to keep my voice down."

"As I've said before, you have the best job ever," Sherry said.

"Hi, Patti," Marla said. "It's been a long time since I've seen you."

"Sister love, how nice," Patti said.

"There are more Oliveris over there." Sherry pointed across the room.

"Are you all ignoring me on purpose?" Warren asked.

"I'm sorry, Warren. It's very nice to see you. This is my sister, Marla. She's on her way home tonight. We're here for her farewell lunch. Are you keeping an eye on your newspaper's intrepid restaurant reviewer?"

He cleared his throat and deepened his voice. "Yes, of course, this is a business lunch." He winked in Sherry's direction. "She was on her way here, so I hooked my wagon to her star to join her in a great meal."

"That's not true. Warren is taking all his employees out to lunch to thank us for putting up with upgrading the computer system and all the inconvenience that entailed. I happened to be going out today, so I think what's really happening is I'm taking *him* out." She gave Warren the stink eye, followed by a warm grin.

"Thank you for your article, Patti. I know it was written under tough office conditions. Not only did you write a wonderful bake-off recap, you went the extra mile and added insightful information on the Story For Glory's first-ever cookie bake-off, held many years ago."

"Did you?" Warren asked. "I'd like to read that. Sounds fascinating. My father was editor of the paper in those days. The bake-off was his idea, as a way to endear the newspaper to the community. The event was a big hit."

"Why did it only run for one year if it was so popular?" Marla asked.

"That I don't know." Patti turned to face Warren. "Do you have any idea?"

"Let me think. What did my father tell me?" Warren paused. "I think it partially had to do with how much it takes to put on a cook-off. So much more than people understand. Look who I'm talking to. Of course Sherry would know that."

"It's true. There are many cook-offs that are one and done because of all the work that goes into organizing cooking competitions," Sherry said. "You said that was part of the reason? Was there more to it?"

"The winner of the first cookie bake-off was Ivy Currier. Within a few months of the contest, the Augustin Marina was destroyed by a fire. Her husband, Lonnie, was the dockmaster, and there were whisperings that the fire was set by Crosby in an attempt to make his father pay for breaking up the Currier family. When a second bake-off was discussed, my father felt it was essential the previous year's winner return to present the new one with the grand prize for the sake of continuity. Suddenly, drawing more attention to the Currier family didn't seem like a good move. Any mention of Ivy in promotional material would be awkward. Rather than deal with any backlash, Dad just didn't schedule a second bake-off. In the blink of an eye, twenty years went by."

"What did you think when you saw Crosby had entered the contest?" Marla asked.

"Nothing at first. I didn't know Crosby Banks and Crosby Currier were the same fellow. To be honest, Gina, my secretary, handled the logistics of the bake-off for the most part, and I only saw the finalized list of contestants when I took it home the night before. I had a suspicion Crosby Banks was related to the Currier family because my paper printed Ivy Banks Currier's obituary months ago. Unusual he would drop the name Currier in favor of his mother's maiden name, but odder things have occurred. When I saw him the day of the bake-off, I was sure he was a Currier. Strong family resemblance. Chef Buckman waited until he was sure Crosby's recipe was nearly identical to Ivy Currier's winning cookie bar recipe before telling me we couldn't give him points, no matter how good his cookie might be."

"Your paper published some rough articles about Crosby in the marina fire's aftermath. Were you at all nervous to see him because of that?" Sherry asked. "I was none the wiser because I'm not much of a boater, and I'm kind of glad. That would have been on my mind while I was judging his cookie."

Warren scoffed. "If I was nervous at facing everyone the paper had ever published a not-so-flattering piece about, I'd never leave my house. I can't live that way. Maybe Crosby entering the bake-off was a way for him to come to terms with the past. The fact that he entered the same recipe as his mother's winning cookie wasn't lost on me."

Patti sat up taller. "Crosby's ex-wife, Rachel, was at the bake-off, as was his father. Maybe as a show of support for Crosby, or maybe as a show of support for Ivy's past win."

"Warren, do you think Rachel had any connection to Crosby's murder?" Sherry asked.

He scraped his fork across the bottom of his bowl of greens. "My father always taught me to let the facts speak for themselves. If you're aware of Rachel having more than a divorce daydream about Crosby not remaining alive, you may be on to something. For me to give an opinion one way or the other, though, would be career suicide."

"Has your father passed away?" Marla asked.

"No, he's down in a senior community in Florida. He's in his nineties."

"If you don't mind me saying so, you're very young to have a ninety-plus-year-old father," Marla said.

"You're right. He was a bachelor until his fifties. Married to his career until my mother convinced him otherwise. Ironically, she died young and he's been single ever since," Warren explained.

Marla elbowed Sherry in the ribs. "I see the waitress delivering our food. We need to get going." She checked her watch. "My ride to the airport shows up in two hours and I haven't had lunch yet."

"See you two soon," Sherry said to Patti and Warren.

She and Marla crossed the dining room and sat down to questions about the length of time they'd taken to make a trip to the ladies' room.

"Let me guess," Don said. "You took so long because you ran into someone who either was a cooking competitor, a suspect in Crosby's murder, or associated with the Community Garden. Or possibly someone from Town Hall who works with you on the newsletter."

Sherry replied, "Yes, I do know many people in town and I have my fingers in many pies, so your guess is a very good one. I ran into Warren Yardsmith, who was a bake-off judge with me, and Patti Mellitt, a food journalist who covers a lot of my cook-offs."

Erno leaned across his plate of food. "You'll have to get used to Sherry's wide world of connections, Don. But she's worth the patience you'll learn to summon up when trying to spend time with her out in public. She's a celebrity."

Sherry aimed a forkful of tropical goodness at her mouth. "I am not, and Dad, you're scaring him."

Sherry offered a bite of her lunch to Don in exchange for a taste of his poke bowl. "After lunch, Dad's dropping me off at the tire center to pick up my car. If you'd like to join me, I'm treating myself to two new front tires, courtesy of someone who forced me to need them sooner rather than later."

"That requires further explanation, and I have a feeling I won't believe what I hear," Don replied. "The answer is, sure, I'll come with you. In exchange for a ride to the train station. I can take another taxi, but with the frequency of schedule changes around here, a ride would be a lot easier."

"Of course. And we have to make sure Marla makes her ride to the airport."

Ruth and Frances emerged from a quiet conference. "Sherry, we have a bet going about Crosby's death."

"What would that bet be?" Sherry asked.

"I say Rachel did it. She's very close to Lonnie and wants the inheritance when his time is up. In the meantime, one less person in the will makes her chances of cashing in better," Frances said.

"That all makes sense." Erno nodded.

"Erno, you should be on my side," Ruth was quick to add.

"And your side is?" Erno asked.

"I knew Ivy," Ruth said. "Not well. I wouldn't call us friends. Acquaintances, yes. I was never a lover of sailing and boating. I didn't run in those social circles. One boat ride a year, on average, fills my ancestral Viking yearnings. What I'm getting at is, the reputation of Lonnie as dockmaster was renowned. He put the marina on the map with the wealthy. His ideas and forward-thinking transformed a simple boat docking station into a fancy destination, where the town could generate revenue year-round. I went to the club for special dinners with my late husband. We loved it."

"Sounds so nice," Marla said.

"It was. One day, it all disappeared. Lonnie was out of a job. Ivy, who was an avid sailor, lost her beloved hobby of sailing and Crosby lost his reputation as a well-liked teacher." Ruth's tone saddened as the story concluded.

"Ivy and Crosby are gone now. Leaving only Lonnie. Are you saying you think Lonnie killed his son?" Sherry asked.

"That's my bet," Ruth said. "Frances says Rachel. I say Lonnie."

"Something to consider," Marla said. "First, let's consider getting the check. After we pay, I'll ride with Ruth and meet you at the Ruggery, Sher." Marla raised her voice. "Sher? Did you hear me?"

Sherry removed her gaze from across the room, where she was tracking the exit of Rachel and Barry. She settled back on Marla. "Yes, yes. I hear you."

The check was paid, and Sherry and Don loaded themselves into Erno's wagon.

Don looked back at Sherry. "You comfortable back there?"

"Depends how much longer the ride is," Sherry replied.

"Could be worse," Erno added. "The good driver got you here in one piece."

"Thank you, Dad. I'll see you at the store in a few minutes. Don't forget to give Amber her takeout lunch."

Don gave Sherry a hand leveraging herself out of the back seat of Erno's car.

"Will do," Erno called through the open window.

"So, what happened to your car exactly?" Don held the door open for Sherry. "I've only heard the abbreviated version of the story."

They took their place in a line of four other customers.

"Something happen to your car?"

Sherry turned her head to see Ray Bease standing behind her in line. "Hi, Ray. I might as well save my breath and only tell this story once, to the both of you."

Ray's gaze shifted from Sherry to Don.

"Don, I'd like you to meet Detective Ray Bease. Ray, this is my friend Don."

The men shook hands and returned their attention to Sherry. She explained the story, beginning with her visit to Sunset Village for the purpose of scouting out volunteer opportunities, a notion she wasn't sure passed muster with Ray, judging by the tight lines forming on his forehead. After Sherry's description of Vitis's tire rescue operation, neither man looked pleased.

"How does this keep happening?" Ray asked.

"Which part of the story are you referring to?" Sherry asked.

"The part where there's an attack on either your personal property or, worse, your well-being."

"Next, please." The man behind the counter stood waiting for Sherry and Don to step forward.

"To be continued," Sherry said.

"Your tires definitely were intentionally compromised," the man with the blue, tire company logoed shirt told Sherry. "You can choose to report it or not, that's up to you and your insurance coverage."

"Thank you." Sherry handed the man her credit card. She faced Don. "Why am I thanking him? I just handed over hundreds of dollars."

"We'll pull up your car. You can wait right over there." He pointed to two empty plastic chairs by the front door.

Ray joined Sherry and Don after he spoke to the man behind the desk.

"I asked the manager for your slashed tires."

"Wait a minute. I might need those to convince my insurance company I didn't cause the damage," Sherry said.

"When I'm done with them, they're all yours."

"Thanks, I think."

"What's your impression of Vitis Costa?" Ray asked.

"He has reason to hold a grudge against the Currier family, yes. Would he help me both times I was in need, at the marina and at Sunset Village, if he were the person who sabotaged the boat and the car? I can't be certain."

"You, Don? Do you have an opinion?"

"Vitis was nothing but professional when we were at the marina. On the other hand, I remember there was a small period of time when he was alone with my boat."

"When was that?" Sherry asked.

"When we were searching for the best-fitting life jackets outside the dockmaster shed. He excused himself and left us to sort out the vests. We found him down at the dock," Don said.

"There was another warning," Sherry said.

Don groaned and Ray sucked in a noisy inhalation.

"Besides the boat and the car?" Don asked.

"Nothing meant for you or me. Sal and Effi Forino, owners of the Shore Cleaners, received one. Effi was in the cookie bake-off. Crosby is a customer of theirs. Can't be a coincidence," Sherry said. "They found a paper under the door of their business somewhere between closing time on Saturday and opening Monday morning. A blocky font spelled out a warning to mind their own business or else."

"Cookies, cook-offs, and Crosby," Ray said.

"Crosby and Sal had a word with each other during the bake-off." Sherry pulled out her phone and began scrolling through her photos.

"If you know about the warning note, I'm guessing you've asked Sal what he and Crosby talked about at the bake-off. If you'd like to share, please do," Ray said.

Sherry found the photo she was looking for. "Sal said Crosby had some dry cleaning to pick up."

Ray laughed so hard his hat fell off. "I'm sorry. That was very funny. Not the grand revelation I was anticipating."

Sherry held her phone in front of Ray's face. "Effi is adamant she doesn't want to draw attention to a situation she doesn't understand. They are very proud people. If their business suffers from bad publicity, they will be devastated."

"If one of them gets hurt, they'll be devastated. Stubborn pride can be an overrated characteristic," Ray said.

"This is the note the Forinos received under their door."

Ray studied the screen. Sherry studied Ray.

When he was done, he fixed his gaze on Sherry. "You need to clean the lens of your phone."

"Ms. Oliveri, your car is out front," the blue-shirted man announced.

"Thank you." Sherry stuffed her phone back in her purse.

Don headed to the door, leaving Ray and Sherry a last moment together.

"Be careful," Ray said. "You know something. And someone knows you know it, and that makes them unhappy. Keep your head up and your eyes open and, most important, we all need to move faster now. It's only a matter of time before . . ."

"Sherry? You coming?" Don urged as he reached the door. "The line of cars is growing."

"Okay, Ray. I hear you." Sherry followed Don out to her car.

Chapter 20

"Am I stepping into a field of landmines?" Don asked.

Sherry avoided Don's gaze. "I don't know what you're talking about."

"I knew you had a well-deserved reputation for solving a few murders, but the realization I may now be in the middle of one is hard to swallow. It may have already cost me a boat, and I'm not sure I'm willing to lose more."

Sherry waited for the streetlight to shine green before she countered his sentiment. "I can see how you'd feel that way. I'm not asking you to stick with me until this case gets resolved if you feel you're not up for the challenge."

"Up for the challenge?" Don's voice raised an octave. "The challenge is finding a murderer. That's not your run-of-the-mill challenge. What if the murderer finds you, or me, first?"

Sherry drove her car down the narrow opening between the Ruggery and Leather & Lace, grimacing when her car's side mirror nearly grazed the shared dumpster. She wedged the car as close to Erno's as would allow the doors to open wide enough to let a body slide through.

"I need to have a word with the woman who owns the lingerie store." Sherry gestured toward a woman hoisting a garbage bag into the giant trash container. "That dumpster needs to find a new place to reside so I can start parking back here again. I'll meet you inside."

Don left the car and opened Sherry's car door for her.

"Nobody's done that for me since my first date with my ex. Thank you."

"See, I am worth your giving up the murder investigation. But I have a strong suspicion you won't. See you inside." Don kissed Sherry's warming cheek.

Sherry locked her car. "Evette?"

The woman closing the lid of the dumpster answered without turning to face Sherry. "Yes?"

"I was wondering if we could relocate the dumpster to its original location. That way I can park my car back here, the way I've done for years."

The pretty young woman stepped back from the dumpster. She could model for her line of lingerie and no one would know she wasn't a professional.

"Your father said he likes the new location. Maybe you and he should discuss the matter before we get the forklift down here."

"Okay," Sherry said.

"Sherry?"

Rachel approached from the street side of the alley, giving Evette her cue to head inside her store. "We have some unfinished business. Wouldn't you say?"

Sherry checked her surroundings. She and Rachel were alone. She could reach into her purse and pull out her phone, she could scream, she could run, or she could stand up to the woman she was sure had issued multiple warnings to her in the last few days for reasons she wasn't quite sure of.

"I'd say I have some unanswered questions for you." Sherry was surprised at the steadiness of her tone.

"I talked to you about finding Crosby's killer and come to learn from Detective Bease that you think *I'm* the killer."

A screech interrupted Sherry's train of thought.

"Sorry," Evette called out. She sent Sherry a wave from across the alleyway. "The hinges on this old door are temperamental."

"That's okay," Sherry yelled back. She steeled her gaze on Rachel. "I don't know if you killed your ex-husband or not. You can't deny you have a motive. You're in Lonnie's will and Crosby's gone now, so more for you."

"I adore Lonnie. He's like a father to me and I would never want any harm to come to him to get my hands on his money. I resent your implication."

"I agree you are caring and attentive to Lonnie. But your bitter attitude toward your ex-husband more than overshadows those warm and fuzzy sentiments. I don't know you well, yet one of the first details of your life you shared with me was what a loser you thought Crosby was. Yes, you shared how close you are to his father, who, in turn, shared with me how he felt Crosby squandered the opportunities he was offered. An opinion, by the way, I don't agree with. When he was my teacher, I found Crosby kind, generous, and inspiring."

Rachel shrugged.

"Add to that, you were on the scene when Don's boat sprung a leak, courtesy of a precise knife cut in the exact spot that would cause a slow leak so that the boat took on water far from the marina. Not to mention you were at Sunset Village with me this morning until you left before me. Imagine my surprise when I found my two front tires slashed in the parking lot after leaving the field trip. Did you have anything to do with any of those mishaps?"

"Why would I be interested in damaging your property? I asked for your help. Do you think I'd ask only to turn around and make it impossible for you to believe in my innocence? You're not making sense."

"Not much of a defense on your behalf."

Rachel made a small circle in the driveway gravel with the toe of her shoe. "Crosby wasn't in Lonnie's will," she said when the circle was complete. "He'd been out of the will for many years. I knew that fact before I married Crosby. I didn't marry Crosby for his family's money, although they were well off. Ivy came from a wealthy family. Word was, they didn't approve of her choice of a dockmaster for a husband. They were hoping for more of an old-money yachtsman."

"Why did Ivy and Lonnie live apart?"

"Ivy was told one too many times Lonnie wasn't worthy of her and she began to believe her parents. I know she still loved Lonnie, despite the pressure to leave him for someone more acceptable. Those were the times."

"So," Sherry softened her tone, "there was no third party involved?"

Rachel's face twisted into a scowl. "That's the thin ice you shouldn't tread on. Whether there was a third party or not has nothing to do with Crosby's death. That's something to stay away from."

Sherry studied Rachel's face. When she wasn't smiling, which was most of the time, she looked older than the midforties Sherry assumed was her age. "Before we stay away from the subject entirely, did you and Crosby break up over a third party?"

"You are persistent, aren't you? Neither Crosby nor I were involved with anyone else. There were plenty of other interfering circumstances keeping us from a happy marriage."

"I know how that goes." Sherry nodded.

"You understand, then? If you've ever been suspected of murder, you'd know how desperate I am to find the real killer."

"Actually, I have, and I do know."

"You have to believe me when I say I didn't kill Crosby. But who did?" Rachel asked.

"I need to show you something." Sherry headed to her car. She opened the rear passenger door and reached inside. "Is this your glove? There's only one right answer."

"Yes, it is." Rachel stepped forward and took the glove from Sherry. "Where'd you find it? I've looked everywhere."

"Your glove was on the deck of Don's boat. Don found it the night his boat was sabotaged. You tell me how it got there."

"I thought I had both gloves that night. The weather was going to get chilly, and any boater will tell you, keeping your head and hands covered is the best way to combat hypothermia. I didn't check for them, though, because

I thought they were in my coat pocket. By the time we left the boat, after docking at the marina, I went to put them on and realized I had lost a glove."

"Did you or Barry set foot on Don's boat while Don, my sister, and I were choosing a life vest at the dockmaster shed?" Sherry asked. "That's the only reasonable deduction I can make. because Don found your glove on his boat's deck. Can you explain, please?"

"I don't think I can explain." Rachel shook her head. "It wasn't me, and I certainly don't think Barry went aboard your boat. Have you asked Vitis? He was walking the dock that night. Maybe he was returning the glove he thought was either yours or your sister's."

"By tossing it on the deck? Doesn't sound plausible."

"Sherry?"

She turned to see Evette leaning out her store's back door. "I just spoke to your father, and he said the dumpster was fine where it is."

"Dad's a traitor," Sherry whispered. "Thank you. Okay," she called out.

"The last point I want to make is that Lonnie didn't kill Crosby," Rachel said.

"I didn't say he did. By the way, you're not speaking about his innocence with much conviction. If you were his lawyer and I were his relative, I'd recommend he fire you and get someone who believed what they were saying."

"I know." Rachel bowed her head. "The thing is, the more investigators learn, the more they might be convinced he not only had the motive, he had the means."

"Maybe he did it, then."

"I'll be honest with you about my fears. I'm afraid Lonnie was the one who set the fire at the Augustin Marina. Out of anger over his crumbling marriage. He let Crosby take the blame because an angry man in his twenties was the obvious scapegoat. Once someone made the suggestion Crosby was the cause of Lonnie's way of life ending in retaliation for letting the marriage dissolve without a fight, the blame game began. The family fell apart as a result. No one spoke of the past, present, or future. Ever. It was horrendously stressful. Whoever was guilty, the end result was the Currier family living in a bubble of shame for years."

"Even if your theory about the fire is correct, what does any of that have to do with Crosby's death? I mean, what happened in the past is the past, wouldn't you agree?" She studied Rachel's relaxing face.

"Have you read a history book lately? The present is basically the past with a modern twist."

"Sounds to me like you're trying to convince yourself Lonnie didn't commit a number of crimes and you're having trouble doing it."

"He may have. He had his reasons. He may have cracked after all these years of suppressing the truth about Crosby's guilt."

"From what you've described, the two haven't had much contact over the years. Had something recently aggravated their relationship?"

"The past is being stirred up by people who don't understand it should be left in the past. Lonnie has suffered enough."

"If the facts of the investigation lead back to Lonnie—well, there's not much I can do about him getting convicted. The same way you may be found guilty because of developments over the last couple of days. How hard are you working to clear your own name?"

The intensity of the frown on Rachel's face sent a chill through Sherry's core.

"Sherry?"

"Yes, Evette?" Out of the corner of Sherry's sight line, Evette was stepping out of her side door.

"I'd like to discuss the dumpster issue further," Evette said.

"I'm in the middle of . . ." Sherry began.

"I'm on my way out," Rachel said. "One last thought. You're not seeing Crosby for who he truly was. Thank you for your time." She turned and walked away down the alleyway between the Ruggery and Evette's store.

Sherry approached Evette. Before she could express her frustration with the woman, Evette smiled.

"I thought you needed some help. I saw that woman pacing back and forth back here before you pulled your car in. I asked her if I could assist her and her reply was rather rude. She said she had pressing business with you and I should mind my own," Evette explained. "When I saw the look on her face when she was speaking to you, I figured I'd provide you with an out if you needed one. If you want to tell me to buzz off, I won't take offense. I'm a straight shooter. You need to know that about me."

"Thank you. I did need an out. I owe you one. Let's leave the dumpster where it is if the location helps you during your construction phase. Then we'll reassess." Sherry sent Evette a grateful grin before making her way to the Ruggery.

"Sherry, finally. What have you been doing out there? Poor Don has been subjected to shop talk for the last ten minutes," Erno said.

"It's so interesting," Don said. "This artistry isn't something you see every day. I'm trying to absorb every pearl of wisdom your father has to offer."

"Dad is the king of pearls of wisdom." Marla laughed.

"I was talking to Rachel, and then to Evette," Sherry said.

"Rachel Currier was outside?" Marla asked.

"Did she change her mind about selling me Crosby's boat?" Don added.

"Yes, Rachel was outside. She just appeared when I was walking from the car. And no, we didn't talk about the boat; sorry."

"Evette is a nice gal," Erno said. "I told her not to worry about moving the dumpster until her construction was complete. You don't mind parking in the municipal lot until then, right, Sher? She mentioned you had a tough time parking in the tight space."

"I'll get used to it. And yes, Evette is very nice."

"What did Rachel have to say?" Marla asked.

"Nothing that makes me sure either she or Lonnie didn't have anything to do with Crosby's death," Sherry said. "Marla, shouldn't we get you home? Your ride will be picking you up in about an hour and a half. Don, what time is your train?"

"I'll check the schedule," Don said.

Marla bid her goodbyes to her father and Ruth. After Sherry edged her car out of the tight parking spot, they set off for Sherry's house.

"Would anyone mind if we stopped at the cleaners for two minutes?" Sherry asked as she slowed her car.

"If we ever went from point A to point B as planned, I'd be flabbergasted," Don said. "Please, do what you need to do."

Sherry checked her rearview mirror.

Marla was peering at her phone. "We have plenty of time. Need us to come inside with you?"

"Nope, thanks. I'll be right back." Sherry backed the car into a spot in front of the store. Sherry went inside Shore Cleaners.

Effi handed the only person in line at the sales counter her dry cleaning. The woman brushed past Sherry with her arms full of plastic-wrapped clothing.

Sherry stepped to the front of the counter. "Hi, Effi."

"Sherry. How nice to see you. Are you dropping off?" Effi scanned Sherry, presumably for any laundry she might be holding.

"Not this time." Sherry raised her empty hands.

"Or last time," Effi added.

Sherry lifted her purse strap from her shoulder and set the bag on the counter. "I've changed my mind. I'd like to take you up on your offer for Ivy's blue wool coat. Retro fashion is back in and this is my chance to be stylish."

Effi squinted in Sherry's direction. "I have to check whether Sal has already given the coat away. We're not a storage facility, you know. I told you that. You should have jumped on the chance when we offered it to you."

Effi's unexpected resistance deflated Sherry's determination to convince the woman of her reason for wanting the coat.

"If you wouldn't mind taking a look, I'd appreciate it. I have plenty of dry cleaning I'll be bringing in later this week," Sherry said.

Without a further word, Effi headed out of sight. She returned a few minutes later to a long line. Sherry was engaged in a conversation with the couple behind her, who'd lamented over this being Sal's day off, but it was their only chance to bring in vacation wear before their cruise ship sailed.

"You're in luck. I found the coat. One word of warning. It's been waiting to be picked up for so long, it may not be as fresh as it was when it was first cleaned. Another reason why we aren't a storage facility." Effi handed over the coat.

Before Sherry draped the plastic-protected garment over her forearm, she pulled some cash from her purse. "This covers the cost of the dry cleaning." She pulled the ticket from the bag and laid it on the counter. "Thank you."

"I knew you'd go back for the coat," Marla said when Sherry returned to the car.

"While you were gone, Marla and I discussed her situation," Don said. "Your sister gave you, your dad, and Amber credit for setting her straight and sending her home to where she belongs."

Sherry cast a fast glance Marla's way. "She told you that?"

"It's true," Marla said. "That's what big sisters are for. Their wisdom. If it weren't for you, I'd probably take the easy route and move home. Instead, I'm going to give my marriage the effort it deserves. Now, would you like to explain what led you to return for the coat?"

"The coat was an excuse." Sherry steered the car onto Augustin's scenic, winding North Avenue, one turn away from her house. "I wanted to get back in there to have another look at the note the Forinos received."

"And did you?" Marla asked.

"I got lucky. It's Sal's day off. Only Effi was working, and for a brief time, I was the only one in the store when she went to find the coat. I was going to snap a photo, but a couple came in as I snatched the note from under the cash register."

"So, you didn't get a picture?" Don asked.

"No. I had to think fast. All I could do was pop the note in my purse. I doubt she'll be revisiting it anytime soon. She knows what it says, and both she and Sal want to keep it a secret."

Chapter 21

"I'm really going to miss Marla." Sherry watched the airport van pull out of her driveway. "Chutney will miss having the extra body in the house for company."

"I'm sorry I have to leave, too." Don put his arm around Sherry.

"We have a half hour before we need to head to the train station. Would you mind if I asked you a favor?"

Don beamed a brilliant smile. "Anything for an Augustin celebrity cook."

"I want your expert boating opinion on a photograph."

Don tipped his head to the side. "Not exactly the favor I had in mind. I wouldn't call myself a boating expert, but I hope I can be of help."

Sherry retrieved her laptop from the kitchen and brought it to the living room couch. She swatted the empty spot next to her and Don obediently sat beside her.

"Take a look at this photo of the marina fire that happened twenty years ago." Sherry adjusted the laptop for better viewing.

Don leaned in and studied the photo.

"What sticks out to you?"

"The interesting pattern of the fire's destruction. I don't know much about the origin of the fire, except that I have heard it may have been intentionally set." His index finger hovered over the section of the photo by the skeleton of a small, outdoor storage structure. "This storage locker is metal and still seems to have the worst damage. I'd say the fire started just outside it. If so, the fire would have traveled down the wooden dock, fed by the old wood, and taken out any boat in its path. Then the fire seems to have lost its fuel. The destruction line stops partway down the dock. Down here, the fire starts up again, or a second fire started up near this giant sailboat. It suffered so much damage it nearly sank."

"Do you think this man owns that huge sailboat?" Sherry pointed to a figure with the slumped posture standing on what remained of the dock, facing the partially submerged boat.

"If he does, he must like Hawaii," Don said.

"What makes you say that?"

The name of the boat, *Ha wah e*."

"I thought letters were missing. Burned off or melted. I never said the name out loud. You're right. Hawaii."

"First time for everything," Don said.

"It could be Lonnie's boat. He and Ivy went to Hawaii on their honeymoon. Rachel told me Crosby's middle name is Kai, which, if I'm not mistaken, is a Hawaiian word."

"Absolutely. Kai means 'the sea,'" Don said.

"How do you know that?"

"When I thought I was on the receiving end of Crosby's boat, I began an intensive research for a new name. The boat was named *Rachel's Way*, and that didn't have any meaning for me. I found so many references to ocean, water, and sea, and Kai was one word that stuck out to me. I wouldn't have used the name, though, because I have no connection to Hawaii, other than that the state is on my travel wish list for a second visit."

"Lonnie was the dockmaster in those days. Explains why this woman in the background is most likely Ivy, his wife. Doesn't explain why she's so intently watching the man, who isn't her husband."

"She does have a serious expression. These old black-and-white photos always seem to capture the mood better than modern color prints. Not sure whether it's the viewer projecting the mood onto the photo to some extent."

"If I had to write a dialogue between the two, I'd have him saying, 'Goodbye, my love.'"

"You're such a romantic." Don glanced at his phone. "I think we'd better get over to the train station. As much as I'd like to help solve the riddles you're involved in, I have a meeting I can't miss and not much wiggle room to get there on time."

"You've helped more than you can imagine. Come on, Chutney. We have a train to catch." Sherry clapped her hands and her willing dog appeared.

Don caught his train back to Long Island with only minutes to spare. As the train chugged away from the station, Sherry's cell phone rang.

"Hi, this is Sherry." She didn't recognize the number, and it didn't conjure up a name from her Contacts list.

"Sherry, this is Rachel Currier." Rachel paused, during

which time Sherry's surprise at learning the identity of the caller left her momentarily mute. "Are you there?"

"Yes. What can I do for you?"

"I answered a call from the Forinos to pick up my mother-in-law's coat from the cleaners, and when I got there, I was told you have it. I admit I was a bit late picking it up, but I'm sure you understand I'd like to have the coat. Sentimental reasons."

Again, Rachel's surprise left Sherry speechless.

"Are you there? We must have a bad connection," Rachel said. There was a hint of desperation in her tone.

"It's your family's coat. You have first dibs on it, even though the Forinos said they made multiple attempts to get a Currier to pick it up and pay for the cleaning. It's here, so whenever you can pick it up I'll leave it on the porch if I won't be home. Just give me a heads-up when you can come by." Sherry was quick to add, "Rachel, there was a note in the pocket. I read it when I thought the coat was mine. It said, 'Aloha, my love.'" Sherry listened for a response. None came. "In Hawaiian, 'aloha' means hello and goodbye."

"In this case, goodbye."

"So, it was your note?"

"It doesn't matter who the note was for, or from," Rachel said in a monotone.

"Rachel, you asked me for help and provided me with no answers. Do you know how frustrating that is?" Sherry's voice picked up a momentum that couldn't be stopped. "Yes, it matters. If you were having an affair, there are plenty of implications, and none of them favor your innocence when it comes to your husband's death. The coat was at the dry cleaners for over six months. If

you divorced because of an affair, this note confirms it."
Sherry ran out of breath.

"Ivy had the affair. She never spoke of it until she was on her deathbed. The name of the man was her closely guarded secret. That was the way it was in that era. The affair ended for the sake of her marriage to Lonnie and her son, Crosby. The damage was done. No one involved ever really recovered. But these things happen. History can't be changed. Crosby was innocent in all the shenanigans between Lonnie and Ivy."

"If the note was Ivy's, and she carried it in her coat pocket all those years, that's sad. Means she was never truly happy."

"I think she was happy enough." Rachel sighed. "Who really is ever truly happy?"

"I am." Sherry waited for an additional comment. None came. "I'm at the Ruggery tomorrow. Would you like to pick it up there? Or I could leave it on my porch."

"I'd rather avoid doing this in public. Would you text me your address, please?"

"Okay." Sherry hesitated while considering whether to give Rachel access to her property. "I'll put the coat on the front porch. It's nicely wrapped in plastic and I paid the cleaning bill."

"Thank you. I'll reimburse you. I have one more question. When Ivy was on her deathbed, she told me about her affair. She'd been carrying the burden of the secret for so long, she felt it had contributed to her health's decline. She stopped short of telling me who she was involved with. Would you be able to confirm who it was?"

"First things first. Can you provide an alibi for your father-in-law during the afternoon of the cookie bake-off? An alibi that would get Lonnie off the suspect list?"

"You know he was with me at the bake-off. I can vouch for that. But not every single moment. He spent most of the time in the bathroom, out of my sight. That point is moot, because Crosby survived the bake-off. There's no association there."

"What did you two do after the bake-off?"

"I took Lonnie back to Sunset Village, as I would after any of our outings."

Sherry considered what Rachel had said.

Rachel cleared her throat. "I'm sorry, I'm mistaken. That day I didn't return him to the Village. Barry gave him a ride. I had an errand to run. Not sure if they went straight back to the Village or took a drive, which is something Lonnie loves to do. Barry would have to tell us what they did after the bake-off. My guess is they did what Lonnie often has me do with him."

"And that is?"

"Drive by his old truck. The vintage truck Vitis drives to work at the marina. He really misses that thing."

"So, you think Barry drove him down to the marina?"

"That's where he has me take him at least once a week."

"Do you have anyone who can vouch for *your* where-abouts the afternoon of the bake-off, because you weren't with Lonnie?" Sherry asked.

"After the bake-off, I grocery shopped, went to the pharmacy, and answered some emails at home." Rachel exhaled. A sign of resignation or distress, Sherry couldn't say. "I have to go. Barry and I are delivering cookies to the homeless shelter and we need to get them there before dinner. Goodbye." The phone went silent.

Sherry sat in her car and watched another train pull into the station, deliver and pick up passengers, then chug away. She checked her car's dashboard clock. She had time before dinner to send an email to Ruth. Whether Ruth would like her idea was another matter. When she arrived home, Sherry crafted the email.

Hi Ruth. I have become very excited since you took me down to the Historical Society. If you would accept my help, I've come up with an idea. I spoke with some people about the upcoming Augustin Marina fire exhibit and, to my surprise, they were interested in possibly contributing to the museum. The only catch was, each requested a private viewing of the exhibit artifacts to know where their contributions would be most useful. I have attached the list of the interested parties and a couple of others I felt should be included, if you agree to the arrangement. An after-hours viewing party makes the most sense. Later this week would work for most, if not all. Let me know what you think. Best, Sherry

She hit the Send button. She found her purse on the front hall table, next to Ivy's plastic-wrapped coat. Distracted from her original task of finding her phone inside her purse, she lifted the plastic off the coat.

"I don't like the smell of dry-cleaning chemicals," she said to Chutney. He also turned up his nose at the acrid odor. She drew the garment closer. "Or is that the slightest smell of smoke?" Sherry pictured the photograph of the woman wearing the exact style coat she was holding. The woman was watching a man next to a charred boat. The boat with the name having a reference to Hawaii.

"Not my problem anymore. Rachel can figure out a way to get rid of the smell. The plastic bag must have trapped the odor, and now it's going to be the devil to remove. No wonder Sal and Effi were so gung ho to get it out of the shop. They did their best, trying to clean the garment. Chutney, are you listening to me?"

Her dog pranced over to his bowl.

"Okay, dinnertime. You know what's most important."

Sherry lay the coat across the antique Shaker stool that sat in the corner of the front hall. She returned, and Chutney went to the kitchen, still poised to chow down, and she gave him a scoop of his crunchy kibble. The sight of her happy pet, snout plunged in his bowl of dinner, reminded Sherry she had one more task to attend to before she could set her sights on her own dinner. She returned to the front hall in search of her purse. Inside it, she found the absconded piece of paper from the Shore Cleaners.

The paper was a little worse for wear after receiving a harsh shove into Sherry's purse when the couple entered the cleaners and Sherry was forced to scrap her plan to photograph, then return, the note. She took the paper to the kitchen table, where she smoothed it out as best she could. Her ringing phone broke her concentration.

"Sherry, it's Ruth. I got your email. I have to say, I was a bit surprised at the urgency to get this all done in the next few days. That being said, I love a challenge, especially if it comes with financial gains for the Historical Society. I've texted and received the green light from the board president. That's the beauty of having only three board members—decisions are made at a faster pace. We've chosen the evening after tomorrow. I emailed an invitation to your list of potential donors, offering them a coveted chance at an early viewing of the marina fire artifacts."

"Ruth, you're amazing. You get things done in a hurry. What's the plan for the evening?"

"At closing time, we'll clear out our day patrons and provide the incoming group with a small reception. Drinks, finger foods, casual yet elegant."

"Sounds nice," Sherry said.

"I'll give a short welcome speech, an introduction to the history of the original Augustin settlement, and how the development of the Augustin Harbor played a pivotal role in the growth and well-being of the town. I'll leave some questions up in the air about the fire. That way the group will be anxious to reconstruct the event through their own eyes, while taking in the exhibition photos, articles, and artifacts."

"How did you brainstorm this over the last fifteen minutes?" Sherry asked.

"We've been thinking of doing something like this for a while. We put it on the back burner because of the holidays, but you've given us an excuse to go ahead and hold the get-together. So, I thank you."

"Glad to be of help. What else can I do?"

"I was thinking about the variety of drinks and snacks. I'll prepare my smoked salmon rolls. Everyone asks me for the recipe when I serve them. I've only shared it once, with a woman who I knew never used her kitchen except to plug in her coffee maker. Sneaky, right? That way I kept a friend, and my recipe remained a closely guarded secret."

Sherry laughed. "I've had your delicious salmon rolls and I can understand why you'd guard the recipe."

"Would you be able to contribute to the snacks? Maybe a delicious and sinful cookie?"

"Baking isn't my strong suit. Don't you need another savory snack? I have some great recipes for appetizers."

"We really don't. Dolly will be bringing a contribution of sorts. You have dibs on a sweet snack. Cookies are the perfect finger food for sugar lovers."

"If you can rise to the challenge by pulling this all together in forty-eight hours, I suppose I can, too. I just hope I don't poison any potential donors with my bad baking."

"Dear, you're being silly. When was the last time your cooking poisoned anyone?" Ruth asked. "I'll have the full head count by tomorrow. I asked for the RSVP to be in by then."

"Very good, Ruth. Great job."

"All thanks to your good idea. Talk to you soon."

"Bye." Sherry brought up her phone's calendar. "Two days." Tomorrow was like any other day—busy. Sherry was now going to have to fit in a trip to the grocery store for baking supplies, which she only stocked for extraordinarily special occasions. She examined her hourly schedule. The best time to shop and bake was the morning; she was working the afternoon shift at the Ruggery. With the new addition to tomorrow's schedule, she needed to squeeze in typing up her completed recipe for Snappy Holiday Butternut Squash Panzanella after she ate dinner. That way she wouldn't be rushed to meet the deadline on the last day submissions were accepted, which coincided with the party.

Dinner would be a chef's salad with any leftovers she found in the refrigerator. Her dressing would be her new and improved chutney balsamic vinaigrette. Her side dish would be a glass of chardonnay, in honor of accomplishing a recipe she had confidence in. If only she could find the same confidence in her list of suspects in the Crosby investigation. She rummaged through the refrigerator. The longer it took to narrow down the field, the higher the chances were someone else might be hurt and threatened, or worse.

Chapter 22

"I've made my grocery list for the Tropical Aloha Bars."

Sherry closed the cupboard door after checking for any cookie ingredients she might have. She only came up with flour, sugar, and vanilla extract. Chutney whined. Sherry glanced at her empty hand.

"I've neglected buying your treats for two days. Sorry, boy. At the top of my grocery list is a big bag of doggy cookies." She leaned across the marble counter and jotted down items on the paper. "I'm not going to bother putting in the guava paste Ivy's recipe calls for. Crosby didn't include the ingredient in his version, so the recipe should still come together without it. The party guests will have to be satisfied with the East Coast version."

Sherry grabbed her purse and gave Chutney the heads-up they were leaving.

"Almost forgot to put out Ivy's coat. Rachel texted she may drive by sometime today or tomorrow."

Sherry scooped up the coat, left the house, and locked the door behind her. She set the coat over the porch stair railing. Chutney scampered over to his favorite bush, made his mark, and followed Sherry to the car. After a short ride to the grocery store, Sherry embarked on a trip down aisle two, baking. List in one hand, handbasket in the other, she checked off each item as she pulled it from the shelf. Shredded coconut, dark chocolate and white chocolate chips, turbinado sugar, macadamia nuts, and old-fashioned oats. She'd find a fresh lime in the produce section. Parchment paper to line the baking pan was in the cooking accessory aisle.

Sherry retraced her steps back to the dairy aisle, where she'd forgotten to pick up butter sticks.

"I know where to find you if I'm ever looking for you," a deep voice sounded over her shoulder.

Sherry lifted her eyes from the expensive, imported Irish butter she was contemplating splurging on.

"Hi, Warren. You saved me from making a rash and costly purchase." She pointed to the colorful box of butter sticks.

"Go for it. Better butter means better flavor. Not a rash choice at all, in my opinion."

Sherry picked up the box, winced at the price, which was double that of her normal brand, and tossed it in her basket. "Glad I didn't see you in the caviar aisle." She laughed.

"I received an invitation to a fundraiser to be held tomorrow night at the Historical Society. I saw your name on the organizing committee."

Sherry nodded. "We hand-selected a group we feel are

interested in Augustin's history and future. Educating the public about how Augustin came to be will make the community more cohesive and knowledgeable about what our future holds."

"Well said. You've convinced me to attend. I'm guessing you'd like the paper to run an article, after the fact, to drum up interest in the exhibit. That's usually the reason I'm on someone's guest list."

"Wouldn't be a bad idea." There was a hint of coyness in Sherry's voice.

"Done."

"If your wife is feeling better, she's, of course, invited."

"Her cough drops are the next item on my list. Unless that cough miraculously is cured in the next two days, I'd say she may have to decline." Warren peered at the butter package Sherry was studying. "The butter reminds me, it's my father's birthday. I'm going to send him a cake. He loves buttercream frosting. They'll make him one at his nursing home, but if I can get a bakery to deliver, that would be my first choice. He's ninety-four today. I wish I could get down to Florida to see him, but with all the upgrades the paper is doing this month, I'm chained to my desk."

"You don't look chained to your desk right now. Ignore me if I'm being rude, but did your father have you when he was older? I'm guessing you're only in your forties."

"How astute of you. Yes, he was fifty-one. He married my mother when he was fifty. She was quite a lot younger. Unusual to have such a gap in age in those days, but not unheard of."

"Anything goes. As long as true love prevails." Sherry scanned the remaining butter choices in the dairy case. She exchanged one butter package for another and placed the expensive choice in her basket.

"I agree. Did I lose you? You seem to be thinking of something else besides my father and butter. True love, perhaps?"

"Oh no. Sorry. I have so many things on my mind."

"I'll let you go. As for me, I don't want to get caught playing hooky. See you tomorrow?" Warren tipped his head and walked away.

"Yes, looking forward to it," Sherry called after him.

Sherry found a lime in the produce section and had to ask for assistance finding the parchment paper. When her basket was full, she lined up to pay. The young man behind the register was in training, the tag on his shirt indicated, so the process was time-consuming. Each bar code was double-checked by a supervisor, leaving Sherry several minutes to review her phone. While she was scrolling through unread emails, a text came in from Ruth, saying the response to the invitation was wonderful and only Erno had declined. Sherry texted back, asking why in the world her father and Ruth's boyfriend had declined to come to an event both were organizing. A moment later, she received a reply from Ruth. Erno said he'd lived through the fire and didn't want to relive the sadness that had consumed him during that time. He would make a donation and that was that.

"Ma'am? You can swipe your credit card now."

Sherry refocused her attention on the young man. "Thank you. You did a great job."

His cheeks flushed a vibrant red. "Thank you."

                          *   *   *

Sherry returned home and got to work preparing the Tropical Aloha Bars. As soon as she laid the ingredients across her counter, her usual spark of kitchen creativity was smothered. There were three items facing her that she seldom included in her recipe creation process. A measuring cup, a sheet of paper with a recipe typed on it, and a timer.

Years of experimentation had given Sherry the confidence that cooking mistakes could be altered and adjusted to yield good results. She knew a loose sauce could easily be tightened any number of ways. Likewise, a thick sauce could be easily thinned without losing the integrity of the recipe. The same method could be applied to mashed potatoes, soups, and stews, but none of those translated to baked goods. Baking required precise measuring, accurate techniques, and unforgiving ingredient balance, all incredibly useful skills in the kitchen. For better or worse, Sherry labeled herself a fly-by-the-seat-of-her-pants cook, whose ingenuity won her the big prizes at competitions. That was foremost on her mind as she reread Ivy's recipe. She had to trust Ivy had written down exactly the way she'd prepared the bars that won her the grand prize years ago or Sherry was going to run into trouble.

Adhering to the typed instructions, she put the dry ingredients in the bowl first. Wet ingredients were added to the dry and, in no time, the prep was done. Ivy's cookie bar batter seemed looser than any cookie batter Sherry had ever worked with. Doubt crept into her head.

One hour later, the Tropical Aloha Bars were baked and on their way to being cool enough to cut into manageable-sized squares. Sherry puffed out her chest as she sampled the first morsel she lifted out of the baking pan.

"Not bad. Not bad at all," she told Chutney.

The dog waited at Sherry's feet for any crumb that might fall his way.

"I may become a baker after all."

Sherry checked the oven clock. "I need to get over to the store. Come on, boy. I'll let these cool until we get back."

"Dad, why did we get so many boxes of yellow wool dye?" Sherry used a box cutter to open the second shipment of dye packets. "Twice as many as any other color we stock."

"You weren't here when Victoria Templeton ordered a second rug. A giant field of daffodils. Beautiful, but I sure hope she doesn't get tired of yellow after living with the rug for the next twenty years."

"As long as it was made by your loving hands, she'll cherish it forever."

"Good morning, fine people." Eileen's lilting voice rang out as the Ruggery's front door opened.

"Good morning, Eileen," Sherry said.

Erno repeated the greeting. "How nice to see you, Eileen. Are you still savoring your big win?"

"More than ever. The newspaper contacted me and gave me the details on my holiday parade float ride. I have to shop for a whole new outfit. All I have is garden wear." Eileen lifted her leg and showed off her utilitarian jeans and ankle-heigh rubber boots.

"You're going to need cookie wear." Erno chuckled.

"If you want to wear a kitchen apron on the float, Sherry's the one to ask. We must have a hundred."

Sherry nodded. "It's true. At almost every cook-off, the contestants receive a sponsors' apron, and I've saved every single one."

"Is there something you'd like us to show you?" Erno asked.

Eileen softened her voice. "You might make fun of me, but I'd like an oval throw rug for my pantry featuring my cookie."

"I love that idea," said Sherry. "That's so special."

"I've never won anything based on talent in my life, and I want to remember the win every time I'm searching for baking ingredients. I brought a photo of my winning cookie platter from the newspaper article. I'd love an exact replica of the photo made into a rug, if possible." Eileen lowered her purse from her shoulder and unclipped the latch. She removed a business-size envelope and handed it to Erno.

He opened it with the greatest of care and removed the folded clipping. "I have to admit, I've had a wide variety of rug-subject requests. Never a cookie. You take the cake, pun intended." Erno giggled at his own joke.

"So, you can do it?" Eileen asked.

"Of course. I'll need six to eight weeks. Probably the slowest cookie ever baked." Again, Erno had amused himself and erupted into a contagious laughing episode.

Eileen and Sherry joined in the laughter.

Erno handed the article and envelope back to Eileen, who waved it off. "You keep the photo as long as you need it. Same colors, everything as is in the photo is what I'd love."

"You've got it." Pride dripped from Erno's words.

"Eileen, I've been meaning to ask you something. Were you in the one-and-only Story For Glory Cookie Bake-off many years ago? The one Ivy Currier won?"

"Huh, yes," Eileen replied without hesitation. "That was quite a spectacle."

"What do you mean?"

"There weren't as many bakers entered—maybe thirty, which I felt gave me a pretty good chance—and the average age of the contestants, I'm guessing, was barely twenty-five. Bakers don't blossom until their forties. Everyone knows that. You're a prime example, dear. No offense, but you haven't hit forty yet, so you have something to look forward to."

"Thank you, I think. Good to know my baking has yet to peak. It has a long way to go to catch up to my cooking. What's your memory of that bake-off?"

"My memory isn't a fond one. It was my first and only bake-off back then. I was young and had all the hope in the world my cookie would win on taste, presentation, and all-out goodness. Turns out those weren't the criteria the judge based his decision on. I entered this year's bake-off as a kind of vindication after all these years. At the time, I wasn't the only baker who felt we were wronged." Eileen's face soured.

"Only one judge?" Erno asked. "I know from Sherry's contests, one judge is highly unusual."

"I know what you're thinking, that I'm a sore loser. Not true," Eileen said. "Ivy was a gorgeous lady. The rest of us paled in comparison. Yes, her Tropical Whatcha-macallit Cookie Bars were good. I tasted one. Not as good as mine, though."

"What you're suggesting doesn't happen in well-run contests," Sherry said.

"You're a touch naïve," Eileen added. "Winning on my second try against her cookie makes it almost all better. With three judges, all impartial. It didn't seem to matter you didn't vote for me. I got the majority vote from the others."

Sherry opened her mouth to respond. The words didn't come.

"Her story wasn't even that good. I remember it perfectly. She simply said the cookie recipe was invented by her to woo the man of her dreams."

"Sounds familiar."

"You've heard the story before?" Eileen asked.

"Same story, different contestant. When we had Crosby over for dinner the night before the bake-off, he told me the story of his recipe, even though I told him I didn't want to hear it and I couldn't comment on it." Sherry listened for any unusual reaction. The more she tried to explain herself, the deeper potential trouble she was getting in to with Eileen for not choosing her as the bake-off winner.

"You had a contestant over for dinner the night before you were to judge him?"

Sherry winced at the incredulous tone of Eileen's voice.

"Let me explain. Crosby stopped into the Ruggery, introduced himself, and before long, Marla and I came to the realization he had been our home economics teacher in high school, a million years ago."

Eileen's eyebrows raised.

"Hold on, though. Give me some credit for showing integrity in maintaining impartiality during the bake-off. Remember, you're my next-door neighbor. The two other judges gave me a look when I mentioned our connection as you approached the judging table. And it wasn't just you and Crosby I was familiar with. I knew most of the contestants, one way or another. Augustin's not that big a town."

"You may have known a lot of the bakers, but did any of them try to flirt with you?" Eileen asked.

Sherry laughed. "Not that I noticed. Wouldn't make a difference if they did."

"Okay, I feel better now. Maybe after all these years, there's a possibility I read the situation wrong." Eileen sighed. "Ivy won the bake-off fair and square. Can't penalize her for being a beauty."

"I think that's a good way to remember it," Sherry said.

"If you'd like to leave a deposit for the cookie rug, I can work up the numbers," Erno inserted into the awkward silence. "Follow me."

Erno led Eileen to the store's lookbooks to begin the process of working up the rug's specifications. Sherry returned to the sales counter and the boxes of daffodil-yellow yarn dye. She unloaded the last box and finalized the inventory sheet. Her phone rang as she flattened the last cardboard box to be taken out to the recycle bin next to the driveway dumpster.

"Hello, Ruth. Do you have the complete list of guests for tomorrow night?"

"I've heard back from everyone on the list you gave me."

"And we have at least one extra, so I hope you'll make lots of salmon rolls."

"Extra?" Ruth asked.

"I had the idea of inviting Vitis Costa, the current Augustin Marina dockmaster. He can give a short talk on the functions of the marina. I urged him to emphasize that, despite the reduced size of the operation today, the town's economy depends in part on a healthy tourist trade, which includes the visiting boaters."

"Good idea. And Lonnie is bringing a plus-one," Ruth said.

"I thought that might happen. Rachel?"

"That's right."

"So, the final count without you and me is . . . ?"

"Somewhere between eleven and fifteen," Ruth said.

"That's a wide range. I'll bring two dozen cookies."

"Dolly will be dressed in her Colonial costume and attending the Colonial kitchen as any dutiful eighteenth-century woman would happily aspire to. You'd fit in perfectly in that era, dear."

"Thank you, I think. See you tomorrow night." Sherry clicked to end the call. She waited by the register as her father and Eileen approached.

"Eileen and I have wrapped up the details of her project. She's very excited. I think you might see her on the cooking contest circuit again sometime soon." Erno opened the door for her.

Her broad grin was accompanied by a wave goodbye.

"Dad, do you think 'aloha' means hello or goodbye?" Sherry asked as her father turned her way.

"Sometimes, you do ask the strangest questions. Let me think. I know it means both, and I also know it means love. It's a pleasant greeting expressing a caring sentiment. Does that help?"

"Imagine you received a card and written inside was a note that read, 'Aloha, my love.' Would you take that as a 'this can't continue' or as a 'nice to see you today, my love' note?" Sherry asked.

"Sadly, the former. Sounds like a line from a movie." Erno softened his tone. "Did you get this note from Don? You know, he's not the only fish in the sea. Although I do consider him a good catch for you."

Sherry pursed her lips. "No, Don didn't send me that note. There was a card inside the pocket of the coat I picked up from the cleaners. The one that belonged to Ivy. Effi and Sal offered it to me when they were about to donate it to a thrift store. When I tried it on, I found a card with those words written on it."

"Not terribly unusual, except for the fact that the note may have been in the pocket for an awfully long time. The elder Curriers went to Hawaii on their honeymoon. Maybe the card was from their time in Hawaii. Maybe the inscription meant goodbye to Hawaii because they loved their trip."

"How do you know they went there on their honeymoon?" Sherry asked.

"That's an easy one. Years later, the islands were the theme of the rug they asked me to make for them. They were married many years by then. I made the rug and they were quite pleased with it. It wasn't laid in their home. Rather, they put it in the yacht club. Unfortunately, the rug was heavily damaged in the marina fire. They contacted me to repair it, then never followed up. I believe it was beyond repair."

"Wonder if the note was from Lonnie to Ivy with the meaning, 'it's been nice, but now it's over?'" Sherry thought out loud. "Or was it from Crosby to Rachel? She wore the coat at some point. Or was the note written by someone else entirely? A third party."

Erno began portioning off packets of yellow dye into groups of three.

"Do you have any idea how long ago the Hawaiian honeymoon was?" Sherry watched her father close his eyes. She assumed he was mentally running through years. She knew he held a vast database of customer information, as if his brain were a Rolodex.

He opened his eyes. "Forty-four."

"That's the number I was hoping you'd come up with."

Chapter 23

The first thing Sherry did when she returned home in the afternoon was remove the freshly baked cookie bars from the pan. The coconutty bars cut nicely, thanks to the addition of parchment paper on the bottom of the baking dish. Ivy's recipe instructions pointed out the necessity of the extra layer between the batter and the baking dish to avoid sticking, and she was spot-on. She must have practiced baking these Tropical Aloha Bars a number of times to get the moist, sweet, crumby texture perfect.

Sherry stacked the bars on a blue dessert plate and covered them with plastic wrap. They would retain their moisture and form until tomorrow afternoon, she hoped. "I wonder why Crosby changed the name of the cookie from Tropical Aloha to Tropical Dream. The recipe itself wasn't changed, for the most part, so why bother changing the name?" Sherry glanced at Chutney, who wasn't able to come up with an answer.

Sherry rinsed her hands and picked up her phone. She began a text then deleted the two words she'd typed. Instead, she found Ray's name in her Contacts and called him.

"Hi, Ray."

"Is this a social call? Must be, because usually you don't even pause long enough to give me time to return the greeting."

"I was gathering my thoughts. I was going to text but had a change of heart. With you, it's all about my presentation."

"Go on." Ray's tone was casual, or he was distracted by multitasking, which was more probable.

"You won't like this question, but here I go. In my opinion, Crosby had a number of family issues. Lonnie doesn't seem particularly broken up over Crosby's death. Lonnie is the first to tell anyone who'll listen that Crosby was a source of disappointment for him. Rachel married a man she thought was her dream, but that dream never came true." Sherry paused. She repeated the word, "dream."

"The name of his bake-off cookies," Ray said. "Tropical Dream Bars."

"That's right. Crosby seemed to have the closest relationship to his mother. People familiar with the situation say Ivy went out of her way to keep Crosby from taking the blame for the Augustin Marina fire. The fire that tore the family apart. Unless I'm mistaken, Ivy and Rachel may have been close, despite Rachel's current negative opinion of Crosby. At least, close enough to share an expensive coat."

"And your question is . . . ?" Ray repeatedly tapped something—a pen perhaps—on a hard surface.

"What would you say if I told you Crosby was a honeymoon baby?"

"I'd say that's interesting and not unheard of, but why are you so focused on what happened decades ago?"

Sherry paused to consider facts versus speculation. Ray would jump at the chance to call her out on any theory she came up with that couldn't be proven with solid evidence. She'd have to stick to the dry facts. She proceeded with caution.

"Crosby's body was found at the marina. The same marina his father worked at until Crosby was in his early twenties."

"Right." The tapping continued.

"If Lonnie were the murderer, seems too obvious he'd return to the marina to dispose of the body. Might as well leave his business card to ensure no one overlooked his guilt."

Ray didn't respond.

"Rachel said Crosby was never much of a sailor. He was considerate enough to buy a boat and name it after his wife, who did enjoy being out on the water. Although he was changing the name of the boat after the divorce. *Sweet Revenge* is yet another calling card. If he got the boat's name changed before Rachel took ownership, she'd have to go through the effort of renaming and repainting the boat, or live with a name that draws suspicion. All because Crosby wanted to get one last dig in on his ex-wife."

"I've seen worse cases of spousal retaliation," Ray said.

"That being said, my gut tells me neither Lonnie nor Rachel killed Crosby. Someone is out to peg them for his murder."

She waited, and Ray stayed silent.

"Have you ever been sailing?" Sherry knew jumping from subject to subject tested Ray's patience, but the method worked best to keep him engaged.

"Reluctantly. Case in point: I had high hopes once when I took a young lady out on a romantic sail with a skilled sailor at the helm. In my mind, the end result would be her labeling me adventurous and she'd throw herself at me."

"How did that work out?"

"I'm single. The plan backfired. She saw the skilled sailor, not me, as the adventurous and attractive catch and threw herself at him. Reinforces the words of Shakespeare, 'to thine own self be true.' I tried to be something I wasn't and it blew up in my face. Live and learn."

"I think you're adventurous in your own way. The right girl is out there for you. Don't give up hope."

"How did this call get to be about my love life anyway? Is that all you wanted to ask?" Ray's tone grew gruff, bringing Sherry to grin.

"That's all. Bye, Ray."

Sherry jotted down the word, "dream," on a scrap of paper. "Chutney, the man is a genius." She reexamined the paper and realized it was the receipt Vitis had found under her car when he was changing the flat tires. "There's a price written down. Was I supposed to pay for those cookies?" Horrified at the thought she had assumed incorrectly Chef Buckman's cookies were a present, she reviewed the receipt. "This isn't mine. But I think I know who made this purchase."

* * *

The next day, gray clouds smothered the sun and the nip in the air was no longer a glancing blow. The weatherman on the television morning news relayed the extended forecast in two words: "cold" and "colder." Winter had arrived. When the time came to leave for the Historical Society, Sherry changed her footwear three times, from boots to shoes to boots and back to shoes. There was a chance for sleet that evening, so Sherry finally decided on carrying her waterproof boots and leaving them in the car, for peace of mind. If what to wear on her feet was the only indecision plaguing her, she would have been quite content.

Arriving at the Historical Society an hour early would give Sherry and Ruth plenty of time to tidy up from the daily visitors before the evening guests arrived. The first thing Sherry saw when she entered the wood-and-stone, Colonial-era building was a candy wrapper on the floor.

"This could spoil the illusion of the seventeen hundreds in a hurry." She picked up the brightly colored, crumpled paper.

"Thank you. That wasn't there last time I swept." Dolly approached with a broom made of a sturdy stick rod with twigs for bristles. She wore a bonnet and a white apron tied over her long, impractical dress. She swept the floor around the front entryway. The inefficient broom stirred up debris rather than containing the dust the way a modern broom would.

The woman peered up from her task. "Sherry, right?"

"Yes. Nice to see you again, Dolly. Thank you for staying on and helping with the donor party."

"It's my home." Dolly didn't break character. "Of

course I'm staying to greet the guests. Welcoming strangers with food and drink is one of my most important roles as a Colonial woman. The visitors may have traveled days to get here, under difficult and dangerous circumstances, and I want to make them feel at home after their tiring journey."

"You're a good host." Sherry lifted her plate of cookies. "Where should I put these?"

"Let's bring them into the kitchen, where I'll transfer them onto a more era-appropriate serving platter. Follow me."

Sherry gave her cookies a forlorn glance as she traced Dolly's footsteps into the kitchen. The overwhelming theme of the room's décor was dark wood. The centerpiece was an oversized brick fireplace, as tall as Dolly. Sherry imagined that she, with her slight build, might have scored the job portraying a Colonial woman for the sole reason of fitting the fireplace's dimensions to perfection. Sherry considered she, herself, would have been categorized an oversized woman hundreds of years ago, thus limiting her potential to find a Colonial husband, as, she had read, males were inches shorter on average back then.

Sherry set her cookie plate on the cloth-covered, wooden table that sat a safe distance back from the fireplace. Dolly set a hammered metal plate next to Sherry's and began transferring the cookies from the modern plate to the hand-forged serving platter of yesteryear.

"Is Ruth here? I thought I saw her car in the lot, unless that was yours."

"Car? What is that? You must be speaking of my horse and wagon. I've put them away for the night." Dolly side-eyed Sherry. "Yes, Mistress Ruth is tidying up the drawing room."

"Thanks. I'll go find her." Sherry left Dolly stacking cookie bars. She hoped Ruth was embracing the modern era. The night was going to be awkward if Sherry was the only host speaking in twenty-first-century lingo.

"Ruth? Are you in here?" Sherry entered the large room adorned with small windows and another fireplace.

Sparsely decorated with only olive green and ivory window treatments, the room matched the kitchen in its austerity and drabness. Antique wooden chairs were set up in two rows facing the unlit fireplace. Candlelight bulbs in lantern cases were hung on the wall to mimic the lighting used before electricity. The wooden floor creaked as Sherry approached Ruth, who was putting the finishing touches on the fireplace tool arrangement.

"Hi, dear. Aren't you excited? If we get some big donations, we can have some wonderful exhibits in the new year. I brought wine and my salmon rolls. Hopefully, you brought some sweet treats." Ruth's midshin-length dress billowed out as she made a lap around the edge of the room, picking up lint specks as she did so.

"I'm very excited."

Ruth came to rest next to Sherry. "I've been meaning to ask you. How did you come up with your list of guests? I did some checking, and, while some are extremely well off, others wouldn't be my pick of someone I'd consider a potentially large donor. Unless they have a strong interest in either the history of Augustin or the preservation of the harbor, I wouldn't understand why you chose some of them."

"It's more about the chemistry of the group. As you said, some have the money and some have the interest in aspects of the Augustin community. Between you, Dolly, and Vitis, one of us ought to be able to convince the others to open their wallets wide. When one makes a pledge, the others will follow suit, mark my words. Before you know it, the society will have donations, the Augustin Marina Restoration Fund may have some donors and, beyond that, there may be a few surprises we didn't count on."

"I trust your judgment. Why don't we get up to the special exhibit storeroom and start bringing down the key pieces? I'm going to bring Dolly along, too, although she may have to break character for a moment to help us." Ruth narrowed her eyes and giggled.

Sherry saw a side of her father's friend she had never seen before. One that was slightly devilish.

"That woman is rather," Ruth tapped her temple, "out there. Born a couple of hundred years too late."

"Lead the way."

The women exited the drawing room and stopped by the kitchen to solicit Dolly's help. She was adjusting the position of the spinning wheel from in front of the massive fireplace to the corner of the room. The spinning wheel had been camouflaging a huge metal caldron hung from the center of the stone hearth. Sherry couldn't resist peering inside.

"That's where the magic happens." Dolly lifted an enormous utensil that appeared to be part ladle, part spatula, part spoon. She stirred the imaginary contents of the giant bowl. "If we had a fire going, I'd most likely be preparing a root vegetable and pork stew. It's my job to keep the fire burning all day and the residual embers glowing throughout the night."

Sherry peered at Ruth, whose kind smile lines spoke of her appreciation for Dolly's enthusiasm for her role.

"Dolly, we don't have the fire going, so would you mind coming upstairs with Sherry and me to choose which exhibit items to bring downstairs? Let's save your stories for the folks coming here in an hour."

Ruth and Dolly made short work of the creaky dark stairs leading up to the special exhibits storage room. Sherry took her time, running her hand along the wall to safeguard herself as she snailed her way up the challenging steps.

"Maybe we'll bring down six or so framed photos, all of the written articles, because there are only four, and as many artifacts as we can carry in the next twenty minutes. Let's start with the photos," Ruth said.

The third floor of the Historical Society's building had low-pitched ceilings, dictated by the steeply pitched roofline. As a result, the taller photos leaning on the wall touched the floor and the ceiling at the same time. Sherry had to be careful not to bump her head when she examined the photos to choose. The process was quick, though, as she had her choices already stored in her brain.

She picked up the photo of the partially submerged yacht and carefully backed into the center of the room, where the ceiling was highest. "I'll take this one downstairs."

"Hold on. I'll join you. I've got one. A map of the harbor, prior to the fire," Dolly said. "That should inspire gifts to restore the natural beauty of the area."

"I'm choosing this photo because the dock has suffered such visible damage," Ruth said. "Did you see this one?"

Sherry lugged her photo over to Ruth and set it by her feet. She studied Ruth's choice.

"I've been thinking a lot about this photo. It caught my eye last time we were here. The fire burned in two different spots. Near the dockmaster shed and farther down the dock toward the boats and clubhouse. There's an undamaged area between the two heavily damaged spots. Unless an ember jumped from the first fire to start a second fire, it definitely looks as if the fire was set deliberately in two locations."

Sherry patted her friend on the back before retrieving her photo from the floor. "Wonder if there was a specific target in mind, rather than the entire marina? Maybe someone tonight can provide some answers. You have a good eye, Ruth."

Ruth puffed out her chest. "That's quite a compliment from an accomplished amateur sleuth such as yourself. Maybe I could help you crack a case one day."

Sherry, Dolly, and Ruth brought the photos downstairs to the drawing room. The centerpiece of the room was the fireplace, a small relative to the kitchen's, which made a perfect backdrop for the evening's speakers. Opposite the fireplace was a long, rectangular table. They lined the photos on that table, making for a dramatic display.

The women returned to the third floor, where Sherry browsed for more photos. She found herself alone in the room when Ruth and Dolly carried the framed articles downstairs. Sherry paced the wall of photos in an uncomfortable crouch. After reaching the last one, she stretched, doubled back, and parked herself in front of a frame containing two side-by-side images. One was the inside of the dockmaster shed. The room was spacious, and the walls were decorated with maps. Beyond an extensive counter was a picture window overlooking the dock, harboring impressive boats. *Wow, Lonnie had a nice workspace in those days*.

In the same frame, next to the photo of the dockmaster shed interior from decades ago, was pictured what Sherry recognized as Vitis's current dockmaster shed. The cramped workspace, the smaller picture window behind the counter, even a portion of the article about the fire on the wall, were all visible. The contrast between the two photos told a story of the extent of the fire's destruction and the inability, or lack of desire, to rebuild the past. Sherry picked up the cumbersome photo, the width of which would make it tricky to navigate the narrow stairs. Before she left the room, she took another look over her shoulder.

A small, easily overlooked photo sat beside a photo of the Augustin firehouse. Sherry set down the photo clutched in her arms and picked up another, framed in distressed wood, embellished with detailed carving. She admired the subject, a single-mast sailboat in rough water. The sail was bulging and the two sailors on board appeared to be fully absorbed in controlling the leaning boat. Both sailors wore hats, one with long hair spilling out. The side of the boat read *Augustin Yacht Club*. Sherry recognized the Augustin Harbor as the backdrop and, in the black-and-white photo, was a gorgeous portrait. Sherry picked up the large frame she had chosen and stacked the second one on top.

"Two more pictures," Sherry announced as she entered the drawing room.

"We'll move on to small knickknacks, such as the ship's clock, that were saved from the fire," Ruth said.

"A clock survived? Where was it?" Sherry asked.

"In the clubhouse, originally. It was removed for repair the day before the fire. Lonnie had it in his truck, so it didn't sustain any fire damage," Ruth said.

"Which is now Vitis's truck," Sherry said. "New dockmaster, same old truck."

"I'd also suggest bringing down some racing medals, a

ship's whistle, the charred boardwalk plank, and the dockmaster log from the month of the fire."

"How in the world did the logbook survive the fire?" Sherry asked.

"Again, it was in Lonnie's truck. Maybe he took it home every night for safekeeping, or to review it. He donated the items, so I imagine he's willing to explain how they were used." Ruth checked her wristwatch. "Let's get a move on. Guests will be showing up soon. Dolly and I need to set out our finger food." Ruth eyed Dolly. "By the way, what did you bring?"

"I was here all day, so I had to bring something I could prepare last night. Ham biscuits. The recipe is from George Washington's era. Involves plenty of lard, as the women of the day would use. Makes the biscuits flaky and moist," Dolly said. "The best recipes are hundreds of years old."

"Sherry invents new recipes all the time and wins competitions with them," Ruth said. "Some would say hers are the best."

"I've heard. Congratulations," Dolly said. "I wonder if there was anything like a cook-off back in the eighteenth century."

"All it takes is a couple of cooks looking to be labeled the best and it's game on. You can't tell me the right to reign supreme using that massive fireplace didn't count for a lot. Might even win you a husband." Ruth laughed at her joke.

"Ruth, please behave yourself." Sherry smiled. She paused. "Did I hear the door open?"

"Hello? Is anyone here?" a deep voice called out.

Chapter 24

Standing inside the door, Vitis was peering around in search of something.

"Good evening, Vitis. This is my friend, Ruth Gadabee. She's a board member of the Historical Society. We're so happy you could say a few words tonight."

Vitis fidgeted with the sleeve of his unironed blue dress shirt. Sherry imagined he had scavenged it from the back of his closet, where he kept his seldom-used collared button-down shirts. He rolled up one sleeve to his elbow, revealing a tattoo of a mermaid on his inner forearm. "Nice to meet you, ma'am."

"Thank you for coming, Vitis. To have the current dockmaster of the marina attend is such a thrill," Ruth said. "Thank you for addressing the guests tonight."

"I hope I can say something interesting. You folks

probably know more about the history of this area than I ever would."

"Don't be silly. People will be hanging on your every word," Ruth said.

"That's what Sherry told me when she invited me." Vitis shifted his gaze to Sherry, who gave him an enthusiastic nod.

"If it's all right with you, we'd like you to speak about the duties of today's dockmaster and the role the marina and harbor play in Augustin's community." Ruth hooked her elbow around Vitis's. "Let's get you a refreshment. Maybe a glass of wine will settle any nerves you might be experiencing." Ruth scanned Vitis from head to toe. "Don't you have a coat?"

"I made a last-minute decision to take an Uber here, just in case I had a drink. The driver was at the door before I could find my dress coat." Vitis smoothed the front of his wrinkled shirt. "It's been a while since I dressed fancy."

Ruth dropped Vitis's elbow. "Drinks are this way. Follow me." Ruth led Sherry and Vitis to the kitchen. "Red or white wine?"

"Red, please," Vitis replied as he quickened his pace.

Ruth uncorked a bottle of malbec. "This okay?"

Vitis nodded and Ruth poured him a glass.

Within fifteen minutes, all the guests arrived and Vitis was on his second glass of wine. Ruth corralled everyone into the kitchen for snacks and beverages. Dolly and Sherry made fast work of serving drinks.

"Ladies and gentlemen," Ruth clanged her wineglass with a fork, "we'd like to invite you all to join us in the drawing room for a few words and a preview of the Augustin Marina fire exhibit the Society is hosting next month. My colleague, Dolly, will be passing out a pamphlet with a donation envelope, should any of you feel inclined to donate to the museum or the refurbishment fund of the Augustin Marina property. Follow me and be sure to bring your glass."

Sherry and Dolly directed the guests to the drawing room. Everyone was given time to view the exhibit pieces before Ruth gave the direction to find a chair. When all were seated, Ruth gave a short greeting and called Sherry up to offer a few words. As Sherry made her way forward to face the guests, Dolly intercepted her with a curl of her finger.

"I can hear your phone continually buzzing inside your purse." She pointed toward the kitchen. "Might be an emergency."

Sherry glanced through the doorway into the adjoining room. Her purse was slung across a hook beside the grand fireplace. She could hear her phone buzzing on its muted ring setting. She paused before continuing to the front of the chairs. "I'll get it in a minute. Thanks.

"Good evening, everyone," Sherry began. "As Ruth said, we invited this select group of Augustin residents here for a special preview of one of the most interesting exhibits the Historical Society has had in years. Despite the ambience of the Historical Society, the Colonial era isn't the only focus of the museum. Next year marks the twentieth anniversary of the Augustin Marina fire."

Sherry's gaze drifted to Lonnie, who was involved in a side conversation with Cap. "Gathered here tonight are two marina dockmasters, a journalist who wrote about the fire, the current manager of the newspaper that covered the story, and others who have firsthand knowledge of the catastrophe. Of course, another underlying reason to gather you all here is to solicit your comments and expertise about what you lived through and what you'd like to see included in the exhibit. Finally, any donations are appreciated but not mandatory. Your presence here tonight is a donation in and of itself. You're all living history. We've asked the current dockmaster, Vitis Costa, to say a few words. Vitis?"

Glass of wine in hand, Vitis and Sherry traded places. When he reached the front of the room, he stayed silent for a moment. His gaze shifted from person to person, lingering longest on Lonnie. Vitis's scruffy facial hair made it difficult to read his expression. He let loose a soft laugh. "I'm the last person in this group who should be sharing stories. But you invited me, and thank you for that. Here we go."

Sherry adjusted her posture to best see the others' reactions. She felt a tap on her shoulder.

"Your phone is still going off. Shouldn't you go check it?" Ruth said. "What if it's Erno?"

"If it were Dad in an emergency, he'd be calling you, too, so I'm not worried." Although Sherry wasn't 100 percent certain she felt that way.

"My phone's in my car," Ruth whispered. "We'd never know until it was too late."

"If that's the case, I'll check my phone as soon as Vitis is done speaking."

Vitis shifted his weight from foot to foot, as if experiencing discomfort standing for an extended length of time. "I took over as dockmaster about six months after the fire. A working dock, a gangway, and boat slips were complete by then, and the marina was back in business." Vitis sipped from his wineglass. "Unfortunately, the job I signed up for never fully materialized, as the bad press from the fire kept the town from investing in the marina's full refurbishment." He paused and let his gaze settle on Cap. "Twenty years later, I'm still hopeful my job will evolve into the full-time one it should be. Hopefully, Augustin will be returned to the esteemed harbor it once was. Thank you."

Vitis returned to his seat with his head bowed. Ruth stood and uttered the beginning of a "thank you" before being interrupted by Lonnie, from the front row.

"I have something to say." Lonnie raised himself out of his chair and pointed to the opposite side of the room. "There's a photo over there of my wife. I cannot let that photo be part of the exhibit." He sat back down. "Make that two photos of her."

"What about the articles that strongly suggest Crosby was a vindictive arsonist?" Penny Nagle stood and pointed to the framed articles. "Mr. Diminsky, how can you sit next to the man whose life you nearly ruined? And, Ruth, how could you have invited these two to the same event, knowing they may be the worst of enemies?"

Tony Nagle joined in. "And incredibly, they arrived together. Talk about forgiveness. Those are the real stories here."

"Thank you for your feedback, everyone. Lonnie, we were really hoping to use those photos." Ruth stood and pointed to the table on which they sat. "That photo captures the fire's destruction. The fact that your wife is in the picture only adds to its authenticity."

Rachel shifted in her seat. "Does anyone know the name of the man in the photo with my mother-in-law?"

"I do of course," said Warren. "That's my father."

"Maxwell Yardsmith," Lonnie said. "He was celebrated for his yacht racing successes."

"Is that his boat?" Victoria Templeton asked. "So sad. Looks like a total loss."

"Total loss. He was devastated." Warren turned his face toward the photo.

"Lonnie, your wife's mighty dressed up to be helping with the cleanup." Effi Forino turned and whispered something in her husband's ear.

"I don't recall what she was doing at that moment. In those days, Ivy was learning how to sail. Unfortunately, after the fire, she lost interest," Lonnie explained.

"She looks mighty interested in Mr. Yardsmith's business," Sal said.

By this time, everyone had turned around to view the photos on the table.

"Warren's father was her instructor?" Penny pointed to the photo of the two sailors in the small sailboat. "That sure looks like the same man as the other photo. In the smaller sailboat. Maybe that's your wife in the boat with him?"

"When he had time, he taught a willing student," Warren said.

"He was no spring chicken. Must have been in his seventies in that photo," Effi said.

"We're getting way off the subject, folks," Ruth announced from her seat.

"Could we take a quick break? I'll check my phone," Sherry told Ruth. "Maybe it's time to put out the cookie bars, too."

Ruth stood. "Folks, we're going to take a few minutes' break. We'll be offering some sweet treats Sherry has cooked up, so take another look at the exhibit and we'll resume very shortly."

Sherry made her way over to her purse. She had eight missed calls. She sidled up to Dolly, who was taking the protective cover from the Tropical Aloha Bars.

"Dolly, I'm running to the ladies' room. I'll be right back."

On the door of the restroom was a diagram of where the Colonial public relieved themselves hundreds of years before. She opened the door warily. Relieved to be treated to indoor plumbing rather than a more authentic replication of an outhouse, Sherry locked the door behind her. She hit the Callback button on her phone and Eileen answered on the first ring. "Hey, Eileen, what's going on? You've called eight times."

"Where have you been? I didn't want to text you in case you were in trouble."

"What are you talking about? Start from the beginning."

"I think someone's out to get you. A car, or rather a truck, circled around the block endlessly after I saw you leave your house. You were dressed so nicely and carrying what looked like a delicious plate of something yummy to eat."

"Yes, my cookies. I'm over at the Historical Society for a small fundraiser. Now, about that truck?"

"It went up and down the street, slowing at your house for many passes. A distinctive rumble caught my attention as I was washing dishes. I opened the window and heard Chutney barking inside. I know he was very worried. I could have used my key to go in to calm him down, but I didn't want the truck to take me out, as they say in the movies. I did go outside for a better look, and I think I scared whoever it was off."

"Would you be able to describe the truck?"

The knob of the bathroom door wobbled and a voice asked if anyone was inside.

"Be right out," Sherry called out.

"Are you in the bathroom?" Eileen asked.

"Yep. Needed some privacy."

"Okay, well, then, let me see. The truck was the exact model my brother had years ago. It was in amazing condition, except for the noisy muffler or engine or whatever makes that annoying rumble men seem to love. Color was medium blue. That royal blue that was so popular decades ago. I was more of a navy-blue type of gal when I was in my heyday."

"With a wide, white stripe running down the side?" Sherry asked.

"Yes. Exactly."

"Vitis's truck. I have to go, Eileen."

"Sherry, please be careful. At least you're somewhere safe, I'm assuming."

Another knock on the door interrupted Eileen's good-bye.

"I hope so," Sherry said.

Eileen ended the call.

Sherry opened the door. Vitis raced in before she could exit. Sherry's phone was nearly knocked out of her hand by a flailing elbow.

"Just in the nick of time. One too many glasses of wine." Vitis slammed the bathroom door as soon as Sherry wedged through to the other side.

She stood staring at the closed door. Sherry gave a knock.

"Busy, be right out." Vitis called from the other side of the door.

"Vitis, where's your truck? You said you took an Uber here?" Sherry called through the door.

"I don't know where the truck is. I don't own it anymore. I sold it yesterday, back to the Curriers. I needed the money and Rachel wanted the truck."

"It wasn't Vitis, it was Rachel," Sherry whispered. Rather than compete with the noise of a flushing toilet by asking another question, she returned to the kitchen. She picked up her tray of cookies and brought them to the drawing room.

Chapter 25

Sherry weaved around the guests' chairs, offering her sweets.

"I'll take a cookie, Sherry. Sal, you take one, too. If Sherry made these, they must be prizewinners." Effi removed two bars from the plate.

Sherry stopped in front of Lonnie and Cap.

"Well, what do you know. Tropical Aloha Bars. These are the ones Ivy won her one-and-only bake-off with," Lonnie said. "This evening is turning out to be all sorts of blasts from my past."

"Is the story correct that she made these cookie bars to woo you into becoming her husband?" Sherry asked.

Lonnie's face drooped into a deep frown. His gaze shifted to Cap. "No, that's not true. She made them for him." Lonnie tipped his head toward the photographs on the table.

"Let me help you." Rachel pulled the plate from Sherry's hands. She lowered her voice to a whisper. "You had to have known these bars would jog memories. Not only of Ivy, but of Crosby, too."

"That's okay, Rachel. You don't need to protect me. What's done is done," Lonnie said. "Ivy had a special fondness for Hawaii. The name of the bars says as much. She was a complicated woman. She thought she knew what she wanted and what was best for her, and they weren't always the same thing. By the time she reconciled those two issues, it was too late. Sherry and I have come to an understanding on the facts. Haven't we?"

"Everyone's back in their seat," Sherry announced. "Let's get this show on the road." She winked at Lonnie.

Ruth made her way to the front of the room. "May I have your attention, please? Thank you again for coming tonight. It's been fascinating hearing your stories of the events surrounding the marina fire and its aftermath. I'd like to encourage a donation to the Historical Society or the Augustin Marina Renovation Fund so we're able to provide the public with more exhibits to educate and entertain. Lastly, I would like to solicit retired journalist Cap Diminsky to close tonight's event with any words he'd like to share."

Cap rose from his seat. Lonnie gave him a gentle push forward.

"There's a reason I'm a writer, not a speaker. But I'll do my best. Here's what I've learned from my time here tonight. Sherry is a great organizer, as is Ruth. Dolly loves what she does, and her enthusiasm is contagious."

Sherry mouthed a thank-you.

Cap continued, "My friend Lonnie had a cushy life as the yacht club's dockmaster."

Lonnie chuckled.

"I can't believe they're friends," Effi was heard saying to Sal.

"I have a new article I'm adding to the collection of Marina fire memorabilia," Cap added. "I can give you a brief recap, so as not to bore you. In the article, I apologize for implicating the Currier family in any way in the fire.

"At the same time, I wanted to pay tribute to the man who paid me to write the story about the marina fire, urging me to push for the public's conviction of Crosby. His name is Maxwell Yardsmith." Cap tipped his head toward Warren. "'Tribute' may not be correct word. I'm a bit rusty, remember? Let me correct myself. The man was a master manipulator who ran a highly respected newspaper. He built himself an undeserved reputation for excellence by having his writers spin stories to create an audience, rather than tell the truth, and I was caught up in the frenzy of its popularity. The current editor-in-chief, his son, Warren, has brought respectability to the newspaper, but as we learned tonight, history cannot be rewritten."

"What are you talking about?" Warren shouted. "Is this some sort of an attempt at a backhanded compliment? If so, Cap needs to go back to journalism school."

"Warren, this evening is dedicated to the memory of Crosby and all he wasn't able to accomplish in life because of you," Cap proclaimed.

"What are you talking about?" Warren begged for an answer.

"Let me put another spin on the story your father had me write. Crosby wasn't an arsonist, Lonnie isn't a murderer, and, oh, by the way, Crosby was your half brother."

A hushed murmur overtook the room.

"I've kept that secret for my pal Lonnie for three years. His dockmaster's logbook was full of documentation of your father and Lonnie's wife's sailing time together. Imagine your job is to watch your wife sail off with her lover and you have to keep that a secret to safeguard their child's well-being. Lonnie brought the logbook home every night so no one would read it. Maxwell held Lonnie emotionally captive, and I hate him for that. If you don't believe me, have a look for yourself." Cap pointed to the well-worn, leather-bound book on the table. "But that wasn't the only secret Lonnie was forced to keep."

"Ridiculous," shouted Warren.

"When Crosby entered the bake-off and showed up with the Tropical Aloha Cookie Bars Ivy made so often for your father, you must have had so many mixed emotions," Sherry said when the silence became unbearable. She joined Cap at his side and faced the stunned guests.

"All I considered was that the man had entered someone else's recipe, so, in my mind, he was disqualified," Warren said. "Yes, I'd had them many times before. My father brought them home after his sailing sessions. Ivy made them as a nice gesture of thanks."

"Your father, Maxwell, was the sole judge in the very first Story For Glory Cookie Bake-off. Ivy's story behind the cookie was that she invented the recipe to woo her suitor, presumably her husband, but she really invented the recipe to say goodbye to her lover. Your father. She never did say goodbye, because they shared Crosby and he was a constant reminder of her dalliance in Hawaii. On her honeymoon." Sherry's gaze passed over Lonnie. "His response, besides choosing her as the winner, was to give her a card saying goodbye. He has it in his hand in the photograph over there. She carried it in her coat pocket until the day she died."

"Okay, I admit my father had a weakness. I'm sorry, Lonnie," Warren said.

"I always suspected. Crosby looked exactly like Maxwell. Maxwell came to Hawaii to break us up. Ivy was weak and couldn't say no to his advances." Lonnie turned to face Warren. "I took the logbook home every night because your father was the Yacht Club's most esteemed member. What the other members didn't know was, before the fire, his debts from overspending on the cost of running his racing yacht had mounted into the five figures. He'd owed the club and marina money for months. The burden of his secrets was wearing on him. He was embarrassed and promised he'd make it all right. I could have taken him down, exposed him, ruined him, but I didn't want to jeopardize my job, the only sure thing in my life. What a foolish mistake on my part." Lonnie shook his head. "Maxwell must have snapped. Nothing in his world was stable. He was in debt, he ran a newspaper based on sketchy practices, his son didn't know he was his father, and he suffered the loss of the love of his life, never to recover. Destroying the Yacht Club, his boat, and the marina was his twisted way of hitting the reset button. He thought destroying the physical evidence of his past was his only option. Collecting the boat insurance was a form of vindication for him. All he needed to do was cast the blame on someone else to safeguard never being caught."

"He blamed Crosby," Rachel said. "Awful."

Sherry stared intently at Rachel, hoping to catch her attention and send her encouragement.

"My father would never burn down the marina, not to mention frame someone else for the deed. There's a very good chance Crosby committed suicide because he's lived with the shame of his actions all these years," Warren said. "The fact that he used the name Banks, not Currier, should have been a red flag he wanted out."

"Yes, it was a nod to his mother," Lonnie said. "And a slight to me."

"See if this scenario makes sense. Crosby came to the bake-off to confront you with evidence of your father setting the marina fire. Namely, what Ivy told him on her deathbed about the contents of the logbook and the boat insurance payment Maxwell said he would use to whisk Ivy away to a new, dream life in Hawaii. Instead, you were able to cool him down long enough to get through the event," Lonnie said. "I heard it all on my way to the men's room at the bake-off. Poor Tia dropped her plate of cookies, halting the contest and giving Warren the chance for a bathroom break. I came upon the explosive confrontation between Warren and Crosby in the hallway. If I hadn't, no telling what would have gone down."

Warren's face bloomed a red hue. "Lonnie was going to publicly slander my father's good name. The past is the past. Let my father live out his final days in dignity. He made a mistake, but that was years ago. Ivy and Lonnie stayed married. Where's the harm? Crosby always thought he was Lonnie's son. What's the problem with that?"

Penny stood. "I'd like to add, Warren came in to my store for very interesting items the day before the bake-off. A box cutter, rope, duct tape, and a crowbar." She nodded to Sherry and gave her a wink. "As you and I discussed, the Dry Goods store keeps a list of purchases we find unusual. Some businesses have register cameras. We have running lists. That's how we stay on top of things." She turned to face Warren. "Sorry, Warren. You made the list."

From the kitchen came a clambering noise. Sherry peered across the room and saw Dolly banging the huge metal cauldron with the ladle. "The police are here."

"Good evening, folks." Ray walked into the drawing room with two uniformed police officers. "Someone dialed nine-one-one from this address but hung up before giving any information." Ray scanned the room, and his gaze came to an abrupt halt when it landed on Sherry's face.

She gave him the slightest of nods.

"Would someone like to explain how we can be of service?"

"We were discussing Warren's reasons for killing Crosby." Sherry was impressed when Ray's expression remained stoic.

"We were not," Warren stated in no uncertain terms. "I didn't kill him. I have no idea what trouble that man was in, nor do I care. Even if we did share the same father, as Sherry insists."

Vitis cleared his throat. "The day Crosby was murdered, Mr. Yardsmith came by the marina and asked to see Crosby's boat. Said he was considering buying it and wanted to do a once-over on it. Against my rules. If it's not your boat, you're not allowed onboard without the owner's written permission. *Rachel's Way* was about to be winterized, and it's my responsibility to keep the vessel safe. He wasn't happy. But he left the grounds. I went to lunch, came back, and found Crosby's body."

"How awful," Mrs. Templeton cried out.

"Looked bad for Mr. Yardsmith, but I had no reason to get involved. I told the detective what had happened, and he agreed with me. The evidence was circumstantial." Vitis shifted his gaze to the detective. "That's what you called it, right?"

Ray nodded.

"The marina sits out there in the wide open. Anyone could have stepped onto the property while I was away at lunch. It was also my father's doughnut delivery day, so I was gone for an extra-long amount of time."

"If you weren't there, you have no idea how Crosby's body ended up at the marina," Warren said.

"True, but then things started happening to Sherry. The boat, then her car. I figured it was no coincidence. I didn't want to be blamed for any of it, although I certainly could be. So, I rethought the evening Mr. Johnstone's boat's pump line was cut. I admit I failed at my job by leaving *Buy-Lo Sell-Hi* unattended while we went in search of life vests. Anyone could have boarded the boat and, if they knew what they were doing, could have made fast work of cutting the pump lines."

"Anyone," Warren repeated.

"I saw you at Sunset Village the day Sherry's car tires were slashed. You were in the parking lot. You asked me why I wasn't at the nature center, because it was almost lunchtime. You seemed to know my routine." Vitis smoothed back his hair. "I had to share my concerns with Sherry."

"What would my reason be for causing damage to Sherry's car and her friend's boat, may I ask?"

"A warning she may be close to discovering Crosby's killer, for one?"

"I wasn't even aware of what she did on her off-time besides enter cook-offs until now." Warren shrugged.

"You must know a lot about the inner workings of a boat, Mr. Yardsmith. Your father was an experienced yachtsman. Some of that knowledge must have rubbed off on you. Like, what pump lines can be cut for a slow leak," Cap said.

"I was around boats fairly often growing up, but nothing about them interested me," Warren said with an air of calm. "I was a journalist, and still am. That was what I learned from my father."

"Does any part of your journalism career entail authoring threatening notes to the Forinos?" Sherry asked.

Sal let out a sigh. "Effi, did you tell Sherry about the note?"

"Yes, I did, and I want to know the answer, Warren," Effi stated.

"What are you talking about?" Warren's voice was pinched. "What threatening note?"

"The article Patti Mellitt submitted for the Town newsletter was printed on your secretary, Gina's, printer. The only working printer in the newsroom while your network has been down. The printout had a distinct track of black ink lines down the right side."

"The printer's seen better days. We'll be purchasing a new one soon," Warren said.

"The point is, those line tracks were on the note you printed and left under the door at the Shore Cleaners last weekend," Sherry said.

"Any number of my employees could have left that note. One printer, many employees."

"Sal told me when you visited the cleaners, you were very interested in Ivy's coat. You saw the coat on the conveyor mechanism when you came in to pick up your sick wife's cleaning. Currier, Culli, alphabetically next to each other."

"Culli?" Mrs. Templeton asked. "Who is Culli?"

Warren produced a noise, but was interrupted by Sal. "Culli Yardsmith. She likes her clothes listed under her first name. Says she's picked up the wrong cleaning too many times. Lots of Yardsmith relatives in the vicinity. No other Cullis on our customer list, so no more mix-ups."

"Sal's making this up. I came into his shop, picked up our cleaning, and that's that. Why would I be interested in another woman's coat?" Warren asked.

"The coat must have been a harsh reminder of your father's poor choices. Sal said you asked him who the coat belonged to."

Sal nodded. "True. Mr. Yardsmith's face turned sheet white when he saw the coat. I told him I couldn't get anyone to pick it up, let alone pay the overdue bill."

"And what did he say to that?" Sherry asked.

"He said, 'Burn the damn thing.'"

"Why would a coat cause such a ruckus?" Victoria Templeton asked.

"Good question. Warren?" Sherry asked. "Is it because growing up you saw Ivy wearing the coat many times? When she was with your father?"

Warren's voice softened. "Listen. Everyone. Relax. You're reading this all wrong. I'm the hero here. Crosby threatened me and my father. Said he had a gun. In his car. At the bake-off. Said he'd take care of me, then go find my father down in Florida. He said before she passed away, his poor mother, Ivy, may she rest in peace, complained my father ruined her life. He never took responsibility for the son he had with her. She said my father promised her a dream world and, in reality, gave her a nightmare. Not true."

"By the way, I have your receipt for the birthday cake you ordered from Pinch and Dash while we were at Eileen's cookie launch." Sherry held up the bill of sale. "Vitis found it under my car the day you slashed my tires. You should be more careful not to leave evidence behind when you threaten people."

Warren's face bloomed an even rosier hue. "You weren't taking my warning to back off. I knew you'd end up hunting down Diminsky, and I got lucky, finding your car there when I did. I'd been looking for days." Warren's voice strengthened to a harsh level of intensity.

"Mr. Yardsmith, I'd like you to come with us down to the station to answer some questions." Ray took a step toward Warren, who, in turn, backed up a step.

"I needed Crosby to go away. To leave my father alone. The man doesn't have much time left. When Crosby showed up at the bake-off, he whispered to me that he was winning for his mother. All her prizes were destroyed the night of the fire, and it was her dream to win them back. The fire my father set. He let her win the bake-off, then he took everything away from her as punishment for not choosing him over Lonnie."

"Let's go down to the station, Mr. Yardsmith. You're under arrest."

Chairs screeched along the floor as the guests rose. Sherry could feel the collective sentiment that if Warren resisted Ray and the officers' attempt to guide him out of the room, panic would reign. Sherry saw Warren ball his hands into fists. Her gaze shifted to Ray's hand, resting on the handle of the gun he revealed with a flick of his blazer. Sherry heard a gasp from Dolly in the kitchen. She turned and saw the woman in the doorway, holding the massive ladle over her head, poised to take down anyone trying to enter. Everyone froze in place until Warren lowered his head.

He was led to the waiting police car by the officers and placed in the back seat. Before Ray pulled his gray sedan out of the Historical Society parking lot, he gave Sherry a tip of his hat. The sleet began to fall as the squad car left the driveway, lights flashing, siren silent.

Chapter 26

"Good morning. I wanted to return this." Sherry handed Effi a piece of paper as the petite woman wrestled with the handle of the cleaner's door. The cold December wind rattled the paper until the hand-off was complete. "It belongs to you. I don't think you'll be needing to hide it under the cash register anymore. It may be one of the stronger pieces of evidence against Warren Yardsmith. Good job."

"You're sure he sent this threat?" Sal peered over his wife's shoulder.

"There's a streak from his printer running down the side of this printout. The same streak was on Patti's bake-off recap article printout. They both used Warren's secretary's printer. All fits together."

"Is there more evidence against Warren?" Sal asked.

"The Nagles will vouch for Warren purchasing the

equipment used to kill Crosby and tie him to the marina's anchor from the Augustin Dry Goods store. Thank goodness for Mrs. Nagle's purchase recording system. Beyond that, I don't think any jury will have trouble convicting Warren of Crosby's murder. Detective Bease and his team are the best at closing the case."

"Thank you. Not sure how you ended up with our note, and I won't even ask." Effi winked. "There are worse things in this world than a paper burglary. Can't wait for the parade. So excited for Eileen."

"We're so lucky to have a great view of the parade from our stores. We don't even have to put on our coats to see everything. Hope Eileen is wearing her long underwear. Have a good day and try to stay warm."

Sherry continued on her way to the Ruggery. Chutney strutted a step behind, wearing his warm, fleece sweater, snapped tight under his belly.

"Hi, Sherry," Mrs. Nagle called out from her doorway.

"Hi, Mrs. Nagle."

"We just got in a shipment of flashlights if you need one. Winter's coming and there's not much daylight after five. You'll need to walk Chutney in the dark. You buy one every year at this time, my list says."

"Thank you. I'll stop by later." Sherry tossed Mrs. Nagle a wave. She continued on until she found herself in front of the Nutmeg News Media Center.

"Good morning, Sherry," said Hans, wearing his blue jacket.

"Hans, how are you?" Sherry greeted the man with a generous smile. She hadn't seen him since Warren was arrested. "How's the mood in the building?"

Hans peered around. He took a step forward and lowered his voice. "Things are great. The mood is festive and spirits are high. Mr. Clifton has done a bang-up job taking over the newsroom. He's the right man for the job."

"Happy to hear it. Keep your eye on my friend Patti. Don't let her past you without a cookie bribe or two."

"Will do. You off to the parade?" Hans asked.

"I told my friend Eileen I'd meet her at her float before her send-off. The parade starts at Town Hall. After it begins, Chutney and I will race back and watch from the store, where it's warm."

"Eileen, the bake-off winner. What a wonderful prize she won. Hope we can have the contest again next year." Hans leaned down and reached into a plastic bag parked next to his leg. He held up a wool glove with a leather palm. "I've been asking everyone who was at the bake-off. Is this yours? Seems as if I've asked everyone else."

"It's not mine, but I have a good idea who it belongs to, and I may be seeing her today. Want me to bring it along in case I do?" Sherry asked.

"That would be a great help." Hans handed the glove to Sherry, who stuffed it in her coat pocket. "Enjoy the parade."

"You, too. Have a great day." Sherry waved and picked up her pace toward Town Hall. As she approached the building, she saw a pickup truck she recognized. The side of the truck sported a banner touting the Augustin Marina Renovation Fund. Judging by the truck's proximity to the mayor's huge, convertible sedan, the retired dockmaster was given the number two spot in the procession. An honor Sherry felt was long overdue.

"How have you been, Lonnie?" Sherry asked. "I haven't seen you since the Historical Society fundraiser. That was quite a night."

Rachel and Cap flanked their friend.

"That was quite a scheme you dreamed up to get Warren to confess." Lonnie put an arm around Rachel on one side and Cap on the other. "I'm glad to be of service."

"Hey, don't forget you got your beloved old truck out of the deal," Cap said.

"When I found out it was Rachel riding around my neighborhood in that truck after you bought it from Vitis, I have to admit, I thought twice about whether Warren was Crosby's killer. My neighbor was certain the driver was stalking me."

"I was looking for your house to collect Ivy's coat. I had just picked up the truck from Vitis, so it was my only mode of transportation. The address you texted me didn't include a house number. I tried to ask a woman on the street, walking a cat on a leash, something I'd never seen before, if she knew you, but she was on the phone and didn't respond. Strange woman. Then I tried to call you, but you didn't pick up."

"You made it awfully hard to trust you, Rachel. When I finally could see past what I thought was your guilt, Warren came into focus. Why did you insist on getting back Ivy's coat and Crosby's boat? I've never had a chance to ask you," Sherry said.

Rachel turned toward Lonnie. "I'd do anything for this guy. Just trying to keep what looked like evidence against him out of sight while you did your sleuthing."

"And the truck?"

"Bought back the truck because he missed it so. Want the coat back? I've already sold the boat to your friend Don."

Sherry grinned. "No thanks. Anyone else would look better in it than me." She reached in her coat pocket. "Is this yours?"

"My gloves must have boomerang powers. I keep losing one and it finds its way back to me. Where was this one?" Rachel asked as she took the glove.

"At the Nutmeg News Media Center," Sherry said.

"Can't be mine, then. The one I lost at the bake-off was brown, not black. And you found that one on Don's boat." Rachel paused. "Do you think Warren found my glove at the bake-off, knew it was mine, and planted it on Don's boat to implicate me? I didn't go on Don's boat, that I'm sure of. As a matter of fact, when we were pulling up to the dock that night, a lone person got off Don's boat."

"We were at the life vest bin up at the dockmaster shed. All of us. The boat should have been empty," Sherry said.

"Had to have been Warren," Rachel said.

"All in an attempt to throw suspicion elsewhere. Didn't work for long," Cap said.

"You know, Maxwell Yardsmith had trouble in his first attempt to burn his boat to get the insurance money. When I showed the photograph of the dock damage to a firewoman, she recognized he had started the fire too far up the dock, by the metal storage shed. The fire didn't travel to his boat, so he had to start a second one farther down the dock. The photo solved the question of why there were two fires. Something the department had pondered for years."

"Ivy knew the truth for a long time, I'm guessing," Lonnie said. "Wanted to protect Maxwell and Crosby at the same time. She had so many secrets."

"Sherry, over here," a voice sang out from the line of parade vehicles and floats. "Sherry!"

"Have a good time in the parade," Sherry said to the three friends climbing into the decades-old truck.

Rachel put on a captain's hat and took the wheel.

"Coming," Sherry called back to Eileen, waving her arms over her head. "Come on, Chutney." She tugged on the leash and trotted down the line of parade participants until she reached the float honoring the Hillsboro County Homeless Shelter and Food Bank.

"Eileen, what a great float." Sherry admired the fruit and vegetable decorations surrounding her neighbor. Perched on a throne at the peak of the display, Eileen was holding an oversized platter of enormous, papier-mâché cookies. "Good luck up there. Hold on tight."

"Eileen looks like she's already having a ball."

Sherry turned around. Patti was coming up behind her. "I'll be riding with her. I'll make sure Augustin's cookie queen doesn't fall off her throne."

"Thanks. She's head of our unofficial neighborhood watch. She needs to stay in one piece to fulfill her duties." Sherry paused. "Did you ever see Crosby at the Food Bank on one of your drop-offs?"

"Many times. He was a solid contributor."

"So, the story of his cookie was believable after all. I should have given him the points." Sherry took a last look at Eileen, who was adjusting her position on her ornate seat. Sherry cupped her hands around her mouth. "Have a great ride. We'll be watching."

Roasted Sweet Potato Panzanella

2 cups country style bread, cubed
3 medium-sized sweet potatoes, peeled, cut in 1-inch
   cubes
3 tablespoons olive oil
2 teaspoons crushed fresh rosemary
$\frac{1}{4}$ teaspoon ground cumin
1 teaspoon fresh grated ginger
$\frac{1}{4}$ teaspoon sea salt
$\frac{1}{4}$ teaspoon ground black pepper
$\frac{1}{4}$ cup green pumpkin seeds (pepitas)
$\frac{1}{2}$ cup chopped smoked mozzarella cheese
$\frac{1}{3}$ cup dried cranberries
4 chopped scallions
$\frac{1}{3}$ cup julienne roasted red pepper

Preheat oven to 425 degrees F.

Place bread cubes on a cookie sheet and bake in oven until golden. Set aside.

Coat potatoes with 3 tablespoons olive oil, then sprinkle with rosemary, cumin, ginger, salt, and pepper and roast in a roasting pan for 40-45 minutes until potatoes are fork tender.

Meanwhile, heat a frying pan or skillet to medium-hot and toast the pumpkin seeds until puffed and golden. Remove seeds to cool on a plate.

In a small bowl combine the mozzarella, cranberries, scallions, and red peppers.

Assemble dish by gently tossing the potatoes, red pepper blend and croutons in a large bowl with enough Warm Chutney Balsamic Dressing (recipe follows) to coat. Top with pepitas and serve.

Warm Chutney Balsamic Dressing

⅓ cup balsamic vinegar
2 tablespoons fresh lemon juice
¼ cup mango chutney
1 tablespoon Dijon mustard
2 cloves garlic, minced
⅓ cup olive oil

Prepare the dressing by placing the vinegar, lemon juice, chutney, mustard, and garlic in a small saucepan and heat to very warm, stirring often. Remove from heat and whisk in ⅓ cup olive oil.

Sherry's Favorite Holiday Cookie Recipe

Candy Cane Kissed Peppermint Patties

14 tablespoons butter, room temperature
¼ cup brown sugar
¼ cup granulated sugar
1 teaspoon vanilla extract
1 egg yolk
1 cup plus 2 tablespoons all-purpose flour
¼ cup Dutch process cocoa
1 cup confectioners' sugar
1 teaspoon peppermint extract
3 tablespoons plus 1 teaspoon light cream
1½ cups semisweet chocolate chips
½ cup crushed candy canes

Preheat the oven to 350 degrees F.

Cream 10 tablespoons of the butter with the sugars in a medium bowl, and then beat in the vanilla and egg yolk. Add the flour and cocoa and beat until smooth. Transfer the dough to wax paper and roll into a 10-by-2-inch log. Wrap and refrigerate 1 hour.

Slice the dough into ¼-inch rounds and flatten gently on a baking sheet. Bake 7 to 8 minutes, and then let cool 10 minutes.

Cream the remaining 4 tablespoons butter with the confectioners' sugar, peppermint extract and 1 teaspoon of the cream until smooth. Spread about 2 teaspoons of peppermint cream each over half of the cookies and close with a plain baked cookie.

Melt the chocolate chips with the remaining cream in a small saucepan, adding more cream to make it smooth but not runny. Spread over half of the cookies and top with the candy canes while the chocolate is still wet.

Connect with U(s)

Visit us online at
KensingtonBooks.com
to read more from your favorite authors, see books
by series, view reading group guides, and more.

Join us on social media

for sneak peeks, chances to win books and prize packs,
and to share your thoughts with other readers.

facebook.com/kensingtonpublishing
twitter.com/kensingtonbooks

Tell us what you think!

To share your thoughts, submit a review,
or sign up for our eNewsletters, please visit:
KensingtonBooks.com/TellUs.